HE WASN'T ABOUT TO GIVE UP EASILY

"Why don't you just get on with it?" Charles voiced the question in a playful tone, and for a moment, Kate was nonplussed.

"W-with what?"

"Seducing me."

"I don't know how," she murmured, turning away as she admitted the awful truth.

"Oh, yes, you do. In fact, you've already begun."

"I have?" she asked incredulously.

"I find your laugh very seductive, as well as your voice. But the first thing about you that seduced me was your air of mystery."

"Air of mystery?" Kate croaked, feeling as mysterious as a plate glass window.

Charles nodded emphatically. "On the surface your cool collectedness is like a very severe business suit. But I know it's only covering the real you, which is silken underwear. Very mysterious and very seductive."

Speechlessly considering some new lingerie, Kate could only blush.

ABOUT THE AUTHOR

A native Texan who claims trailblazing pioneers as her ancestors, Cara West still resides in the Lone Star State with her two sons and a menagerie of pets. Charles Sheffield, the hero of *There Is a Season*, is Cara's fantasy of the ideal mate, and she hints that there's a great deal of herself in the character of Kate Hennessey. Their tender love story is Cara's second Superromance.

Books by Cara West

HARLEQUIN SUPERROMANCE
259–NOW THERE'S TOMORROW

Cara West

THERE IS A SEASON

Harlequin Books

TORONTO • NEW YORK • LONDON
AMSTERDAM • PARIS • SYDNEY • HAMBURG
STOCKHOLM • ATHENS • TOKYO • MILAN

Published March 1988

First printing January 1988

ISBN 0-373-70299-X

To Pam...
who never thought I was crazy

CHAPTER ONE

The body lay on the floor of the library...

Randolph doesn't have a library....

The body lay on the floor of the kitchen...in a pool of blood, arms and legs spread out. A blank stare of surprise was a death mask on the too-handsome features.

Needs more...

The body...lay in a pool of thickening blood on the polished floor of the kitchen. A butcher knife, clotted with red, had impaled *impaled?* the countertop. A blank stare of surprise was a death mask on the too-handsome features. *Of the body, not the countertop dummy!* The stale remains of a sandwich were strewn about the head like a bizarre funeral wreath...

Argh! Die, Randolph! Die!

The phone rang beside Kate, and relieved, she turned away from the unblinking screen of her computer.

"Hello."

"You got a minute?" The speaker was Lynn, an old friend. "I thought you might be writing."

"Not so you'd notice. I've finished one page in the last hour. Randolph won't die, and I'm ready to strangle him.

But Rebecca, the murderer, is a ninny and can't work up her courage to do the deed at all. I was about to quit for the night, anyway. I start the new job tomorrow."

"That's one of the reasons I called, to wish you luck. Nervous?"

"Always. It's one of the joys of being a temporary. That and having too little time and too little money."

"What's this assignment going to be?"

"Different. I'm taking over for a church secretary who's on a leave of absence. Don't snicker. I know I'm not the type. But it's an Episcopal church and they're not interested in my religious convictions. They want me for my maturity. The first temp the agency sent was a sweet young thing who left in five days. If I work out, it could turn into a long-term assignment. The hours are perfect—nine to four. I can chauffeur Michael to and from school. Therefore, I intend to be on my most circumspect behavior."

"That should be different."

"Watch it, dear. Long friendship only entitles you to certain privileges."

Lynn laughed. "Listen, that's not the only reason I called. Hank and I wondered—" she paused and her tone was coaxing "—if you could go out to dinner with us this Friday night."

Kate was immediately suspicious. "Hank, you and who else?"

"Well, Hank is entertaining a business colleague I'd like you to meet. Tall, dark and forty-five. Divorced five years. I think you'd be interested."

"Lynn," Kate pleaded, "don't do this to me. You know I'm a disaster on a blind date. I'd probably choke on a lettuce leaf. Besides, I'm not interested and don't plan to be." Her refusal was firm. Lynn ignored it.

"Kate, I won't take no for an answer. You're a good-looking, loving, intelligent woman, and you're missing half of life. You need connections, a relationship. Not to mention sex. Sex is fun, remember?"

"Vaguely," Kate said dryly. She was touched by Lynn's words and hid behind humor. "I thought you said this was a dinner date? What else did you have in mind for the evening?"

"Why nothing, Kate!" Lynn sounded like an injured innocent. She paused, then continued. "Later, of course... after you get to know each other..."

Kate snorted skeptically.

Lynn was undeterred. "Trust me, Kate. I swear this one's a winner."

"Oh, I trust you all right. It's men I'm wary of. They're delightful, don't get me wrong. I'm very, very fond of them. I just don't trust them. They either go off to war and get killed, or stay home and have a heart attack. Or they go through a midlife crisis, buy a Porsche and run away with a twenty-year-old. Or... they fall into a bottle and can't get out.... Anyway," Kate said decisively, "I'm through with all that. I'm thirty-eight years old and too hassled for mating behavior. I have two kids, a dog, a cat, an ex-husband and twenty-three gray hairs—but who's counting? Not to mention a mortgage and a stack of bills that looks like the Leaning Tower of Pisa. And an unfinished mystery novel with a victim who won't die."

"I don't need any more problems. I certainly don't need a relationship. I haven't the time. Although... I would consider a sex object, if you have one in stock. Say, around twenty-three, more brawn than brains... with some endurance. Someone who simply adores older women. Find this person for me and I'll take him on a two-week cruise to the

Island of Majorca.'' Kate grew dreamy. ''They say the Mediterranean sun has aphrodisiac qualities.''

''I think a cruise could be arranged,'' Lynn said. ''But why only two weeks?''

''That's my limit for sexual orgies.''

''Yeah, you talk a good line,'' Lynn countered, ''but you live like a nun and have for three years.''

''Five, but who's counting?''

''Anyway,'' Lynn continued, determined to make her point, ''if I did find you a sex object, you'd run like crazy.''

''Well, the poor child would probably need a mother more than a temptress. But I'm too profane to be a nun.'' Kate referred back to Lynn's earlier teasing.

''We've established that you're not a nun. So what about Friday?''

''Oh, Lynn, please, don't play Cupid. You haven't the figure for it.'' She took another tack. ''Besides...eligible men with a hint of gray at their temples are rare birds. And I'm not in the mood to go hunting. No, I'll just settle back with an old Cary Grant film and resign myself to my fate.'' Kate was a connoisseur of vintage movies and prized her VCR above almost all else.

''An old movie won't rub your back for you,'' Lynn reminded her.

''That may be true. But it presents fewer problems than a live-in masseur.''

''Oh, I don't know,'' Lynn purred. ''Hank comes in handy on occasion.''

Kate laughed. ''Hank's an exception. Face it, Lynn, you got lucky the second time around. *And* it didn't hurt that you look more like a Barbie doll than an English professor with a specialty in Jane Austen.''

''Hank's friend may be an exception, too,'' Lynn reminded her. ''It's worth a try. As for my playing Cupid, it's time you got used to it. You've been divorced two years and separated for three. We won't even go into the years before that." Her tone betrayed the residue of long-ago anger. Then she went into what Kate called her steamroller act.

"You're ready for a love life. You're just gun-shy. And I've only begun my matchmaking campaign. It's a good friend's duty."

"And you're just filled with the milk of human kindness," Kate murmured, to no avail.

"That's me, kid. A regular Girl Scout."

"That's not what I call it. Sounds more like pandering to me."

But Lynn overrode Kate's muttering. "I won't take no for an answer, Kate. I've already told you that. But I will take a 'maybe.' Sleep on it. Call me tomorrow or the next day. That way you can tell me about the new job. In the meantime, I'll think of some new methods of persuasion."

On that ominous note, the two exchanged farewells and the phone call ended.

Still thinking of Lynn and Hank, Kate turned back to her computer and patted it fondly. The machine had practically been a gift from Lynn and her husband. Hank, the head of a software firm, had helped Kate buy the machine below cost.

"You're a marvelous creature," she said softly, not above coaxing flattery and a bit of magical thinking. Maybe Rebecca, the cowardly murderer, had taken matters into her own hands and run over Randolph with her Mercedes. But Kate's compliment had fallen on deaf electrodes. The screen stared back dumbly. The body hadn't moved.

Sighing wearily, she quit the unfinished chapter and turned off the switch. The screen went gray to match her mood. Some nights all the words fit together, her mind hummed, and the excitement built inside her as the story flowed. When that happened, the rejection slips, the hard work, the chronic self-doubt were all worth it.

But tonight the words hadn't come, and no amount of electronic wizardry could substitute for an original thought. She was preoccupied with the job tomorrow...and Michael's homework...and the car insurance bill.

The thought of her younger son set Kate to worrying. He hadn't come to her with a question in an hour. That probably meant he'd given up on his algebra and escaped between his headphones, a rock tape in his cassette player. Already, in late September, the struggle with school had begun, the old stresses and strains resurfacing.

Michael was a good kid—generous, bright, creative. But just beneath the surface he was unhappy and angry, both with her and with Kevin, his father, for their failed marriage. Evidence of this showed up in Michael's grades, his evasiveness with her, his ambivalence toward Kevin. Her ex-husband didn't have to face Michael's ambivalence on a daily basis the way she did. Kate felt the old bitterness stirring. Then it died away. It was impossible to remain bitter when she felt so much pity for the shell of a person that Kevin had become.

She turned that thought aside and glanced at her watch. Clark should be home from work by now. It was after nine.

Kate smiled. Clark, her older son, was the sort of child who lulls a parent into a false sense of competency. Industrious, even-tempered, the one who brought home the As. He was a freshman at the University of Texas and held down a part-time job as a checker at the nearby supermarket. He'd made peace with his father and visited him often. Kevin had helped Clark resuscitate his ancient Volkswagen just last week.

No...don't think about Kevin. Yet, Kate felt her thoughts circling. At least Kevin was no longer her responsibility. Not that he'd ever been. She'd learned that lesson the hard way.

For so long she'd had rescue fantasies—of saving their marriage, of saving Kevin, of saving some part of the man she'd met and fallen in love with at nineteen. But that man had disappeared into a haze of alcohol and it had been difficult to let go of the past and her illusions. For too long she'd bought into the guilt Kevin laid on her for his problems. Now she didn't.

In their fifteen years of marriage, Kevin had never been overtly abusive to her or the kids. But as the years wore on, his ability to love had shriveled away despite her unwillingness to admit it. Until there'd been no love left. At least not for her. Only blame for all the despair and emptiness that had engulfed him.

He'd walked out the door one day, searching for an elusive peace, leaving the three of them behind. Now, alone in his apartment with a well-stocked liquor cabinet and his private demons to keep him company, perhaps still blaming Kate for the wreckage of his life, Kevin was quietly and rather desperately drinking himself to death.

They'd negotiated a standing truce. Kevin had done the decent thing when they'd divorced and given her the house. She had an adequate support check for the boys. She was thankful he was functional enough to hold down his job as a chemist.

It was better than the job she had, Kate remembered, feeling discouraged. Sometimes she wondered if maybe she should have gone back to teaching, making the bill collectors happy. But all she'd wanted was work that paid enough to put bread on the table. She'd committed herself to writing, however quixotic a goal that might be. It was the personal dream she nurtured.

Sometimes the thought of that dream was the only thing keeping her sane. That and the lesson life had taught her—to take each day as it came.

There'd been a time when she wasn't sure she could face the coming days. But she had faced them, and she was stronger for it. The days had turned into months and into years. If now those years seemed to be trudging by with a certain monotony, at least she knew how to cope.

Except, where was she going to find the money for the car insurance?

And how was she ever going to extinguish, finally, the old yearnings that came upon her when she was depressed or vulnerable? The longing for a certain touch, a private satiny caress that told her she was special and desired as a woman.

The heat of remembered passion would spread through Kate, frustrating her, a craving that wouldn't die. Her need for Kevin was truly dead. He'd successfully killed it. But her need for someone who cared, especially for her, was harder to extinguish.

The hunger for someone who understood her as well as lusted for her couldn't be satisfied, and Kate hated such treacherous feelings. They only tore at her peace and control.

She wasn't lonely. There were family and friends who loved her. Yet sometimes she felt so very alone and incomplete.

Kate sighed wearily, rubbing at her eyes, then caught herself up short.

"Self-pity is an ancient curse that makes an old confusion worse," she said aloud, paraphrasing Theodore Roethke, one of her favorite poets. Then she silently reminded herself that in the other room there was a kid who was flunking algebra. She'd do well to tend her *X*s and *Y*s and keep her cool with Michael for once.

And repress the dangerous yearnings.

NEXT MORNING in her car, searching out the address of her new workplace Kate, felt cheerier. For once the Austin, Texas, traffic had cooperated and made the drive a pleasant one. Last night's algebra had gone well enough and Michael finally seemed to be grasping concepts. When Kate had gone to bed at eleven-thirty, she hadn't been haunted by one of her old anxiety dreams.

She often had them before she started a new job, but they'd lessened lately. And just now, the ride to school had been amiable. She and Michael had little enough time together to just be friends. She treasured those moments.

Kate sniffed the fresh air. The hint of fall must be part of her brightened outlook, she decided. After the blast-oven heat of a Texas summer, the sixty-eight-degree morning felt invigorating. She could even view this new assignment with ironic amusement. Working as a secretary to a minister was no stranger than some of the other positions she'd held. She'd been placed everywhere from a travel agency to a one-man solar-heating firm, the headquarters of which were the company president's back bedroom.

Connie, her mother, who prayed for Kate on a daily basis, would no doubt be pleased by this particular job. Connie, bless her dear devout soul, never despaired of rescuing her children from their varying degrees of agnosticism.

Smiling, Kate turned the car onto a tree-covered street. Following the agency's directions she drove a block and a half, and there, just where it was supposed to be, was Emmanuel Episcopal Church.

The group of buildings before her nestled peacefully under spreading pecan trees. The sanctuary was small and conventional looking in the style of modern church architecture. It lacked, fortunately, some of the excesses of tradition. The roof was tall, slanted and vaguely gothic. The windows were patterned with panes of roughly cut stained glass. A plain cross hung above the large double oaken doors. And what appeared to be offices and Sunday school rooms were in a long, low, one-story building that stood nearby. The structures were built of native stone and wood, creating a scene both restful and unpretentious. And the location was only fifteen minutes from her home in west Austin. Very convenient.

Kate sat in the car for a moment, gathering her wits. She was wearing her standard first-day work uniform—a simple gray suit, rose blouse, black pumps and a clutch purse. She aimed for a conservative effect rather than a severe one. There was no need to intimidate other staff. After a week she'd have a better feel for the office's unwritten dress code.

Her only adornments were silver stud earrings, a businesslike watch, and a pleasantly competent smile, designed to calm the jitters of a new employer and to hide her own.

As Kate opened her car door, she glanced at her instructions one last time. She was to report to a Father Sheffield. Calling the clergyman by his title might prove to be her first difficulty.

She checked her watch. Three minutes to nine. Climbing from the car, she walked resolutely toward the one-story building. As she approached, a door opened and a pleasant man in his early fifties greeted her with a smile. Maybe addressing this man as Father wouldn't be so difficult. He had an open, friendly face, framed by graying temples. He looked a little like Spencer Tracy as the priest in *Boys' Town*. She warmed to his pastoral air.

He spoke. "You must be Kate Hennessey. Our temporary secretary."

"Yes. And you're Father Sheffield. It's nice to meet you." Kate held out her hand.

"Well, no," he explained apologetically as they shook. "I'm Dan Crighton, the senior warden. Father Sheffield asked me to be here this morning because he had an emergency at the hospital. One of our parishioners was in an accident."

"I'm sorry. Is it bad?"

"Charles doesn't think so. But he felt he needed to be there."

"Of course. It was kind of you to meet me."

"It was the least I could do."

She heard a further hint of apology. Uh-oh. That was usually a sign the job was rough. Was it the work or the rector? She'd know soon enough.

Dan showed her into a reception area that was pleasant, if cramped and cluttered. At least, beside her desk was a window looking out on the children's playground. She wondered if there was a church-run preschool. The daily accompaniment of four-year-olds would be fun.

She glanced at the typewriter. Good. It was electric and correcting, not like some of the antiques she'd encountered. Then she spotted a genuine high-tech antique, in the form of an ancient copying machine nearby.

Tough times ahead. The copier looked finicky and unreliable. Apparently a new one was too extravagant for the budget.

Remember, Kate placated herself, the assignment should be quiet and peaceful.

"Ah," Dan met her eyes as he paused. "I . . . don't know how much the agency told you about what happened to the last girl they sent out."

"Only that perhaps she was a little young."

"Yes. Well, she got a shock the third day she was here. We have a clothing bazaar," he explained mysteriously, "where we sell or give away used clothing."

Kate nodded her understanding.

"We're not that far from downtown, and transients drop in here from time to time. We also provide a food kitchen on a regular basis."

Kate applauded such charitable efforts, as she wondered where this was leading.

"Anyway...one of the needier ones asked for a shirt and a pair of pants. He changed into them in front of the temporary, our music director, and three lady members of the clothing drive." Dan reddened slightly. "He wasn't wearing underwear."

"I see." *Quiet?* She revised her opinion. "Well, don't worry. I don't shock or scare easily."

He grinned. "I'm glad. Contrary to popular myth, parish secretaries do not lead sheltered lives."

This time Kate's smile was genuine. She liked this man and hoped she'd be working with him.

"I also want to warn you," he added in a resolute tone, "that this is a very hectic time of year. In October, we conduct the E.M.C." He caught himself. "The Every Member Census. It's our annual pledge drive. Then, of course, in November and December come the Thanksgiving and Christmas seasons and the beginning of the church calendar. Also very busy. Unfortunately, Phoebe, our regular secretary, had to quit just now. Her..." he cleared his throat, "her mother was taken ill, and Phoebe felt she should stay home with her."

During their busiest season?

There were undercurrents. Kate could feel them. But then every office had its share of undercurrents, petty feuds and jealousies. Kate had trained herself to ignore them.

"However," he went on, "Phoebe said to tell you to feel free to call her if you had any questions."

"Thank you. I appreciate that, and I hope to catch on to the routine quickly."

"I'm sure you will." His voice held obvious relief. She'd passed the first test.

"Things are more complicated this year since Charles, Father Sheffield, that is, is still learning the routine."

"Is he a new rector?" That was all she needed. An idealistic young minister, fresh from the sheltering arms of the local seminary.

"Charles is an exchange priest," Dan explained. "From London. The American Episcopal Church is affiliated with the C. of E., the Church of England," he elaborated, seeing her blank expression. "Our regular rector, Father Palmer, is spending a year in Father Sheffield's parish and Charles is spending a year here. He's been in Austin since June."

"That sounds interesting. How did he survive our summer?"

She and Dan shared understanding looks.

"Stoically. He can't wait for fall."

"Didn't you tell him this *was* fall?"

"Yes. But he doesn't believe me."

They laughed. Dan glanced at her quizzically. He was already beginning to wonder about her. Kate recognized the look. She didn't fit the profile of the standard temp. In two or three weeks the curiosity would intensify, and she'd have to explain herself.

Not everything. But enough to provide a reference point for her fellow workers. Kate was in no rush to hurry the process, so she smiled at Dan blandly.

He sensed the subtle withdrawal and became business-like again. "Anyway, we thought today I'd take you around. Show you the layout. Explain the kind of phone calls you'll be getting. I've made a list of the staff and the Vestry. We're a small parish, only a hundred and fifty families. You'll learn everybody's name soon enough. Charles has written out a weekly schedule for you so you'll know what the job entails. Thursday or Friday is soon enough to tackle the E.M.C."

"Sounds good." Kate was all business. She was ready to dig in.

For the next hour and a half they followed Dan's itinerary. At the end of that time, Kate's head felt stuffed with new information. But she was pleased. The job had variety and would wear well. Kate was just thankful Dan had a clear, orderly mind that formulated precise instructions. Oh, that Father Sheffield's would be the same!

Kate was an expert on bosses—good, bad and indifferent. Unfortunately, she had her doubts about this one. Especially after she'd had a glimpse at his study. It resembled a file room run amuck. Stacks of papers and books covered every surface, grouped with no apparent rhyme or reason. With her luck, Father Sheffield would be the professorial type, absent-minded and scattered.

She could picture him already: pushing fifty, with a vague air, a genteel paunch, a bosomy wife and grandkids. She was surprised she hadn't seen snapshots of his family scattered around his office, but then they were probably playing hide-and-seek amongst the debris.

"Hullo, Dan. I'm glad to see you're still here. Is this our rescuing angel?"

Even as Dan looked up smiling at the speaker, the voice Kate heard resonated in her mind. Firm, warm and exquisitely English, it didn't begin to match the mental image she'd just conjured up. Kate felt a warning prickle before she even turned around. When she did, she felt as if she'd been poleaxed.

Because standing before her, in a clerical collar, in case there was any lingering doubt, was Father Sheffield. He was undoubtedly one of the sexiest, most attractive males she'd ever met. Of course, that was only if you liked tall, lean, blond-haired men with beautiful smiles, intense blue eyes and gorgeous noses!

Peter O'Toole. That's who he reminded her of. In *Lawrence of Arabia*. Thoughts of kindly, silver-haired Spencer Tracy vanished.

"Mrs. Hennessey, I'm Father Sheffield." He held out his hand and she shook it briefly, hoping frantically that her shaken composure didn't show.

Charles was certainly studying her, in a kindly, unobtrusive way. He liked what he saw. The woman before him was tall, trim and brunette. A young looking thirty-five. She knew how to dress. No jangling bracelets like the formidable Phoebe. No makeup to speak of either. He liked the look of her face. It reflected strength, maturity and an unflappable manner. Certainly she was an improvement over the last temp, who'd shown signs of hysteria from the beginning. The blank look he'd seen just a moment ago was probably first-day nerves. He set out to put Mrs. Hennessey at ease.

"I'm sorry I couldn't be here to meet you, but I know Dan's deputized well."

"Yes, he's been a great help. And he explained about the emergency at the hospital. I hope it wasn't too serious."

Nice voice, Charles thought. Low and a little husky. She seemed self-assured. Another plus. "As it turned out, no. Actually, this is part of my ordinary schedule. I make hospital rounds in the morning. It's usually ten by the time I arrive here, so at least your day begins in peace and quiet." He gave Kate a friendly smile.

Her heart thudded wildly. Her answering smile felt a little weak. "Is that a threat for what the rest of the day has in store?"

He laughed. She was quick. He liked that, too. "Not so much a threat as a warning. Has Dan told you why our last temporary left? I asked him to break the news to you before you heard it elsewhere."

"Yes. And I assured him I don't shock or frighten easily."

"Good. Two admirable qualities in an assistant. Dan—" he held out his hand "—thanks for showing Mrs. Hennessey around. I know I've kept you from work."

"I had time coming to me, it was no problem." They shook hands and Dan turned to leave.

Panic swept over Kate.

No, don't go! Don't leave me with this man... Get hold of yourself, Hennessey. This man is your boss.

A hint of Kate's inner turmoil must have shown, because, as Dan said his goodbyes, he felt compelled to add, "Don't worry...I'm sure you'll get the hang of everything." He grinned. "Despite Charles's crack about a rescuing angel, we don't expect miracles. This is, after all, the Episcopal Church. I'll see you later in the week."

And like a betraying Judas, Dan turned her over for trial.

Charles broke the awkward silence. "Did I receive any phone calls? I'm expecting one from Lieutenant Eccles of the Austin Police Department."

Kate's brows rose involuntarily.

Charles saw and explained. "I work with him on a pilot project, handling family disturbance calls."

"I see," Kate said, not seeing at all. "No, Lieutenant Eccles didn't call, but a Mrs. Bingley and a Millicent did, F-Father Sheffield. I wrote down the messages." She reached for the telephone notepad, smiling brightly to cover her stammer. "Is Millicent your wife?" Immediately, Kate felt her color rising. What had possessed her to ask such a question?

Charles chuckled, unaware of her embarrassment. "No, although if I were forty years older, I'd marry her in a minute. Millicent Greer is the oldest member of the parish, a fact she takes very seriously. You'll meet her before the meeting of The Daughters of the King on the second Wednesday of the month. She'll make it a point to introduce herself. Has Dan given you a list of the organizations that use our facilities? He did give you a schedule, didn't he?"

"Yes." She shuffled through the papers Dan had provided, awkwardly scattering them over the desk. Her struggle to assume a businesslike demeanor hadn't been entirely successful. Her kids always told her she had a poker face. Where was it when the stakes were high?

"Good." He sounded patient. "I have some typing I need completed. You'll find it in the tray with examples to guide you. I'll be in my office, if you need me."

Kate nodded dumbly. With an encouraging smile, Charles left her to go into the inner office, closing the door behind him.

And Kate sank down into the chair behind her desk, folded her arms and stared into space, shaking her head at her chaotic wayward thoughts.

She remembered the conversation with Lynn last night on the phone and laughed out loud before she could stop herself. She'd taken Lynn's search out of her friend's hands. Kate had found her "sex object." He was pushing forty, and he was a priest.

CHAPTER TWO

"PORK CHOPS AGAIN?" Clark sniffed the air fastidiously as he sauntered through the kitchen that evening. "B-o-or-ring! When are you going to use that cookbook I gave you for your birthday?"

Kate made a face at her older son. "That was no gift. It was a comment on my culinary skills. Why don't you take over the cooking *and* the cookbook? I saw an interesting recipe in the entrée section for salt codfish hash with tomatoes and garlic. That should be exciting enough."

Clark raised his hands in mock innocence. "Okay, okay, I was just asking. Pork chops are fine with me. You know I'll eat anything." He grinned infectiously, pleased with his own wit.

Kate grimaced and asked, "Have you seen Michael? Supper's almost ready."

Clark shrugged. "I guess he's in his room. The door's closed."

"Tell him to come to the table, please."

Michael was hiding out. His vanishing act, Kate called it. She wondered if something had happened at school today. Then sniffing the air as Clark had done, she rushed to rescue the forgotten pork chops.

Clark was right. Her meals were plain and only inadvertently exciting. As a cook she made an excellent typist. After today, she wasn't even sure of that.

To say the afternoon had been a disaster would be stretching a point. Kate had just felt like a disaster when she'd left at four.

She'd managed the work Charles Sheffield had provided, and the phone duties were a snap compared to the other switchboards she'd handled. But when her new boss was in the room, her competent facade cracked.

He was just so distractingly attractive. And sexy. And oblivious. Or was that a carefully built-up defense against swooning female parishioners? Either way, it only added to his appeal.

She hadn't been able to keep her mind on her typing. It kept creeping back to...Father Sheffield. He was over six feet. At five eight Kate had a built-in tape measure. And he had the lean frame and grace of an athlete. His sunburned skin and corn-colored hair also told her he'd spent time outdoors in the Texas sun.

His hands were almost her undoing. They were strong and sensitive looking, with long narrow fingers. The hands of an aesthete. Yet when he used them to explain the quirks of the copy machine, she'd noticed the rough calluses on his palms.

In midafternoon, Father Sheffield left for an hour and Kate recovered her poise. Then his unexpected return took her straight out of her chair. He couldn't have failed to notice the strange behavior. His deliberate kindness told her that.

Now as Kate set the table for dinner, she decided she had to get a grip on herself—or quit the assignment. Despite the blare of the evening newscast, a scorched meal and a lippy kid, she couldn't get her new boss off her mind. She had this inane desire to giggle like a lovesick adolescent as she tossed the dinner salad. And she was, after all, a sensible woman.

AT THAT MOMENT, Kate Hennessey, sensible woman, was the last thing on Charles's mind. As he rode through the early evening in the police patrol car beside Lieutenant Nolan Eccles, his thoughts were preoccupied with the wrenching drama at the address they'd just left in one of the poorest sections of East Austin.

The call had come in over the police radio as a family disturbance, the kind they'd been set up to handle. When Nolan and Charles had arrived, they'd found a group of distressed neighbors, milling around the dusty front yard, unwilling witnesses to the unfolding crisis. Four disheveled children crouched together on the stoop of a cramped five-room house, grimy with poverty.

The husband and wife were in the center of the crowd, shouting at each other in rage and despair. The neighbors told them she'd taken after him with a baseball bat and the fight had spilled out into the yard. Nobody knew why it had happened, but it had happened before.

"One of these days, someone's gonna get killed," the man from next door warned Nolan grimly.

This time, however, Charles and Nolan had arrived in time to defuse the fight and make strategic phone calls. A grandparent had come to take the children away. The couple had consented, reluctantly, to go to the mental health clinic for counseling, only after Nolan cautioned them he'd be following up on their agreement. And a sister from down the block had taken the wife over to her house, so that the couple could cool off separately.

Despite the successful intervention, Charles felt a sense of frustration, inadequacy, and the same fear the next-door neighbor had expressed.

Just before the wife left with her sister, Charles had asked if he could come again to visit. She'd given him a hard look and a wary "Okay." He couldn't blame her. Her life had

probably been filled with a succession of agency-type social workers who meant well, but who had neither the time
nor the resources to make a difference. Maybe one of the
church outreach programs could provide the personalized
help and nurturing these people needed. There had to be
some way he could steer the six lives away from their colli-
sion course with tragedy.

Reliving the scene, Charles rubbed a hand over his face.
Nolan glanced over at him. "I know. It's only a matter of
time before that family explodes like a bomb."

"There's so much to be done. A lifetime of pain and failure to overcome. I'm not sure of the best way to help."

"I thought you preachers had all the answers."

Charles smiled ruefully and shook his head. "Hardly. A
few of them perhaps—if you believe as I do. But concrete
solutions are harder to come by."

"You're not going to get theological on me?"

"I wouldn't think of it." Charles laughed.

A comfortable silence fell between the two men. Over the
last three months of working together, they'd come to share
a mutual respect and affection. Nolan Eccles, black and
raised in East Austin himself, had been skeptical that a
genteel English clergyman could comprehend the stresses
and strains of the families they'd be working with. Charles
had recognized that skepticism and had known when he
proposed the project that one of his jobs would be to prove
to the other man's satisfaction that he could be as tough and
pragmatic as the work demanded.

Charles had seen that same skepticism before, when he'd
initiated a similar project in the heart of London. Police
were the same the world over, Charles thought wryly. It
made no difference whether it was a British bobby or a
Texas cop. Poverty, too, was just the same in a London slum

or an Austin ghetto. And just as intractable to piecemeal intervention.

Charles stared out the window broodingly. Nolan glanced at his profile, but stayed silent, knowing that for his colleague this time of self-doubt inevitably followed the period of high tension.

Nolan had often wondered, once he'd seen Charles in action, if the man had any idea how much difference his intervention made in the tense domestic scenes. The fact that Charles came from a different world proved to be irrelevant, because he brought a compelling strength and understanding of people that crossed the barriers of culture and race.

Charisma, that's what Charles had. Nolan chuckled, knowing that Charles would have detested the description. But charisma didn't completely explain his success.

Charles radiated commitment and inner peace. Those in need turned to him instinctively. Nolan had found himself doing so on more than one occasion. It was an unnerving discovery for a man who considered himself tough and self-sufficient.

He glanced over again and saw Charles's mood was lightening.

"How's the inspector coming?" Nolan asked as he slowed down for a stoplight. "Is he learning the ways of American police work?"

Charles was ready for a diversion. "He's beginning to speak the lingo, after an initial period of culture shock. I've followed up on your suggestions about the type of case he should handle. There's already a spot of trouble, however. He finds one of the female suspects very appealing. American women are, you know. It must be their air of breezy self-assurance. They're one of your natural wonders."

Nolan chuckled. "I'll be sure and tell my wife you said that. So...the inspector's human. After reading your other five books, I was beginning to wonder."

"He's human all right. He's just overworked. And leery of anyone who'd fall in love with an image rather than the person behind it."

Nolan had a feeling he'd just found out something important about the man sitting next to him. "I know what you're getting at," he agreed. "I've had women come on to me just because of the badge. Does that happen to you? Because of that collar you wear?"

Charles smiled noncommittally, but Nolan had his answer.

"Are you ever tempted," he asked, "in spite of that collar?"

This time Charles laughed and answered honestly, "Certain women attract me, if that's what you're asking. I'm just as human as Inspector Jeffries. With no inclinations to become a monk. But this collar, as you put it, carries responsibilities. I can't take it lightly," he said as he glanced at his companion, "any more than you do that badge."

Nolan acknowledged the point and admitted candidly, "I'm just glad I'm married. It simplifies things."

"Yes."

"Your wife died, didn't she?"

"Seven years ago."

"Have you ever thought...?"

"Of becoming involved again? With the right woman, yes."

"Maybe you'll meet one of those sexy American ladies you were talking about."

"Maybe..." Charles said offhandedly. Then a curious thing happened. An image flitted through his mind of Kate Hennessey, standing in his study that afternoon waiting for instructions, her air of self-sufficiency fitting her like a glove. In spite of first-day nerves. It was interesting to speculate if that cool air was all there was to her. Charles was brought back to the moment by Nolan's return to an earlier topic.

"Is Jeffries going to make love with his suspect and complicate the plot?"

Charles shook his head maddeningly. "To find that out, you'll have to read the book."

"Don't I get any perks as technical consultant?"

Charles smiled blandly and didn't answer.

Nolan sighed. "I guess I should be content to know the author. When I found out you were William Fitzgerald—"

"When I swore you to secrecy, you mean..." Charles's forceful reminder was interrupted by the police radio.

"All units in the area. There's been an assault on 3rd Street and Rio Grande. Do you copy?"

Nolan reached for his hand set. "This is Lieutenant Eccles. We're at 3rd and I-35, proceeding to the scene."

They arrived within minutes, and Charles spotted the small circle of people on the sidewalk beside an entrance to an alley. The group parted for the law officer and the priest.

A Good Samaritan, kneeling beside the injured man, stood to greet the two and began to speak animatedly to Nolan. Charles took his place beside the victim, sprawled on the bloodstained sidewalk.

He was young, Charles noted, around thirty years old. And handsome, if his face hadn't been battered by his attackers. He was dressed in a business suit and tie and he'd probably just left his place of employment.

Charles listened to the explanation being offered by the witness as he assessed the damage. A gash in the man's head had bled profusely, possibly from a fall to the pavement. It was hard to tell from the soaked shirt the extent of other injuries.

"He was in that restaurant," the Good Samaritan said as he pointed. "Same as me. Left five minutes before I did. When I came out, two men had him up against this wall, beating him. When they saw me, they ran. Lucky I came out when I did. Otherwise, he might be dead by now."

But Charles didn't think so. By this time, he'd made a quick check for stab or gunshot wounds. There were none. Apparently fists had been the only weapons used.

The young man stirred in pain. Charles put a hand on his arm. "It's okay. An ambulance will be here shortly."

Charles's voice must have reached the victim, because his eyes flickered open and slowly focused on the concerned face leaning over him. He caught sight of the clerical collar, and the blank expression turned to one of panic. "Father...? Am I dying? Where am I?"

"You're not dying. That's not why I'm here. We're outside the restaurant, waiting for an ambulance." Tension seemed to ease out of the arm Charles touched as he spoke. Still, the man kept his eyes glued to Charles anxiously.

"Why are you here?"

"I was with the police officer who came."

"The police..." Fright washed over the bruised and bloodied features, followed by a spasm of pain.

"Shhh. Don't move. I know you're hurting, but help's on its way."

The man nodded slightly. His hand groped for Charles's, as though he drew strength from him.

Someone from the restaurant handed Charles a wet towel. He gently wiped away the grime and blood, then placed a cool compress over the gash in the victim's forehead.

A slow moan escaped the man's lips. "I think...they broke my ribs." His breathing was labored. "Father... you...won't leave me? I'm scared."

"I won't leave. Lie still. The paramedics are here. I'll ride with you to the hospital." The man nodded and Charles stepped back to make way for the medical team.

They conferred hurriedly as they examined the victim. "Head injury. Concussion. Ribs. Might have punctured a lung." After strapping on a stabilizing harness, they secured him to the stretcher and wheeled him to the waiting van.

"Father...are you still there?" The breathing was shallower, more labored. There was an edge of panic in the man's voice. The medics exchanged looks, met Charles's questioning one. The message was exchanged.

"I'm here," Charles spoke quietly. "Don't talk. I'm here beside you. Nolan," he called out, "I'll be at the hospital." And Charles climbed into the rear of the van.

"I'll meet you there," Nolan answered, "as soon as a backup comes to take statements."

And the Emergency Medical System vehicle sped through the downtown canyons of Austin, sirens blaring. Within minutes they'd pulled up to the emergency entrance of Brackenridge Hospital and the victim had been rushed into one of the trauma units.

Charles stepped back out of the way as the trauma team began to work with purposeful haste. But the victim held his hand tightly. His anxiety seemed to linger, and in an obscure way, Charles had become his talisman against the dark that crowded in around confused senses.

"Was he robbed?" one of the doctors asked brusquely. "See if you can find some identification."

Charles searched the suit that had been cut off and found a wallet. It contained a Texas driver's license and fifty dollars in cash. The license told him the man's name was Gregory Arnold. He leaned over the man and asked quietly, "Can you tell me your name?"

"Greg. Greg Arnold. My wife...someone needs to call my wife." His look beseeched Charles. "Will you? The number's 555-4098. Don't frighten her."

"I'll handle it. Greg, I'm not a Catholic priest. I'm Anglican. Do you want me to find a priest?"

"For last rites? A final confession?" Greg's face twisted. He laughed weakly, a laugh that was a gasp turning into a groan. "No...you'll do...unless..."

The doctor nearby heard the implied question. "He'll be okay, I think. Although we need X-rays to be sure. Someone gave him a good working over."

"Do you have any idea who that someone was? Did you get a good look at them?" The voice belonged to Nolan Eccles. He'd walked up quietly behind Charles and was studying Arnold keenly.

Greg's lashes flickered, his eyes avoided theirs. His lids closed and he turned his head away with a whisper. "No...I don't have any idea who did it. It hurts, Doc, my chest hurts."

"That's enough questioning for now," Nolan was warned on cue. "You can have him after we're through here. After he's rested. Although I don't think he'll be much good to you until tomorrow. You going to call his wife?"

"I am," Charles answered. He handed Greg's wallet to Nolan and went to find the phone, his mind racing with questions. The same questions he suspected were in Nolan's mind. Because he'd seen from the start the pervading tension that hovered in Greg Arnold's face. Tension that underlay the pain.

But no bewilderment. The kind you'd sense in an innocent victim after he'd been attacked randomly. From the looks of the billfold, robbery wasn't the intent. And just now when Nolan had asked Greg if he could identify his attackers, Charles had known, just as he was certain Nolan knew, that the man's denial had been a lie.

He put all his questions aside, concentrating instead on the coming phone call. Preparing his words carefully as he listened to the ring.

A woman's voice answered, "Hello?"

"Mrs. Arnold?"

"Yes...this is Jill Arnold." There was a slight pause. "Who are you? What do you want?" Charles sensed tension and immediate fear at the sound of a stranger's voice.

"My name's Charles Sheffield, Mrs. Arnold. Your husband's been in an accident. He's conscious and he's going to be okay. But he's at Brackenridge Hospital and he wanted me to call you."

Charles heard a small gasp. "An accident? What kind of an accident? Are you the police?"

"No, I'm a minister working with the police. Your husband was assaulted, Mrs. Arnold. But someone came along in time to scare away the attackers. At Greg's request, I rode with him to the hospital, and just now he asked me to call you. So you see, he's quite lucid."

"Assaulted? Oh! I...I was afraid this would happen. Oh, God...!"

"Mrs. Arnold, would you like someone to come for you? I can send over a police officer."

"No, no! Don't do that." Charles heard fear again, a struggle for control. "I'll manage something."

"I don't think you should drive yourself, Mrs. Arnold. I know Lieutenant Eccles would be glad to come."

"I...I'll get a ride. It'll be quicker. I'll be there in fifteen minutes. Just as soon as I get my neighbor to babysit the children. Tell Greg I'm coming. Are you...are you sure he's okay?"

"Yes. And I'll be here waiting when you arrive, to fill you in." Charles's calm assurance seemed to do its job. He heard the small click of the receiver.

Fifteen minutes later, he spotted a young woman climbing out of a car and hurrying toward the entrance. She was young, pretty and obviously distressed. He took a chance and walked toward her.

"Mrs. Arnold?"

"Yes..." Jill Arnold took in Charles's appearance and panicked. "Wha—who are you? Where is Greg? Is there something they didn't tell me?"

Charles sorted out her questions. "I'm Charles Sheffield, the minister who called you. Greg's in X-ray. We should be hearing news on him soon. But I assure you he was still conscious when they left with him. Why don't we sit down in the waiting room so I can tell you what I know? Lieutenant Eccles will be here to ask you questions shortly, to find out if you have any idea why this might have happened."

Charles had done what he intended.

He'd warned Mrs. Arnold of what was coming.

Nolan would be upset. But there were times when Nolan's and Charles's duties diverged. This woman's composure was as fragile as glass, and Charles couldn't allow her to face the lieutenant's questioning unprepared.

Jill's eyes widened as she realized the implications of Charles's words. There was a tense silence. "Yes..." she finally said, stumbling, "I...I need to sit down. This is quite a shock for me."

"I'm sure it is." Charles helped her to a chair in one corner where they could talk in peace.

He asked an important question. "Mrs. Arnold, is Greg Roman Catholic? I thought perhaps he might be, because of the way he asked me to stay with him. At any rate, Father Benjamin's on duty at the hospital today. It would be easy enough to page him."

Jill's smile was bleak. "Greg was raised Catholic. But he's not much of anything now. The children and I attend mass regularly. Greg won't go." She stared into Charles's face curiously. "He asked you to stay with him? I'm surprised." As she continued to search his face, her expression changed subtly. "No, I'm not. Thank you for being here. I couldn't face this alone."

"Is there anyone I can call for *you*? Your parish priest, perhaps?"

"No. No one. Greg wouldn't see him, and I'm not sure I could face him, either."

Jill had slipped once more, her words all too revealing, just as they'd been on the phone. Charles was glad Nolan wasn't there to hear the conversation.

"Would you like me to go over what I know?" he asked.

"Yes, please."

Charles had outlined the bare facts when Eccles found them.

"Is this Mrs. Arnold?" Nolan asked sharply as he studied the seated woman.

"Yes. I was explaining what's happened up to now."

"For which I'm sure she's grateful."

Charles heard the ironic note in the lieutenant's voice. He followed Nolan's stare and saw that the short time he and Jill Arnold had spent together had steadied her. The young woman wore an air of tight control.

"I wonder if you can tell us why this might have happened to your husband?" Nolan asked her gently enough.

"I have no idea," Jill came back immediately. "Was he robbed?"

Charles realized it was the first time she'd even asked.

"No," Nolan answered carefully. "His billfold and papers were intact."

This time she responded to Nolan's implied query with a helpless shrug. He'd hit a dead end.

"Do you have any idea why Mr. Arnold might have been at that restaurant?" he pressed her. "Does he eat there often? Why hadn't he come home for supper?"

"Greg sometimes catches a quick bite in town when he's working late. He's with a public relations firm. I have no idea why he was at that particular restaurant."

"I see. And he'd called you to let you know he was working late?"

"Yes."

Nolan's eyes narrowed at the unadorned answers. He knew as well as Charles she was hiding something. And he'd detected her subterfuge without nearly as many clues as Charles already had in his possession.

Nolan was just about to follow another line of questioning when the attending physician appeared.

"Lieutenant Eccles, is this Mrs. Arnold?" Nolan nodded briefly as Jill got to her feet.

"Greg—where is he? Can I see him now?" she inquired frantically.

"Yes, he's asking for you. You can come with me up to his room."

"His room? How badly is he hurt?"

"He's suffered a mild concussion and lacerations and bruises on his face. They look worse than they really are. His internal organs are also bruised, but nothing that won't heal. The only serious damage is three broken ribs. One punctured his lung, and we'll have to keep a close watch on him for two or three days. We sedated him, lieutenant, because of the pain, so I don't think he'll be much use to you. Shall we go, Mrs. Arnold?''

"Yes." She started to follow the doctor, then looked to Charles.

"Do you want me to go with you?" Charles asked, sensing her need.

"Yes." She bit back the word, and substituted others. "Perhaps Greg would like to see you, to thank you for all you've done."

"I'll be glad to come." Charles put his hand under her elbow in a gesture of support, and she leaned into it gratefully as they followed the doctor.

"We'll all go," Nolan spoke smoothly as he caught up with them. "I'd like to see Greg to get an idea of when he can make a statement."

Charles felt the muscles in Jill's arm twitch. She glanced anxiously at him. He answered her look with a bracing smile as the three of them followed their guide to the sixth floor and Greg's room. Only the physician was oblivious to the undercurrents.

He gave his patient a brisk bedside greeting.

Greg's answer was a cautious grimace emerging from a swollen face complete with two black eyes. But his look of pain had faded as a result of the injection he'd been given, and he was hovering on the edge of sleep.

Yet his eyes searched for something or someone until he found her. "Jill...honey...you're here." One of his hands reached out to her. "I'm sorry...this is all my fault..."

Jill hurried to the bedside and clasped his hand with both of hers. "I'm here, Greg. I'm staying with you. Just lie still and let the medication work. Lieutenant Eccles from the police department is here with me, darling." There was silence as her warning hung in the air. "He wants a statement. But the doctor's told him you needed rest, and that's just what you're going to have." She sounded determined. "Father Sheffield's here, too, sweetheart. Do you remember him?"

Greg's look flickered warily over Nolan and came to rest on Charles. He grinned faintly and spoke. "Yeah...I never got to thank you." He took a labored breath, and after a moment continued, "Let me tell you, when I came to and saw you were a priest, I thought I was a goner. You almost scared me to death."

Despite the pain and distorted features, Charles sensed charm in Arnold as well as good looks. And a skittery nervousness, regardless of the sedation.

"That's one reason I came in with you," Charles answered lightly. "It was the least I could do. Your wife's right, you need rest. Why don't I drop by in the morning on my regular rounds and see how you're progressing?"

Jill turned to him quickly. "Yes, we'd like that." She looked to Greg for confirmation.

Greg grinned lopsidedly. "Sure. Why not? Jill could use the company."

Charles reached inside his coat. "Here's where you can reach me if you need me between now and then." He spoke to Jill, handing her his card. "I mean that. Call me anytime."

"I will. And thanks for all you've done." Charles took the hand she offered him. It was cold as ice.

All this time, Nolan had been content to watch and wait by the door. Now, Jill Arnold turned to him, her eyes not quite meeting his. She nodded and murmured goodbye. It was the first time since they'd come to the room that she'd directly acknowledged his presence.

"I'll see you later, Mrs. Arnold." Nolan offered his own smooth farewell.

As soon as they reached the elevator, he turned to Charles. "They're hiding something."

"Yes."

The two men rode down in silence. As they got out, Nolan said, "I might have gotten it out of her, if you hadn't coached her first."

"I didn't coach her," Charles replied calmly. "You know me better than that. And you wouldn't have gotten a thing out of her except a crying bout if I hadn't spoken with her. Which is the last thing she needs right now."

"Hmph," was Nolan's grudging response. He walked toward the exit with Charles beside him. "That restaurant is known to the police," he informed Charles tersely. Charles raised his eyebrow but said nothing. "It's a place where you can make a quick bet. Football primarily, both college and the pros. I'm making a discreet check on Arnold. We'll know soon enough if he's into gambling. That should give us a better idea of what's going down."

"Aren't you forgetting something?" Charles asked, after a moment. "Greg Arnold was the victim. He's not on trial."

Nolan's expression registered Charles's point. But he countered forcefully, "You're forgetting something, too. There's a reason why Arnold was singled out for this assault. I have an idea what that reason was. The sooner I find out for sure, the safer he'll be."

Grim-faced and silent, the two men made their way back to the patrol car.

CHAPTER THREE

THE NEXT DAY Charles made good his promise to visit Greg. Though still in pain, the younger man proved as charming as Charles had intuited the night before. He was also quick on the uptake and evasive.

Greg's wife, Jill, provided a stark contrast to Greg. Her drawn mouth indicated the weariness of a night spent by her husband's bedside. And the tension that lay just beneath her brittle calm was almost palpable in the hospital room.

Charles was thoughtful as he drove back to Emmanuel around ten o'clock that morning. When he arrived, he filled Kate in on the Arnolds' situation and alerted her that one of them might call.

They didn't. But Nolan phoned later and reported that during police questioning, Greg had revealed nothing.

The rest of the day was busy but uneventful.

Kate, having prepared herself for Charles's effect on her, suffered only a mild internal tremor at his arrival, and was rather pleased when she left that afternoon having managed the day with no overt acts of foolishness. She decided that being infatuated with the oblivious Charles Sheffield added a certain spice to life.

She was even prepared for Lynn's unexpected visit that evening after supper.

"Hank's out of town and Emma's at kickball practice," Lynn explained breezily, referring to her husband and her ten-year-old daughter. "So I thought I'd throw on something and come over to find out how the new job was treating you.''

Since Lynn looked her usual dazzling self in a casual white outfit, the term ''throw on'' was ironic. Lynn never went anywhere without expertly applied makeup, impossibly long eyelashes and faintly glistening nails. Kate was sure Lynn would look stunning strapped on a stretcher being wheeled into major surgery.

The two women made an incongruous pair. But twelve years, childbirth, two divorces and one subsequent remarriage had cemented the friendship.

They both knew Lynn's purpose in coming. Lynn began, however, with a diversionary tactic. ''So, how were the first two days on the job?''

With a cryptic expression, Kate let the silence linger. She'd decided on tactics of her own.

''Kate? Your job? Has it gone smoothly? Do you think it'll work out?''

Now Kate went into her act, clasping her hands together and assuming a moonstruck expression. ''I think I'm in love.''

''What . . . ?''

Kate went on speaking, ignoring Lynn's bleated question. ''I am working for the most gorgeous specimen of manhood I've ever had the privilege to meet.''

''At a church?''

''Yes.''

Lynn drew a deep breath. ''You'd better start at the beginning.''

Kate got down to particulars. ''He's tall, blond and British.''

''But he's a priest!''

''An Episcopal priest. There's a big difference. They marry, you know.''

Lynn raised her eyebrows. "Is he? Married, that is? Or does he like women?"

"Keep it clean," Kate warned her. "He likes women all right, he's just blind to their snares."

Lynn's voice was stern. "Is this a joke?"

"Yes!" Kate leaned back in her chair, grinning broadly. "A joke on me. I've developed a crush. On my boss, no less. I saw the funny side of it today. I may start wearing horn-rimmed glasses and sensible shoes, and hide my love away under *L* in the files, and serve him faithfully forever, or for eight months, whichever comes first, never letting him know that his loyal, efficient, mousy secretary has been burning with desire for his gorgeous body from the moment she laid eyes on it."

"Mousy? You couldn't be mousy if you tried."

Kate cocked her head. "Don't you think so?"

"You're crazy. That's what I think. Or bluffing." Lynn leaned forward on her elbows and scrutinized Kate. "Does this gorgeous specimen of manhood show any interest in kind?"

"Don't be ridiculous." Kate waved a hand in dismissal. "I told you, he doesn't even know I'm alive. I take that back. He suspects I'm mildly neurotic, but the best of the lot. At least, I don't squeal at naked men."

Lynn's look was blank. "What did you say?"

Kate laughed. "It seems a transient wandered into the church offices and flashed a few of the ladies along with the girl I replaced. I think Father Sheffield's afraid that if I don't work out, the agency will give up on him. But I have to get a grip on myself. I'm having a hard time calling him 'Father.' And I still have a tendency to drool."

"Which you're doing now," Lynn commented dryly. She changed the subject. "Are you going out with us Friday night?"

Kate struck a pose. "I can't possibly think of another man. Charles Sheffield fills my thoughts."

"Very convenient."

"Can I help it if I've developed an undying passion? No, wait, I know what you're going to say..." Kate stopped Lynn before she could make one of her patented responses. A silence fell between them.

When Kate spoke next, she was candid. "Lynn, I know your motives are pure, even if your scheming isn't. And I love you for caring. I just don't want to go on a blind date, crush or no crush." She took a deep breath and continued. "But I'll tell you, I've never before been so attracted to a man as I am to Charles Sheffield. It's unnerving. The only reason I can see the humor is because he doesn't reciprocate."

"Have you thought maybe that's why the whole thing happened?" Lynn's remark was astute.

Kate made a face at her. "Don't try to analyze me."

"It's a thought."

Kate put on a pained expression. "I expected you to be happy for me. You're always saying I need romance in my life."

"A real romance. Not a fantasy."

"Is that what Charles is, a fantasy figure?" Kate asked thoughtfully. She came back down to earth. "Well, not to worry. Within a week, I'll find out he slurps his coffee, has warts and is 'holier than thou.' Then there I'll be, reduced to my usual mundane cares. Will that make you happy?"

Lynn leaned back and an inscrutable expression crossed her face. "I tell you what would make me happy. For this blond preacher man to crack that protective shell you've built around you." She grinned. "And you the original heathen. If he manages that trick, my faith in miracles will be confirmed."

KATE FOUND HERSELF remembering their conversation the next morning. Charles was far from sanctimonious, Kate had already decided. In fact, he seemed to be one of the least judgmental men she'd met. So far she hadn't discovered any warts.

Still, after three days of exposure to him, Charles hadn't managed to crack her shell. Only, little by little he was stripping her of her protective coloring.

The two of them had been wrestling with the printing of the coming Sunday's service. The copier had balked and now their hands were black with the fine powder it required.

Looking down at his smudged fingers, Charles smiled at her ruefully. "I've been meaning to ask, what's a nice girl like you doing in a place like this?"

His remark was unexpected, and Kate laughed spontaneously, the laughter animating her face. "A misspent life, no doubt." Kate shook her head sadly, "And nothing to show for it."

Charles saw the hint of a friendlier, relaxed Kate, and he liked the look of her. So he followed up lightly, "Not even fine memories?"

"Actually," Kate explained, "I've led a very staid existence."

He tutted softly. "Sins of omission. The least satisfying kind."

"And the least dangerous," she came back tartly. "If you want to know the truth, I've been too busy to get into trouble."

"Doing what?"

Her look expressed surprise. He noted that, too. "Oh," she hedged, "being a wife and mother. Bouncing around from career to career. I used to teach school, among other things."

"You're divorced, aren't you?"

"Yes."

"How old are your children? Boys or girls?"

"Fifteen and eighteen. I have two boys. That is, I think that's what they are. That or alien creatures from another planet who have taken over my house."

He grinned as if he understood and she found herself saying, "Since I don't speak the language of the male adolescent, I'm never sure. But then, they don't understand me very well either, so we're even."

Charles nodded gravely, as if he sympathized, and she tried to adopt a lighter tone, wondering how revealing her remark had been.

"Still, we manage," she ended, fighting a sudden urge to pour out her troubles. "Our worst fights come over the VCR. I could watch Fred Astaire and Ginger Rogers dance into the night. All they want to see is *Road Warriors* and *The Terminator*."

"You like old movies?" Charles looked pleased.

"The older the better."

He wiped his hands absently. "We share a weakness. The parsonage has a cassette recorder, and the first month I was here, I went mad in your video stores. You have such a selection to choose from."

"I call my video player an instrument of the devil. The first month we had it, I watched twenty movies. Have you ever seen *Wings*?"

Charles shook his head, enjoying the sound of her voice and the expressiveness of her attractive face as she discussed a favorite topic.

"It's the only silent to win the Best Picture Oscar. It was very moving. I cried at the end."

"I'm more a sucker for your American Westerns."

"Oh, you British, you romanticize the West. Has Texas proven to be everything you imagined?"

"Everything and more," he answered diplomatically. And then slipped back to their earlier conversation. "So tell me, why aren't you still teaching?"

It could get tricky working for Charles, Kate realized. It was part of his job to get people to open up to him. She saw that he did it well.

Should she answer? Why not? If they were going to be working together long, which Kate sincerely hoped they would, they might as well be friends. And friends shared themselves just as Charles and she were doing. Taking a deep breath, Kate plunged. "Six years ago, I did a foolish thing. I sat down to write 'the great American novel.'"

Charles showed complete surprise, and then his expression became one of satisfied comprehension. As though for the first time the depths he'd sensed in Kate made sense.

"And did you?" he asked.

"I tried. Oh my, I tried. But if you're asking if I succeeded? No. All I produced for my efforts were 450 pages of melodramatic drivel."

"But by that time it was too late."

She was surprised by his astuteness. "How did you know?"

"I know that writing is addictive."

"Very addictive. You must do a little."

"Some."

"Well, my output is increasing. Three novels so far. The great American disaster and two mysteries. That's where I decided to concentrate my efforts." She grimaced. "So far without success. No publishing house is beating a path to my door. My *mother* thinks I'm wonderful," she added brightly. "America's answer to Agatha Christie."

Charles laughed. This time when he looked at her there was genuine amusement in his face and a disconcerting imp of mischief as though he were privy to a joke.

"So, you're a writer. That makes things clearer."

"Oh? What do you mean by that?"

He turned so that they faced each other and he answered honestly, "You aren't what I expected, Ms Hennessey. Especially after the first girl the agency sent."

You're not what I expected either! But Kate wisely kept this observation to herself. Instead, she gazed back at him innocently.

Charles caught the laughter in her eyes. Eyes that were a clear green and widely set under well-defined eyebrows. His pulse jerked irregularly, and he suddenly realized how very attracted he was to Kate Hennessey. His physical awareness of her took him by surprise. He wondered if the awareness showed.

Filing the reaction away to mull over later, he smiled down at her pleasantly and asked, "May I call you Kate? Contrary to myth, we English aren't that formal. And I hope we'll be working together until I leave. That is, by the way, a fervent plea that you not desert us."

Kate bowed her head in modest assent, secretly thrilled with the request. "Certainly, call me Kate. And I'd like to stay. The hours are good for me. They allow me to chauffeur Michael, my younger son, back and forth to school."

"And please call me Charles," he went on smoothly. "I've noticed you have trouble saying 'Father Sheffield,' and it isn't necessary for you to do so."

For the first time in their conversation, Kate blushed. Was that all he'd noticed?

Yes. Kate was sure of it. Because when she ventured a covert look his way, she found an expression on his face as open and guileless as a lamb's.

THE NEXT TWO WEEKS went smoothly. Working with Charles was a pleasure, even if Kate did have to struggle to suppress her volatile emotions.

He hadn't, unfortunately for her peace of mind, revealed any major flaws. He didn't slurp his coffee, he had no annoying mannerisms, and he was proving himself to be a considerate, patient, intelligent boss. True, his office lay in chronic disarray. Kate couldn't have found anything in it if she'd tried. She'd learned, however, that there was a peculiar order to the mess, at least in Charles's mind. And she'd stopped being astonished when he managed to hunt down an elusive item.

Nor did he have any physical deficiencies for her to dwell on. He played tennis and handball regularly and climbed rocks for recreation. To Kate, who struggled through an aerobics class out of pure vanity, such pursuits showed a disgusting tendency toward perfection.

Her grudging bow to good health had been to quit smoking last year. She still craved the occasional cigarette. He'd probably never had the nasty habit.

But for all that, she couldn't work up an antagonism. Not when Charles looked at her with those clear blue eyes, and she felt as though she were drowning.

If anything, Kate was growing quietly and more surely besotted. And it was hard to keep thinking of him as a mere fantasy figure. His physical presence was too real. When he leaned over her to explain a project, his nearness was palpable. Their least contact with each other had the shock of electricity.

And he wasn't as oblivious to her presence as she'd thought. On more than one occasion, she discovered him studying her, an odd, disconcerting gleam in his eyes.

When she recognized the look, it was difficult to remain collected. Not to respond. On several levels. Most of them forbidden.

Kate was determined, however, not to give Charles reason to be wary. The job was going too well. She'd settled in nicely. And it was a relief to know she'd be at one assignment drawing a steady paycheck.

She'd also, unexpectedly, found herself enjoying the place. The ebb and flow of the church activities around her had a comforting bustle to them. She delighted in the sewing circle, the clothing drive, the Women's Altar Guild, and the church food kitchen.

As Dan had said, it was a small and friendly parish. She already knew many of the members' names and something about them. She'd had several chats with Phil, the half-time music director. And she'd been intrigued to learn that the female education director was working toward ordination as a priest.

Neither Jill nor Greg Arnold had phoned asking for Charles, which worried Charles.

Nor had the estimable Phoebe called Kate offering assistance, for which Kate was relieved. She'd yet to meet her predecessor. From hints that had been dropped by Phil and the others, she wasn't looking forward to the encounter.

She did meet the dowager Millicent, however, during the second week of October when the Daughters of the King convened.

Kate knew immediately who Millicent was when she appeared at the office door, wearing a flowered voile dress, a sun hat and sensible walking shoes below shapely, hose-covered ankles. Lavender cologne wafted about her faintly.

Millicent was a beauty, even in her late eighties. She had snow-white hair coiled into a braid around her head, and translucent skin artfully rouged along the cheekbones. Her light hazel eyes had a clarity that belied her age.

The tinge of blue around Millicent's lips and her look of fragility alarmed Kate, however. Millicent was walking slowly and deliberately, with the aid of a cane. Her breathing was hurried, and Kate hastened to settle her into a chair.

"Can't make that hill up to the church as well as I used to," the older woman admitted, out of breath.

"Shouldn't you have parked closer?" Kate asked in concern.

"Parked? I walked. My home's only two blocks away. The day I can't walk to Emmanuel is the day I die. And I promised Father Palmer I'd be here next July for his homecoming." Her voice was clear, young-sounding and a trifle tart, which explained why she'd fooled Kate over the phone that first day. Her tone was a startling contrast to her delicate appearance. This gentle-looking lady had a few sharp edges. She looked at Kate keenly. "Don't you dare tell Charles how I got here. I'm under orders to call when I need a ride."

"Well, I'm no snitch," Kate said with a smile. "But it sounds like I should add my orders to his."

"Like that, is it?"

Kate nodded solemnly.

The old lady grinned at her wickedly. "So, you're the temporary help. I guess you know who I am."

That was Kate's cue and she knew her lines, "You're Millicent Greer, Emmanuel's senior parishioner. I'm delighted to meet you."

Millicent gave a satisfied nod. "I've been wanting to meet you, too, young lady. Ever since I heard your voice on the phone."

"My voice?" Kate faltered.

"It's low and attractive. A good deal more inviting than Phoebe's, the woman you're filling in for."

Kate blushed at the unexpected compliment. Millicent examined her face, liking what she saw. "You're much better looking than Phoebe, too. Of course, she can give you fifteen years. Just how old are you?"

"I b-beg your pardon?" Kate managed to ask, feeling like Alice with the Red Queen.

"Don't blame you, Kate, dear. Never admit your age. Even when you're as old as I, the years don't matter. It's what's up here," she said, pointing to her head, "and in here," touching her breast, "that counts."

As she finished her pronouncement, Millicent tilted her head. "Yes, I expect you're an improvement on Phoebe all the way around. Charles must have sent up prayers to get you. He and Phoebe went round and round from the minute he arrived. Her 'sick mother'—my sainted aunt!" she exclaimed in a disconcerting tone of voice. It was all Kate could do to keep a straight face. "Phoebe just has her nose out of joint because Charles won't follow orders. That's why she quit when she did. It was spite, pure and simple.

"Phoebe thinks that because she helped found this parish, she should run it and she pretty near does. Led the first Rector around by the nose. Drove him to an early grave. Best thing Win Palmer did was to escape to England for a year. Let Dan and Charles handle her."

"I'm not sure..." Kate was uncomfortable and uncertain as to how to stem the tide of information.

"You think I'm gossiping, but I'm not. Don't believe in gossip." She grinned. "At least not much. But someone needs to warn you about Phoebe, and I guess I'm the one. Charles can't and Dan's too diplomatic."

Having spoken her piece, Millicent continued her study of Kate. "Nice eyes. They're green, aren't they?"

"Yes," Kate murmured.

"Nice hair, too. Natural looking, not lacquered. Stand up so I can take a look at you. I like a woman who has meat on her bones. Men do, too, for all those starving models."

At this point, Kate broke into helpless laughter, "You're outrageous, you know that? They should have warned me about *you*."

Millicent beamed with satisfaction. "Nice laugh, too. When you let yourself go." With lightning speed she changed topics, to one more dangerous than Kate's appearance.

"So. How do you like our British pastor? Is he good-looking or am I a saint? Have you seen him in his robes? He'll knock your socks off. That's why I make every service. If I were fifty years younger, I'd take up with him. Unfortunately, when I was that age, we weren't supposed to have fun."

Kate shook her head, smiling at Millicent's irreverence. There was no way she was going to wade into this conversation.

"Of course, the dear man needs to be married," Millicent commented judiciously. "He's been a widower too long. His wife died of cancer when she was thirty-two."

"Oh," Kate's smile faded. A chill ran through her. "How...how old was he?"

"Thirty-five. He's forty-two now."

So, Charles was a widower. He had a past.

Strange how up to now Kate had avoided facing that reality.

And it was a past tinged with tragedy. Knowing that made him more human to her in a tangible way. She wondered what kind of woman he'd loved and married, and how long it had taken him to recover from her death.

"She couldn't have any children either." Millicent seemed intent on sharing her cache of knowledge. "So he was left with nothing but memories."

"Not even fine memories?" Charles had asked her.

Millicent rambled on, missing the strange look Kate wore. "Charles would have made a good father. Better than most I know."

She changed the subject and caught Kate up short. "Has he been out on any police calls lately?"

"Yes. I mean, he and Lieutenant Eccles have met several times." Kate stopped herself from an indiscretion, realizing that Millicent was pumping her.

"Did he tell you what he does with Lieutenant Eccles?"

"He's talked to me a little about family crisis intervention."

Millicent shook her head in disapproval. "I say he's going to get himself shot one of these days. This is wild and woolly America, where the handguns outnumber the people. Charles should leave danger to the police. You warn him to be careful."

"Me?" Kate asked. "I don't think anything I say would carry any weight."

"Hmmph. Then what good are you?"

"Well," Kate smiled, on to Millicent's game. "I *can* type. And I don't talk back. Which probably suits Charles just fine."

Millicent looked at her slyly. "So...you call him Charles, do you?"

Kate blushed a bright red, exasperated with herself for lowering her guard. Millicent was no fool and saw a good deal more than was comfortable. Kate tried to retrieve the situation.

"Not being one of the congregation, 'Father' was hard to say."

"Especially when you don't think of him as a 'father figure.' That is the expression, isn't it? I can never get this modern jargon straight."

"I believe that's the correct expression," Kate murmured. "But I haven't needed a 'father figure' in some time."

"Are you married? I don't see a ring."

Kate decided Millicent would make a great interrogator. She knew just when to slip in a probe. No wonder she could recite Charles's history in detail.

Kate thought about dodging the question, but realized that was futile. By hook or by crook, Millicent was determined to add Kate's story to her collection.

"I'm divorced." Kate didn't elaborate. But Millicent was undeterred.

"How did we luck into such a bright girl as you, working for a temporary service?"

This time Kate was saved by the bell. Or rather by the mingled voices of the other women arriving. They gathered around the queenly Millicent like ladies of the court. She presented Kate to each of them and then led her retinue to the library where they met.

After the office emptied, Kate took a minute to recover. She felt like a punch-drunk fighter in the middle of a fight. She knew she had better prepare for the coming round after the meeting had ended.

Something made Kate glance up. Charles was standing at the door, studying her expression. It was hard to tell what he was thinking. But something in his face—plus the remembered conversation with Millicent—made Kate squirm uncomfortably.

Charles didn't speak. Only his brow rose questioningly. Kate decided the gesture was a device to make sinners confess.

"You should have prepared me for Millicent," Kate muttered. "She's a secret weapon."

"Ahhh, now I understand the befuddled look. I hadn't seen it before. You usually wear an air of supreme competence. I'm often intimidated." His tone belied his words.

"That's exactly as it should be," Kate came back smartly. "A good secretary knows how to keep her boss in his place."

LATER THAT WEEK on Friday afternoon, he reminded her of her remark.

"Being a good secretary, do you think you could keep me chained to my desk for an hour? I can't seem to find a surface, and somewhere I've misplaced a sermon I'd like you to type."

"Let me haul out my chain-the-boss-to-the-desk kit," Kate joked, "and I'll see what I can manage." She knew better than to ask him if he wanted to be disturbed. Charles made it a point to be available for calls or visitors.

"I'll be in there somewhere amongst the debris if anyone wants me." He gestured in the general direction of his office, echoing her thoughts. "Will you promise," he asked solemnly, "that if I ever call for help, you'll come running? It'll be a signal that I've finally been trapped."

Kate smiled. "Now I know why you spend so little time in your office. You've created a monster. I'd clean it for you if I knew where to start. Would you like me to volunteer for hazardous duty?"

Charles pondered the offer. "One of these days, I may take you up on that, when we're better acquainted."

Kate gazed at him, questioning.

He met her eyes. "You've heard of skeletons in the closet. Mine are in that room. I'm not sure I'm ready for you to learn them. You have me cowed enough already."

"It's all a bluff. At home, I'm totally disorganized."

"That comforts me. I was afraid you were perfect." The glint in his eyes distracted Kate.

She shook her head. "No chance of that."

He breathed an elaborate sigh of relief. "You've taken a great weight off my mind."

As Kate stared at him suspiciously, Charles squared his shoulders and marched resolutely into the study.

Moments later, Dan phoned and asked to speak to him. It was a short conversation and Charles immediately reappeared. "I have to leave. Dan wants to talk with me about tomorrow's meeting of the Vestry. I probably won't have returned by four, so just lock up when you go."

"But what about your sermon? I thought you needed me to type it."

"I'll take care of it later." Detecting Kate's concern, he added, "I'm not as helpless as I look. I can find my way around a typewriter. Besides, you have to pick up Michael."

He waved a pleasant goodbye and left Kate with solitude settling around her.

CHAPTER FOUR

THE OFFICE SEEMED suddenly empty without Charles. Kate had learned that Friday afternoons represented the lull before the weekend activities. The lull today had a lonely edge to it.

Phil had finished his daily organ practice, so the sound of glorious music could no longer be heard from the sanctuary across the yard. The other staff had left at noon. Only the cheerful squeals of the kindergarten children outside interrupted the silence. Somehow their faint laughter added to Kate's feeling of isolation.

For the first time since she'd taken this job, Kate felt at loose ends and restless. The pledge letters had been mailed out and Phoebe's unfinished work had been completed. Kate's only duty at the moment was to answer the telephone, take messages and wrestle with the realization that she wouldn't see Charles until Monday. She was irritated by her morose reaction.

It was just as well Charles had demurred at her offer to tackle his study. She wasn't sure she wanted to handle his papers, his personal things. He already intruded into her thoughts far more than was healthy. Her crush was getting out of hand. She'd do well to keep a safer distance.

Kate stood and walked around the office aimlessly, running her hands over the mild clutter. She'd give the reception area a good cleaning and reorganize the files. It would be sweet revenge on the infamous Phoebe, who, she'd discovered, employed a strange and peculiar filing system.

But instead of digging into the task, Kate went to stare out the window at the preschoolers playing. Watching them brought back memories. Her two boys had been that age once, not many years ago. Happily secure in their small world.

It had been a different world, a different life. Standing here now, Kate wasn't sure if she'd been a different woman then. A very young, naive woman as Kate remembered.

Was anything left of that naive young girl? Kate wasn't sure she could answer the troubling question. She felt lonely and anxious when she thought about the unpaid bills, Michael's upcoming report card, the manuscript she was struggling to finish.

The sound of a ringing telephone pierced her mood, and she reached for the receiver, eager for the diversion. When the caller turned out to be Lynn, it seemed the answer to a prayer. They hadn't checked in with each other for a while. Kate settled back comfortably in her chair as they chatted.

"I hated to call you at work."

"I'm glad you did. I was feeling sorry for myself. I need a stern lecture."

"How about having dinner with us at the house tonight, instead? The kids are invited."

"Anyone else coming to this impromptu dinner party?" Kate asked warily.

"No, I promise. This is just family."

"In that case, I accept, gratefully. I'm as sick of my cooking as the boys are."

There was a companionable silence, then Lynn said quietly, "I really liked him, Kate. Hank's friend. I think you'd have liked him, too."

Now that the evening had come and gone and Lynn seemed to have accepted defeat, Kate could be magnanimous. "I'm sure I would've. Maybe I'll get to meet him one day."

"How about next weekend?" Lynn suggested quickly. "We're giving a small party. I'll be hurt if you don't come. Hank's friend has already accepted an invitation."

Kate shook her head helplessly at Lynn's underhanded methods. Then she had an idea. She leaned back in her chair, her mood greatly improving. "I'd love to come to your party." Kate rocked the chair idly. "Maybe I'll ask Charles if he'd come with me. Would you mind if I furnished my own escort?"

Kate sensed Lynn's instant alertness. She could almost hear her friend's mind racing.

"I wouldn't mind at all," Lynn said, after a moment. "It'll give me a chance to look him over. So you call him Charles, do you? And you know him well enough to ask him out? What happened to the mousy secretary bit?"

"I've decided I'm not the mousy type. Instead, I think I'll try my hand at being a seductress." Kate kicked off one high heel and took time to admire a trim calf and ankle. "It's a new role for me," she admitted, "but I bet I could get the hang of it. I'm a bright girl."

From somewhere, a thought bubbled up in her, and she asked Lynn an all-important question. "Do you realize, Lynn, how many men I've never gone to bed with? Think about them. Concert pianists. Downhill skiers. Accountants. Tall, dark, handsome spies, foreign or domestic. Do you realize how staid and uneventful my life has been? How depressingly chaste?"

"That's just what I've been telling you," Lynn retorted. "So what are you going to do about it?"

Lynn's question spurred her on. "I've never made love with a minister for that matter. But here's my chance. Why shouldn't I take it?"

"Words, words, words."

Kate knew Lynn was baiting her. Still, she couldn't resist the next remark. "You say I'm all talk and no action. What if I decided to seduce Charles?" Kate dropped her voice down a register and lingered over the words, "And had a wild, *passionate* affair with him?"

Kate's husky tones dissolved into a giggle, and she had to catch her breath before adding, "I could give him to me as sort of a present. Christmas is coming. Why don't I wrap him up and put him under my tree? I deserve a reward for thirty-eight years of virtuous living. How does that sound to you?"

"It's an interesting proposition."

But the words weren't Lynn's, and they hadn't come over the telephone wires.

Stunned, Kate dropped the receiver and swiveled around in her chair. When she saw the speaker she jumped up jerkily, her knees threatening to give way beneath her.

Charles was standing not ten feet away.

There was obvious amusement in his face and something else. But Kate was in no condition to discern the fine points of his expression.

For the first time in her memory she was speechless. And rooted to where she stood. She wasn't sure she could have moved even if she had given in to the wild impulse to run and then keep running.

She certainly wasn't capable of retrieving the telephone receiver, and dimly she heard Lynn's voice squawking her name.

Charles diagnosed the situation and went to pick up the receiver himself. His action was the only one that could have spurred Kate to movement, but by the time she'd lunged for the phone, Charles had already begun an introduction.

"This is Charles Sheffield speaking."

Kate heard the loud cackle of Lynn's laughter from where she was standing. "And you're Lynn," he continued pleasantly. "A friend of Kate's, I gather."

Now Lynn's voice was an indistinct murmur. Charles listened attentively. From his occasional responses, Kate pieced together the conversation.

"A party. Yes, I heard Kate mention it. I'd love to come. Next Friday. Around eight. I look forward to meeting you." He placed the receiver back in its cradle and turned back to face Kate with an interested look. He was curious, Kate decided in a flash of temper, as to how she was going to maneuver out of this fine mess she'd got herself into.

Where was his supposed compassion? Why couldn't he say something that would erase the last few minutes? How much had he heard?

A million explanations were swimming around in Kate's mind. She couldn't organize them into speech. The words that did pop out of her mouth were startling.

"W-what did you say?"

He raised a brow as he obliged her question. "I said I'd love to come to Lynn's party and I looked forward to meeting her."

"No. Before that. Before—that is, after..."

The light dawned and a smile hovered. "Oh, I see. I said it was an interesting proposition. One of the most interesting I've had."

If it was possible, Kate reddened more deeply than before. Charles found himself studying her. Her expressive features registered both confusion and embarrassment. He wondered if she realized how young and vulnerable she looked, standing there, her eyes wide, her lips trembling slightly. Did she have any idea how desirable she was? He noted the increase in his pulse rate. This time it came as no surprise.

He should say something to ease Kate's embarrassment, but Charles was much too intrigued to see how she would handle the delicate contretemps.

Kate grinned weakly. "Lynn's an old friend." He nodded as if in understanding. The gesture failed to soothe her. "She thinks the world should congregate two by two. I'm a challenge to her." *No, no! That isn't the thing to say!* "We joke a lot." *Feeble, very feeble!*

Kate felt another spurt of anger and gave in to it, dangerously. "Damn you, Charles! What are you doing here? You told me not to expect you back!"

His expression was suspiciously meek. "Dan had an emergency at work, so we agreed to meet later."

"Why didn't you let me know you'd returned? I suppose you heard everything!"

The meek expression vanished. He had the audacity to grin and moved to prop his lean frame against her desk, placing him in entirely too close proximity. "Well, I'd certainly have hated to miss anything. But I decided somewhere around the 'wild, passionate affair' that since I might be called upon to play a role in it, I ought to be more than just an innocent bystander."

Kate tried to overcome her mortification in order to think. How could she have been so careless? So indiscreet.

As much as Kate hated to say the words, she forced them out of lips that had stiffened into a travesty of composure. "I'm sorry, of course, that you had to overhear that ridiculous conversation. I've enjoyed the work here very much, but in light of my foolishness, I'm sure you'd rather have someone else take over."

"Is that what it is, foolishness? Don't," he commanded softly. She wasn't sure what he meant until he clarified, "Don't run away and hide behind that guard of yours. It's intimidating, I admit. But it won't work. I've caught on to you." He smiled at her faintly. "You've blown your cover as you Yanks say."

Their eyes met. Kate read something in his that threw her into confusion. She looked away. She felt a frisson of forbidden excitement run down her spine and reacted to it with a tart comeback. "My 'guard,' as you put it, is an old and trusted friend. I wouldn't part with it."

"A staid and uneventful life. Wasn't that how you described it to Lynn? Sins of omission." He shook his head. "That was quite a list you made. I can understand the concert pianist better than the downhill skier." She blushed furiously. "But spies? A singularly duplicitous trade. Ah, well, I guess there's no accounting for tastes."

Riled, she spoke sarcastically. "Whereas a 'man of the cloth' comes prepackaged with honesty."

Charles shrugged. "I admit I couldn't give you any guarantees. But I hope there'd be honesty between us. I'm not sure you could be dishonest if you tried, Kate Hennessey. Don't try to be with me, now."

"I...I don't understand what you're saying," she hedged, trying to beat a retreat.

But he wouldn't allow it. "We were discussing a wild, passionate affair. I think we should explore the possibilities."

There was a stunned silence, before Kate reacted wildly.

"What did you say? No, wait! I heard it!" She put up her hands and literally backed away from him. "This has gone far enough. It was only a joke. I don't have room in my life for any—" she floundered for a moment "—wild, passionate anythings. It's manageable now, barely. My life, that is.

And I don't intend to have it cluttered with affairs, honest or otherwise."

"Lynn's right, you are all talk and no action."

Kate's mouth gaped open at his observation.

Charles grinned at her shocked expression. "You know, just because I'm a minister, doesn't mean I'm not a normal, healthy male."

"I'd noticed..." she muttered.

He went on smoothly, "With normal male urges."

"Well, you can just take your male urges and..."

He waited expectantly for her to continue, but words failed her again. Then, if matters weren't bad enough, her honesty tricked her into saying, "I admit, I'm attracted to you."

"And likewise," he assured her. "I've been gradually becoming aware of that fact. Just now, you called my attention to it."

"I? Called your attention...?"

"Yes. You have nice legs." He glanced down at them approvingly, noting that one foot was still bare. His eyes moved back up to meet hers. "Among other things."

Kate flushed beet red. And suddenly realized that not only did she feel like a fool, she felt like a woman. A desirable woman. It was an intoxicating emotion, one she hadn't felt in years. And she was fluttery with the unfamiliar, dangerous sensation.

"I...uh, I'm feeling ridiculous." She turned away from him awkwardly to stare blindly at the wall.

"On you, it's charming." His voice from behind her was infinitely tender. Its tone shook her to the core.

A fine job she was doing of extricating herself! And Charles was being no help at all.

She turned around to him, her control strung out, her voice flat with effort. "Look, the joke's over. You've had your fun."

Charles looked as if she'd struck him.

Still, his voice was quiet as he protested, "Kate, I'd never do that. I'd never make fun of you."

Kate found herself trembling. "I know. I'm sorry. I . . . I didn't mean it that way." Her voice was a whisper. It rose suspiciously, "But why did you have to spoil everything? I was enjoying a safe, pleasant adolescent fantasy. Perfectly harmless. It reminded me of the foolish girl I used to be. Why couldn't you let it be?"

"Because you're not an adolescent. And neither am I. And safe, pleasant fantasies aren't nearly as enjoyable as the real thing." Charles studied Kate closely. "Kate—you haven't lost the girl you were. She's still inside you. A little wiser perhaps."

"Is she?" Kate's tone was bleak. "Sometimes, I wonder . . ."

"Because you don't take care of Kate. She's been neglected. You spend all your time fretting and worrying about everyone else and being afraid."

"Afraid?" Kate's voice went up an octave. "Of what?"

"Of me, for one thing."

"Don't be ridiculous! How can I be afraid of you? I'd decided to seduce you."

"I remember. So, why don't you get on with it?"

"W-with what?"

"Seducing me."

There was a long silence while they stared at each other. Charles's challenge hung in the air, frightening Kate with all its implications. She tried to hold his gaze but failed. Finally, she turned away, unable to face him.

"I don't know how," she muttered, admitting the awful truth.

She sensed him move closer.

"What was that?" he prompted softly.

"I *said* I don't know how!"

"Yes, you do."

His comment forced her to turn around.

"Do I?" she asked, her expression owlish.

"You've already begun."

"I have?" There was a childlike bewilderment in her voice.

"I find your laugh very seductive. As well as your voice. But the first thing about you that intrigued me was your air of mystery."

"Air of mystery?" Kate croaked, feeling about as mysterious as a plate-glass window.

"Yes." His look was tender.

Kate knew he was teasing her. Before she'd realized it, she smiled in response.

"Those first few days," he explained solemnly, "you were cool and collected. Even prim."

"Oh, never that!" Kate countered.

He nodded his head, refusing to back down. "But *not* mousy. On the contrary. Your cool collectedness was like a severe business suit covering silken underwear. I knew it wasn't the real you."

"Silken underwear isn't the real me either!" Kate protested, thinking back to the sensible cotton bra and panties she'd put on that morning. She decided her skin was going to be tinted a permanent shade of red.

"Pity."

Kate gasped as he went on smoothly, "Fortunately, it didn't take long for me to glimpse the real you."

"It's all your fault," Kate grumbled. But Charles heard the undertone of humor.

"Oh?"

"You kept smiling at me with that blasted grin of yours. What was I supposed to do? You're too easy to talk to. You slip past my guard," she said, acknowledging his earlier re-mark. "And you don't have warts! It's not fair! Why do you have to be so damned attractive?"

Charles grinned and Kate couldn't keep herself from joining him.

"So..." he asked in a mild voice, as though they were carrying on a perfectly normal conversation, "what's your next move going to be?"

He'd lost her again. "I don't follow you."

"The next move in the seduction."

"Oh. Well," Kate tried to sound offhand, "I'll have to think about that. These things should be planned very carefully. I wouldn't want to make a tactical mistake."

"I could give you a few pointers."

"Could you?" Kate retorted, fighting a sinking feeling. "Have you been seduced before?"

"No." Charles's face was very placid as he assured her. "Never."

"But women have tried." Now why had she blurted that out?

"Not many. And before it was over, they found I wasn't worth the effort."

Sure they had!

But Kate was relieved. Charles had just given her a way out of their meaningless banter. "Well—in that case, I guess I'll have to reconsider." She waved her hand airily. "Being a novice and all, I wouldn't want to try my hand at too dif-ficult a project. I'd lose my self-confidence and be scarred for life." She gave him a bright smile, convinced she'd wrapped up matters neatly.

"It won't be," he assured her, resurrecting her confu-sion. "Difficult, that is. I think you'll find it very easy. Your self-confidence won't suffer a bit."

Kate's eyes narrowed. Folding her arms over her breasts, she decided to call his bluff. "Okay, wise guy. How do you propose I go about it? What about those pointers you mentioned?"

Charles looked thoughtful. Kate wasn't deceived. She felt hollow inside as she waited for him to speak.

"To begin with," he explained slowly, "you might be a little skittish. Unsure of yourself. That'll bring out those male urges. And of course, your vulnerability should show, despite your best efforts to hide it. That'll arouse my protective instincts."

He caught his breath, and said huskily, "Yes... look at me just that way, with your lashes sweeping down to conceal your awareness. When you do that, Kate, you're very desirable."

Kate stumbled backward against a crowded bookcase, threatening to topple it as she stuttered, "Yes. Well, I...I'll work on it. Those are enough pointers for today. I'm a slow learner. I wouldn't want to rush into anything and f-fall on my face."

She straightened her back resolutely, steadied the books and smiled tremulously. Hers was an unconsciously gallant pose, and Charles found it endearing.

"I told you not to worry about that. Trust me." He said the words gently. Their effect was unintended.

Because right before his eyes, the vulnerable Kate vanished. In the blink of an eye. Leaving a wall. A well-defended blank wall, where once there'd been a woman.

"Kate? What did I say? You're frightened. What happened?"

Kate didn't pretend she hadn't understood. The smile she gave him this time was a tight one.

"I've gone home, which is where all prudent girls should be. Out of mischief." She elaborately glanced at her watch.

"Yes, I do have to go. It's four o'clock. I'll be late for Michael."

She took a deep breath as if to summon up courage. "I don't suppose it would do any good to apologize again for my behavior."

"No." Charles's voice was implacable.

"I still think it would be better if you found someone else."

"To have a wild, passionate affair with?" he asked silkily.

"No," she snapped. "To be your secretary."

"You'll do just fine," he assured her, a wealth of meaning in his voice.

"Well, I can promise you, it won't happen again."

"What won't?"

Kate was feeling giddy again and fought the sensation. "Any indiscreet behavior."

She picked up her purse to leave, forcing herself to make a dignified exit. She'd have done better to beat a hasty retreat, because then she wouldn't have heard the words he uttered softly.

"If I have anything to say about it, there will be."

She swung around to face him, goaded beyond measure. "Charles!"

"Kate?"

"Mom?"

It was the second time in an hour a male voice had the power to strike Kate dumb. She turned around aghast to find her older son standing at the door staring at both of them with an odd look on his face.

"C-Clark? How did you find me?"

Clark's look grew even more peculiar. He walked forward slowly. "You wrote down this address when you gave me the phone number. Remember? I didn't have any trouble finding the place."

"Of course not. I didn't mean that. I was just wondering—" Kate cut short her own disjointed words. "Charl—Father Sheffield, I'd like you to meet my son, Clark. Clark, this is Father Sheffield."

"How do you do, sir?" Clark said politely, holding out his hand.

Charles shook it. "Fine and you?"

"Fine." An awkward silence fell. Kate wondered how she was going to break it.

Charles filled the breach. "Kate's told me about you. I've been hoping we'd meet."

"Oh?" Clark glanced at him warily and gave his mother a dirty look, suspecting her of the worst.

Kate assumed an innocent expression, searching frantically through her memory for an instance of maternal indiscretion, while at the same time cursing Charles silently. Why had he called her Kate? That would only make Clark suspicious.

Charles read the exchange between parent and child and salved Clark's injured pride. "Actually, I had a hidden motive for wanting to meet you, Clark. Kate mentioned you play handball. Do you use the university courts?"

Clark relaxed a little. "I do when there's one available and when I can scare up a match."

Charles nodded. "I have the same trouble. Father Palmer lent me the use of his membership in a racquetball club while I'm here, but I've had poor luck finding a handball opponent. Are you game?"

Since Clark yearned for the use of a club's facilities to indulge his athletic prowess, Charles had uttered the magic words. His look of suspicion vanished to be replaced by a revealing eagerness. "Sure, I'll take you on." He looked at Charles covertly, this time assessing the competition.

Charles noticed and grinned. "It'll be youth versus cunning. How does tomorrow morning sound?"

"Sounds great. I ought to warn you, sir. I came in third in the last intramural tournament I entered."

"I'll try to give you a good game," Charles promised, with a meek note in his voice.

Kate looked at him keenly. She had a feeling he'd give Clark more than that. But she didn't dwell on her speculations. Things were happening too fast.

"Clark?" she said abruptly. "Don't you have to work tomorrow?"

"Yeah, but not until one." He turned to Charles. "I could meet you at...say nine-thirty in the morning...if that suits you?"

"That suits me fine." Charles wrote down the name and address of the club on a slip of paper and handed it to Clark.

Kate saw Clark's eyes widen when he glanced down at the writing. The facility was probably a good one. Charles couldn't have devised a better way to initiate a friendship with her older son. Was this planned?

She studied Charles suspiciously before addressing her offspring. "What did you need to see me about, Clark?"

"I just wanted to let you know I wouldn't be home for supper. A bunch of us are going to grab a pizza then go listen to a reggae band."

"You could have called me to tell me that." Kate spoke more sharply than she'd intended, and Clark glanced at her again oddly, before his expression turned sheepish. "That's true. But I couldn't borrow twenty dollars from you over the phone. I don't get paid until Monday. How about it, dear old Mom?" He smiled at her winningly. "I'm a good risk."

"You're lucky I have twenty to lend you," Kate muttered as she delved into her purse. "You're also lucky I was still here."

"Yeah, I know. I was kind of expecting you to be gone by now." This time his expression was positively speculative, and it managed to include Charles.

Kate felt uneasy. Clark was a normally myopic eighteen-year-old, but he was no dunce. The charged atmosphere between Charles and her when Clark entered the room would have been spotted by even a casual observer.

Kate hid her emotions behind a determined briskness. "I was just leaving." She began to herd Clark out the door.

Charles ended the conversation pleasantly. "Goodbye, Clark. I'll see you tomorrow."

"Sure thing."

"And Kate." His eyes held hers. "I'll see you later."

"Sure thing," she muttered.

Somehow Charles suspected her reappearance at the church on Monday morning was anything but a surety. The weekend would be a restless one for Kate, he predicted.

As well as for himself. A physical workout with Clark would serve more than one purpose.

CHAPTER FIVE

"I'M SORRY to be late," Kate apologized when she arrived, fifteen minutes later at Michael's school. As he slid into the car beside her she explained her tardiness. "Clark came by the church to mooch twenty dollars and held me up."

She'd been distracted driving across town, the details of the incredible scene with Charles swirling around in her mind. Still, when she saw her son standing forlornly on the sidewalk of the semideserted school grounds, Kate's emotional antenna had immediately honed in on his distress signals.

Michael accepted her apology with a shrug. "That's okay. I had to turn in work after school." Slouching down in the seat, he stared at the road ahead, a set expression on his face.

"Looks like you had a rough day," she commented sympathetically.

Michael shrugged again, "Kind of..."

Kate struggled to penetrate his mood. "Well, relax. The weekend's here. If you don't have too much homework, maybe we'll plan something fun for tomorrow or the next day. Do you have a lot to do?" Kate asked and immediately sensed her error.

Michael's mouth tightened. "Mom, don't start on that already. Can't you get off my back for once?"

His defensiveness frustrated Kate, as did her own inopportune question. Hadn't she suspected he was already upset? It wouldn't help the situation for them to wrangle. Kate settled into what she hoped was an understanding silence.

After several moments, Michael turned to her apologetically. "Sorry about that. Just call me Mike, the attack dog."

"Michael, the attack dog," Kate corrected him straight-faced. "You know I hate the name Mike."

They grinned at each other, declaring a truce.

And Kate realized again how much she loved Michael's smile. It was slightly lopsided, completely honest and lit up his face. And his flashes of wit, self-deprecating and ironic, were sometimes astonishingly perceptive.

"For what it's worth," Kate offered in a conciliatory tone, "you can chew on me sometimes. That's what mothers are for. Just as long as you remember I *can* scar and I do bite back."

The silence between them was more relaxed this time, and when Michael spoke again, it was to make his own peace offering. "Maybe we can go somewhere tomorrow. Drive to Zilker Gardens or out to Bastrop State Park. You remember when the family used to do that—you and Dad and Clark and I?"

Kate's throat tightened at the wistful question. "Sure I remember. Those were good times, weren't they?" She paused, gathering her thoughts. "Michael...don't be afraid of the past. Or mistrust your memories because of everything that's happened. Do you know what I'm trying to say?"

"I guess I do," Michael mumbled. "Only I wish it didn't hurt sometimes to think about it."

"Yes—but isn't that true of all good memories? I mean," she began, trying to make a point, "you can never relive them, so there's always the sense of loss. But what if we didn't have good memories? That would mean all our todays would be sad ones. Besides—those memories are yours, like a private treasure. And there'll be many more, I promise."

"If you say so." Michael looked almost despondent. So much for her philosophizing.

"Hey, listen." Kate attempted to change the subject brightly. "Why wait till tomorrow? Let's splurge tonight. How does take-out fried chicken sound?"

"Gee, Mom, that's pretty extravagant. What about Clark? He hates fried chicken."

"Clark won't be home. It's just you and me, kid. Later, we'll go by the video store and check out a couple of movies, pop popcorn and make a gala evening of it."

There went her writing time, but Michael had brightened.

"Okay," he agreed. "As long as you don't burn the popcorn."

"I like charcoaled popcorn," Kate announced haughtily. "It's an original recipe."

"I guess that means I pick the movies." His was a threat and Kate knew it. "How about *Jaws* and *The Texas Chain Saw Massacre*?"

"Oh, no, you don't," Kate groaned. "We each get a pick. I want *Dark Victory* with Bette Davis."

"Is it in black and white?" Michael asked suspiciously, a child of the modern age.

"Oh, yes. A tragic love story. I always cry."

It was Michael's turn to groan. "Maybe we could compromise."

"Hitchcock?"

"And a Bond movie."

They sealed the bargain with a handshake just as Kate pulled into their drive.

When they went inside Kate sorted through the mail and found Michael's report card. Suddenly, she knew the reason for his earlier depression. He studied her as she read the grades.

Michael had failed algebra. He was also perilously close to flunking two other subjects. The sick sensation Kate felt in the pit of her stomach was an all-too-familiar feeling these days with her younger son.

What to do? She'd exhausted her repertoire—lectures, assistance, cajolery, disregard. She'd even ventured a few rather more original tactics. Nothing seemed to work.

Suddenly, Kate's tiredness went to the bone.

"Because you don't take care of Kate...she's been neglected...you spend all your time fretting and worrying about everyone else and being afraid..."

"Do you think I'm chicken?" Kate blurted out. "You know—scared all the time?"

Michael looked puzzled, trying to assimilate the question. But he was quick on the uptake, Kate gave him that.

After only a second, he answered with a question of his own. "About me, you mean? About how you are as a mother?"

"Oh, not just that. About everything. Do you think I'm anxious, tense? A worrywart?"

"Well, you're not exactly laid back, if that's what you mean." Michael's tone was wry.

It made her chuckle, albeit weakly. "I guess I'm not. Well, tonight I'll chill out. Is that how you say it? Although, it'll be a struggle."

"You can do it, Mom. I have faith in you."

"I have faith in you, too, Michael," Kate said quietly. "Even though I don't always show it. Somehow, we'll muddle through."

Their eyes met, and some of the tension left Michael's face.

"You know, we have to talk about this tomorrow." Kate waved the grade slip gently to match her even words.

Michael nodded glumly, but seemed resigned.

"And Monday, I'll call to set up a conference with your algebra teacher."

Again, her words were expected, and Michael shrugged, signaling his acceptance.

"And your dad needs to know. Maybe he can help. The three of us should sit down and talk about it."

This time Michael stiffened. Kate noticed, but let it pass.

"Tonight, however, we'll pig out on chicken, popcorn and mindless movies. Let's make like a tree and leaf."

Michael grimaced on cue at her terrible pun and went on to more important matters. "I want a three-piece dinner, corn on the cob, two biscuits, a large coke. And a pudding cup."

As they started out the door, he threw a companionable arm around Kate's shoulders and patted her affectionately. The small endearing gesture tightened her throat. Maybe she'd been wrong to put off the time of reckoning, but somehow Kate didn't think so.

For Kate, the entire weekend turned out to be like her conversation with Michael Friday evening—full of odd turns of emotion, yet tinged with a refreshing kind of honesty.

That first night, she and Michael indulged in a case of the sillies, all in the name of good, clean fun. Saturday was a different story. Nerve wracking described it accurately.

Not that the morning didn't have a lighter side, starting with breakfast. It was all Kate could do to act natural as she fried Clark's bacon and eggs prior to his handball engagement. When he returned two hours later, sweaty and red-faced, she attempted a casual interrogation, with little success. Kate could cheerfully have wrung the neck of her laconic offspring. The thought occurred to her that she'd raised a sadist.

Finally, Clark broke down and confessed. "He beat me, Mom, two matches to one. I'm not sure he didn't go easy on me." Clark swatted the air with his open palm. "I can learn a lot from him, he's given me pointers. We're playing again next Saturday." Clark's voice held admiration and respect. "It's hard to believe Charles is a preacher."

Charles?

"I don't think you should call him Charles, Clark. It shows a lack of respect."

"That's what he asked me to call him," Clark protested. "He said if I thought of him as Father Sheffield, it might affect my game. Take away my killer instinct. Actually," he admitted, "I use 'sir' most of the time."

Clark glanced at Kate slyly. The look was a rare one for her normally guileless son. "You know, Mom, he's pretty neat. You must like working for him."

An understatement.

Charles was making a clean sweep of the Hennessey family.

"He's excellent to work for," Kate replied tonelessly. "A patient, understanding employer."

She could be as laconic as Clark. Only for Kate that took effort. Clark smirked knowingly, but dropped the subject, leaving Kate feeling deeply grateful. Maybe she hadn't raised a sadist after all.

Charles wasn't mentioned again, but he was constantly in Kate's thoughts. Especially, later, after she talked with Kevin.

The bad-news phone call to the boys' father was the major hurdle she faced. It was becoming a ritual. In fact, Kate wondered if Michael didn't unconsciously set up situations that drew Kevin and her together, uniting them in their concern for him.

When her ex-husband came by Saturday evening, Kate was shocked by his appearance. The lines in Kevin's face were deep. He was thinner and he'd aged. As they talked, Kate sensed his store of emotional strength had diminished.

Then Kate realized she'd conjured up Charles's image as a comparison. The stark contrast between the two men left her feeling unnerved.

But the discussion went well enough, Kevin agreeing to work with Michael two nights a week on his assignments. Kate could see Michael was ambivalent about the arrangements. He didn't like to visit his father's apartment, but Kate didn't know what she could do about that.

On Sunday evening Kate sat at her desk, reading over the scene she was creating.

Rebecca stared down at Randolph wildly. He groaned, began to stir, and the throbbing in Rebecca's head intensified with panic. She'd had no idea killing someone would take so much effort! Or be so messy!

What a klutz...

What if Randolph came to and lunged for her?

Rebecca glanced frantically around for yet another weapon, but none presented itself.

And then the germ of an idea formed in her mind, calming it with purpose. If she could just manage to carry out the plan. Rebecca's dainty features sharpened into a feral expression. She squatted down to catch hold of Randolph's twitching hands. And slowly but surely she began to drag the body toward the door, leaving a trail of red in her wake.

Hooray! Rebecca was finally getting the hang of it.

Kate leaned back, mildly pleased with her efforts. The writing session had gone strangely today. Usually she could block out extraneous matters when she was working. In fact, the writing was a kind of escape. That hadn't happened this time. She'd had bursts of creativity, followed by flights of thoughts. She was remembering Friday, the events of yesterday. She was trying to avoid facing tomorrow.

In some ways, Kate decided, the last two days had been typical ones in the life of the Hennessey family. She'd played her accustomed roles—harried housekeeper, indifferent cook, single mother, sometime author.

And yet, this weekend had been different. Because *she* was different, no longer merely the sum of the same old parts.

She felt a continual sense of breathless desire because a man had said he desired her. When she looked in the mirror, she discovered a woman with a wide-eyed air of surprise. That woman was unfamiliar and intriguing, because a man had told her how intrigued he was.

Kate's life was no longer defined by the same well-trodden boundaries. She had unknown territory within her to explore if only she weren't so scared.

She *was* scared and she knew it and had almost decided to call in sick, directing the agency to send a replacement.

"Trust me..."

Charles's words had thrown up a wall between them when he'd spoken them Friday afternoon. Now, curiously, their echo in her mind kept Kate from going straight into hiding.

Instead, she felt a kind of fluttering acceptance of what the next day might bring, if she could just get through their initial meeting.

CHARLES MADE the meeting easy. He greeted her with a friendly nod and two hours' worth of correspondence. They slipped into a discussion of the upcoming week's activities, almost as if the conversation on Friday had never happened.

Kate wasn't sure how to react. Did she detect a prick of disappointment within herself at Charles's casual manner? What on earth had she expected?

She looked up from the Order of Service they were arranging.

Charles smiled at her, a deep, warm smile, holding subtle invitation.

And Kate's heart thumped noisily against her ribs.

Now was she afraid? Oh, no, it wasn't fear that had set her to trembling, but rather anticipation.

Kate smiled back at him, tentatively, and felt from his look as if she'd given him a rare gift, one, she realized intuitively, he would handle with care.

She was amazed that the rest of the day proved so normal. The clock on her desk showed three-thirty before the unusual happened. The parish office had a female visitor.

"Is Father Sheffield here?" the woman asked. "I know I don't have an appointment, but he gave me this card and said I could come by to see him anytime. I'm Jill Arnold."

Jill was thin. Dark circles smudged her eyes. Her face was white with strain, and she looked as if she were holding herself together with the greatest effort.

Kate remembered the story Charles had told her about the Arnolds. She knew he'd been worried about them both.

"Have a seat, Mrs. Arnold." Kate gestured toward the couch invitingly. "You don't need an appointment. I'll tell Father Sheffield you're here."

Even as Kate spoke, Charles came out of his study. "Jill, I thought I heard your voice. How are Greg and the children doing?"

"That...that's what I'd hoped to see you about," Jill began bravely.

She swayed, her body started to crumple and Kate moved instinctively to catch her before she fell to the floor.

Charles dove to take Jill's extra weight and together they maneuvered her onto the couch.

"Get some water," Charles instructed Kate, "and a wet towel, please."

Kate brought them back hurriedly.

Charles placed the compress to Jill's head and her eyes opened.

"What happened?"

"You fainted," Charles answered. Jill tried to struggle up. "Don't do that just yet," he cautioned her.

Jill's look wandered to Kate. She asked dazedly, "Who are you?"

"I'm Kate Hennessey, Father Sheffield's secretary."

"It...it's nice to meet you. I'm sorry about this." Jill's polite words were touching.

"Don't apologize. You've been under stress. Father Sheffield told me your husband was in the hospital." Jill's eyes flickered with pain, and Kate suggested, "Why don't you have a sip of water before you try to talk?"

She handed the glass to Jill who did as she was instructed. Color seeped back into Jill's face. After a moment, she struggled to a sitting position, her distress evident. "I'm so embarrassed. I-I've never fainted like this before."

"Did you eat lunch?" Charles asked perceptively.

"No. I—"

"Breakfast?"

Jill shook her head. "I wasn't hungry. I haven't been. I've been so worried." Jill's voice cracked, and Kate's heart went out to her.

"I had to talk to someone." Jill looked beseechingly at Charles. "You were so kind to us. I thought..."

Charles responded immediately, "You can talk to me."

"It's just that...I don't know where to turn. All the money's gone. And Greg owes so much to those people. They'll kill him if he doesn't pay them!"

Tears were beginning to fall down Jill's cheeks. "And he's lost his job. His manager found out he was gambling... and..."

Jill burst into sobs.

Kate reacted immediately, gathering the woman into her arms and patting her shoulder. Jill slumped against her in an unconscious gesture of trust.

It was five minutes before the tears abated. Jill must have had a wealth of them inside, aching to come out. Kate's and Charles's kindness had broken the dam of her control.

But finally, there were only wrenching shudders that grew softer and softer as Jill became calmer.

She was the first of the trio to speak. "This has been quite a day. Not only do I faint, I also break down. I haven't cried in a long time. I guess I was afraid to."

"Sometimes," Kate said from long experience, "crying's the only thing that helps. Clears away the cobwebs."

Jill shrugged limply. "It doesn't solve anything."

"But it helps to put you in the proper frame of mind to try to find solutions."

"It also helps make the talking easier," Charles added. "Are you ready to do that yet?"

"I don't know. But I have to. To somebody. The card with your name on it seemed to be the answer. I can't go to my family. They're furious with Greg already. Our friends are, too—what friends we have left. They can't understand that with Greg, the gambling is a compulsion. He's tried to quit before."

Kate stood, feeling like an intruder. "I'll leave now so you and Father Sheffield can have some privacy."

But when Jill looked at her entreatingly, Kate hesitated. "Unless," Kate said uncertainly, "you'd like me to stay?"

Kate had discovered during the past few weeks that as Charles's secretary she became an extension of him in people's eyes. She'd already been privy to several heartfelt confidences. But Kate wasn't sure how Charles felt about her becoming involved with the Arnolds' troubles.

"I...I would like you to stay," Jill ventured. "But I don't want to bother you."

"It's no bother," Kate said firmly. "I'll be glad to listen."

Charles looked at her approvingly.

Jill smiled timidly. "I appreciate what you're doing. I miss having a woman to confide in. My mother...we used to be able to talk...but not now. And my best friend moved out of town last year. I've been so alone." Which helped explain her earlier trust.

"You're not alone." Kate sat back down beside Jill. "We're here to help in any way we can."

Jill took a deep breath. "I'm not sure where to start."

"Why don't I help you?" Charles offered. "You said Greg gambles."

Jill looked wary. "I have a feeling you already suspected that."

Charles nodded, honestly. "It's what Lieutenant Eccles suspected, too. The Copper Dragon restaurant, where he was assaulted, is known to police as a place to make illegal bets."

"Lieutenant Eccles," Jill said bitterly, "doesn't care what happens to Greg. He just wants to find out what Greg knows. He doesn't care that Greg could get killed."

"Is that why Greg was beaten up?" Charles asked. "Because he threatened to go to the police?"

Jill laughed bitterly. "No. I wish I could say it was for such a noble cause. Greg was worked over because he owes over a hundred thousand dollars in gambling debts. And he doesn't have the money to cancel them. Those goons were reminding him what happens to people who don't pay up."

A hundred thousand dollars! Kate tried to keep the shock from registering on her face.

Charles asked the question Kate was afraid to ask. "Does Greg have any way of getting the money?"

"No." Jill's voice was bleak. "We've borrowed all we can from his parents, his brothers. Our friends. We owe over fifty thousand in loans. The last time, Greg went to my father, and Dad gave him twenty thousand dollars from his retirement account. Greg swore then he'd never gamble again."

She paused. "But he can't help himself. It's a sickness. I knew he'd started betting on the football pools. Greg thinks he can hide it from me, but I can always tell. He gets higher than a kite when he's winning. Then when he loses he gets horribly depressed. He always loses sooner or later."

"This time, when Greg couldn't make up the difference, he went to his manager in desperation. He thought he could charm him into a loan. Greg's very charming. Very bright. He can talk himself out of almost any jam. But not this time. His boss said no and fired him. Now all we have to live on is my teaching salary, and a good part of that goes to child care. There's no way we can possibly pay off the hundred thousand with what I make. We don't even have enough food..." Jill stopped herself, and blinked rapidly, the tears threatening.

Kate fished out a tissue for her from the box on the desk. Jill took it gratefully and dabbed at her eyes.

"Go on," Charles prompted her.

"I can't. Greg would kill me."

"Go on with what you were saying." Charles sounded authoritative.

Jill's head bowed. "Greg found out where I'd hidden the grocery money. He was going to make one last bet. This time, he knew he'd backed a winner. As usual, he was wrong." Jill stopped speaking, her bitterness filling the tense silence.

"This isn't the way it was supposed to be," she said, after a few moments. "When I met Greg in college, I-thought he was wonderful. Tall, blond, good-looking, intelligent and ambitious, a big man on campus. He swept me off my feet. Oh, I knew he gambled on the side. But I thought it was a phase like beer busts and reckless driving. He told me that after we were married he'd cut all that out. We were going to make it big together, become the all-American family. Now—look at us! We're behind on our rent, our house was repossessed. Greg doesn't have a job. He owes a fortune. And there's no food to put on the table for our two children."

Jill's voice cracked with despair. "I love Greg, truly I do. But I hate him, too, for what he's done to us. What he's doing to himself! I just don't think I can take it anymore! My parents want me to leave him. I think maybe they're right." Jill shuddered and rubbed her face with trembling hands.

Kate sat quietly. Charles remained silent for a moment also, allowing the words to settle so that he wouldn't have to fight through them to reach the distraught woman. Then he asked, practically, "That's not something you have to decide right now, is it, Jill? That's something you, Greg, and I can talk about later. Let's take first things first. We have a food kitchen here at Emmanuel. Why don't we put together a sack or two of groceries?"

"Oh," Jill held out a protesting palm. "I don't think I could. I'm not ready to accept charity. If Greg found out he'd be furious. He's a proud man. He'd accuse me of asking for a handout."

Anger welled in Kate. It was all she could do not to articulate her rage.

Fortunately, Charles knew what to say. "Jill, charity's not a dirty word. It's simply people caring for other people, helping them when they need help. We all need help sooner or later. Sometimes, the bravest thing we can do is to accept that help. As for Greg—he's ill, you've said so yourself. Gambling can be an addiction, just like alcohol or drugs. Because he's in the grip of that addiction, he can't be trusted emotionally. You mustn't live your life dependent on his feelings. You have to be the responsible one, for yourself and the children. The responsible move is to get the help the four of you need to keep going. You were right to come here."

"I've been wanting to since before Greg was discharged from the hospital. You were so kind to us then, even though you must have noticed something was wrong.

"Besides, Greg seemed to like you. His taste in companions doesn't usually run to clergymen. But he could tell you weren't judgmental. And I could see you weren't easily fooled. I guess I hoped, maybe, that you could sit down with Greg and get him to open up. He's so defensive. I can't talk to him anymore. I spend half my time angry and the other half frightened—of what he might do to himself."

For the first time, Jill asked Charles directly, "Will you see him, if I can get him to come in?"

"Yes. Or I could go to him."

"Greg may not be willing to discuss all that's happened."

"He may not. And I can't make him, Jill, if that's the case. But he needs to know you can't go on the same way. And that with or without him...you're going to get assistance."

"Yes. That's the other thing I need. Support. When he's found out what I've done."

"Is he home now?"

Jill shook her head. "He hasn't been home all day. I've called several times from school. He might not come home till late tonight. I'm never sure where he's been.

"I'm a fourth-grade teacher," Jill explained to Kate. "This morning, I asked the daycare center if I could pick Lance and Dane, our twins, up late. That's when I knew I'd decided to see you."

"You know, Jill. Emmanuel has a daycare program with subsidized rates. You could enroll the twins here inexpensively."

Jill looked grateful. "I'd like that."

"Good," Charles said. "We'll arrange it before we sack the groceries."

"You've helped me so much already. I don't know how to thank you."

Kate settled one of her hands over Jill's comfortingly. "You can do that by letting us continue to help."

CHAPTER SIX

KATE'S WORDS elicited another one of Charles's approving looks. The two of them had formed a mutual admiration society, Kate decided whimsically, because she was impressed with the concrete way he went about addressing Jill's needs.

As he took Jill out to enroll the twins, Kate went to the kitchen and began sacking staples. When Charles and Jill reappeared, the three of them loaded groceries into the car.

Jill was still too fragile to face Greg alone, so Kate had devised a plan. She'd ride with Jill to the daycare center, and they'd meet Charles at the couple's apartment, just on the off chance that Greg was home. Later, Charles could drop Kate back at her car.

Kate called Clark and asked him to pick up Michael. Thirty minutes later, Charles appeared at the Arnolds' front door, laden with the perishables the family still needed. He'd taken the opportunity Kate had presented him with to swing by the supermarket. Kate suspected that the money for the perishables had come out of Charles's own pocket, but she knew better than to ask.

There was no evidence of Greg. He hadn't left a note saying where he'd gone, what he was doing or when he'd be back. After a light conversation while they put groceries away and a cup of coffee with Jill, Kate and Charles left.

The ride back to the church was quiet. They'd pulled into Emmanuel's parking lot before Charles spoke. "I want to thank you for today. Jill needed you as much as she did me."

He dropped his hand over hers on the seat between them and laced their fingers together. The simple gesture of friendship evoked a complicated reaction. Kate knew it was just that, a friendly gesture, and she was pleased to have been of help. But it was the first time Charles had deliberately touched her, and the firm male contact jerked at her pulse, making her tremble slightly. To cover up the response Kate talked.

"I didn't mind. She's young and lonely. I remember a little of what it means to be that alone. And I was luckier than she. I had understanding family and friends for support."

"During the divorce, you mean?" Their hands were still entwined. He must have felt her trembling. She could have slipped her hand away, opened the car door and said goodbye. She didn't.

Instead, she took a deep breath. "Yes. And before."

Darkness was settling around them. The street light nearby had just flickered on and cast shadows into the car. Charles's features were dimly outlined, just as hers were hard to read. Somehow, that made what she had to say easier.

"My ex-husband is an alcoholic, although he's never admitted he has a problem. As hard as life is for Jill now, it'll be harder if Greg refuses to seek help. You will try to help him, won't you? For Jill and the children's sake?"

"I'll do as much as Greg allows."

"Kevin, my ex-husband, has never accepted treatment."

Charles's thumb stroked hers as though he were offering comfort. She realized how her words must have sounded. "I'm reconciled to that, of course. I'd come to terms with it before the divorce. I'm not still wondering what I could have done differently. But it hurts because of Clark and Michael. I know Michael's struggling with his father's drinking. I guess that's why I feel empathy for Jill. Life'll have more hard knocks for her and the kids."

"Life has hard knocks for everyone."

"I know. The trouble is, we usually don't see them coming."

"Sometimes, that's better. I knew for two years that my wife, Sarah, was dying of cancer. Two years can be an instant and an eternity when you're facing suffering and death."

Kate swallowed hard and uttered inadequate words. "I'm sorry. You must have loved her very much."

"I did. She was a good, kind woman. Before it was over, she'd found peace within herself and helped me find it. I grieved for her. Just as you grieved over the death of your marriage. Are you through grieving, Kate?"

"Yes…yes, I am. The marriage died a slow death. I held on stubbornly. But by the time of the divorce, I was prepared." Except life wasn't that simple. There was still a ghost on the periphery of her children's lives. She was frightened at what the future might hold for them.

"How badly are you scarred, Kate?" His quiet voice reached out to her in the darkness.

"Life scars everyone, Charles." Kate's voice shook a little. "It's the nature of the beast. I had to accept at the end that I'd become an alcoholic's wife. Overprotecting Kevin, playing the family peacemaker. I wasn't happy with the role I'd assumed. But I swore the breakup of the marriage wouldn't leave me bitter. I wanted to grow from what had happened and not be consumed by regret. I hope I've managed that."

"You have. You're like Sarah. There's no bitterness in your makeup, but the scars are there. You find it very hard to trust people. To trust me. To trust yourself."

In a reflex motion, Kate jerked her hand away. The other one moved to the door handle. Charles reached out and caught her wrist loosely. Kate couldn't break away. She couldn't look at him, either.

"Life has lessons to teach us," she said through stiff lips. "That's what the hard knocks are for. Our job is to learn them."

"Is fear one of those lessons?"

"Caution."

"And mistrust?"

"Charles, please..."

"Kate, don't run." His voice was very quiet, yet it had the power to arrest her movement. After a moment, she shook her head wordlessly and let go of the door handle.

Charles knew he'd won a small battle. He prepared for the next one. "Please understand. I know trust isn't a commodity to be bought and sold by the highest bidder. Yours is very precious to me. I don't expect you to offer it as you would a smile. I'm just asking you to stay, to let me into your life. Don't draw mistrust around you like a protective cloak. It won't protect you, Kate, you'll suffocate inside."

Kate heard the sound of harsh breathing, only to realize it was her own. She felt as though she was suffocating now. She was confused and torn and far too aware of Charles's nearness.

"Kate, look at me. You wouldn't have a smile handy? Right now I could use one."

Kate turned to him and smiled tremulously.

He leaned back and dropped her wrist, breaking the current between them. She relaxed slightly.

"Have dinner with me tonight," he suggested lightly. Kate tensed again.

"I can't. Michael and Clark are probably home by now, wondering what's happened to me. And wondering where their supper is."

"We'll include them. How do they like Mexican food? It's one of the local cuisines I've developed a passion for."

"No." Her response sounded starker than she'd intended. "I mean...I don't think it would be a good idea just yet."

"Clark likes me, you know."

"He's awestruck. Any forty-year-old who can whip Clark at handball has earned his amazed admiration."

Charles chuckled. "I like him, too. You've done a nice job."

"Clark's one of those kids who makes it look easy." There was a small silence.

Charles renewed his dinner request. "It's my way of repaying you for your help with Jill. That's something the boys can understand."

But that isn't the way they'll take it, Kate thought. Not when they already sensed the atmosphere that surrounded the two adults.

"I don't think so."

"Is it Michael?"

She didn't answer.

Charles sighed. "He'll have to meet me one of these days. I don't plan on going away."

Not for seven months. The thought set off an ache deep inside Kate.

She shook her head vaguely. "I'd rather wait."

"Until Friday then."

Kate glanced at him, surprised.

"Don't you remember?" Charles asked smoothly. "We have a date for Lynn's party."

"Oh, I—"

"It was your idea. Lynn expects me to escort you." He leaned toward her, trying to decipher her expression. Knowing already that she was hesitant. He reached out and touched her chin, captured it lightly with his fingers and turned her face so that she had to look at him. "Don't run."

Kate's lids fluttered shut. His fingers tightened. Her lashes flew up and the intensity she saw in his eyes made her feel weak and giddy. She wanted to run. Straight into his arms.

Instead, she murmured, "No, I won't. Until Friday then."

Suddenly, afraid of the urges that were threatening to overpower her, she fumbled for the door latch and slipped out of the car, muttering a goodbye.

"And show up for work tomorrow, too." The sound of Charles's teasing words followed her as she walked to her car. "I'm beginning to think the office can't function without you."

FRIDAY CAME amidst a haze of anxious anticipation, mingled with guilt. Though, for heaven's sake, Kate reflected, she hadn't done anything to feel guilty about! Except she hadn't told the boys about her date. Though, for heaven's sake, what was there to tell them?

"I'm being picked up by a man tonight. We're going to a party."

Hmmm.

She'd have to find a better way to announce the momentous occasion.

Kate stirred the spaghetti sauce that evening and discovered it was sticking to the bottom of the pan. The pasta boiling away on the next burner still had a crunchy texture.

She sighed, impatient with supper, with herself and with her ludicrous, self-imposed dilemma.

Clark sat at the table working on one of his innumerable projects. Clark always had to be creating something, repairing something, or tearing something apart. Otherwise, he was bored.

Michael, more easily entertained, was stretched out on the floor of the living room watching a *Mash* rerun.

Kate didn't want to blurt out her news twice. And as nervous as she was, she needed ample time in which to dress.

"Clark, clear the table, please. Michael," she called out, "supper's ready." She'd exaggerated about the meal but still, her purpose was accomplished. Michael ambled in moments later looking expectant. She tested the spaghetti. It still had a crunch.

"I'm going out tonight in an hour. Lynn's giving a party."

"We don't have to go, do we?" Michael asked.

"No. In fact, you weren't invited."

"That's cool," Clark said. "I'm going to a movie. Me and Gene."

"Gene and I."

"Oh . . . you're going too?" This was standard repartee. Kate looked over at Michael. "You have any plans?"

"Me and Jimmy," he said, stealing a glance at his mother, "were thinking of throwing the Frisbee down at the park. Later we'll come back and play games on the computer."

She couldn't show favoritism. "Jimmy and I."

"Gosh, Mom, how can you go to a movie, a party and down to the park all at the same time? That's pretty clever."

She'd raised a couple of clowns. "I'm a very clever mother, hadn't you noticed?" Pouring the steaming pasta into the colander in the sink to be rinsed, she tried to inform them of her date in the same tone. "I'm so clever I finagled a ride to Lynn's party."

"Who with?" Not that Michael was really interested.

"Charles—that is, Father Sheffield, is coming by. He was invited, and I agreed to show him the way to Lynn's house." This was surely one of her more clever lines. Kate smiled at Michael brightly. "If you're back from the park, you can meet him. He's very nice, as Clark can tell you."

She studied her sons covertly. Michael looked curious. Teasing speculation was written all over Clark's face.

"Yeah, he's nice," Clark drawled. "He's also single. Come on, Mom, don't try to kid a kidder. You've got a real live date with him." He punched his brother in the side. "Mom's got a *date*. And wait till you see him." He grinned at Kate. "I'm proud of you, Mom. There's life in the old girl yet." He burst into raucous laughter.

"I beg your pardon." Kate's chin was high. "I'm not old. You're not funny. And this isn't a date. Not exactly." She tried to gauge her younger son's reaction. Michael's face had gone immobile. Suddenly, she couldn't cope with burgeoning teenage censure.

"You go on down to the park, Michael. There's no need to meet Charles. It's not important." She started out of the room. "But eat your supper first. I have to bathe and dress." Kate had decided to forgo the spaghetti. She was so nervous she couldn't eat a bite.

"Hey, Mom," Clark called after her. "Do a little something extra to yourself." He waved at her elaborately. "Get dolled up. We don't wanna scare the man away."

She pointed a finger at her son. "*You* will pay." And then she proceeded on wobbly legs to the bathroom.

Get dolled up. Easier said than done.

But later, when Kate inspected herself nervously in the floor-length mirror in her bedroom, she could say she'd given it her best effort. The dress she wore was five years old, but still looked new. After all, it hadn't gotten much wear in the past five years. And the lines were classic.

It had long narrow sleeves, a high neck, a fitted waist and a full skirt that brushed against her legs sensuously. The material had been its selling point—a rich rose-patterned silk. The color flattered her brunette complexion and was striking enough that she needed no adornment, only teardrop rhinestone earrings, which cast out a rainbow of light.

She hadn't needed blusher, either. There was already too much hectic color in her cheeks. Kate pressed a hand to still the butterflies in her stomach. She'd been right when she told Lynn she wasn't ready for mating behavior. This frantic state of mind was worse than she'd experienced when she'd gone to her high school prom with the boy voted "most likely to succeed." She'd had a crush on him for months, and she couldn't believe her luck when he'd asked *her* to the event of the season.

Her luck had turned dismal, Kate recalled. She'd spilled punch on her escort's dinner jacket, ripped the hem on her formal while dancing the frug, and—what was his name, anyway?—hadn't even tried to feel her up when they'd parked outside her house at the end of the evening. Not that he could have found her in amongst the waist cincher, petticoats and yards of tulle ruffles, anyway. What's-his-name had never asked her out again. Her life had been blighted. She'd felt like a discarded woman at sixteen.

Kate expected that this evening held similar joys in store.

There was a knock at her bedroom door. Clark's face slipped around it gleefully.

"Mother, dear. The Reverend Sheffield, your escort, is waiting."

Kate gave him a dirty look, sent her reflection one last despairing glance, grabbed her evening purse and followed Clark down the hallway to the living room.

The atmosphere was strained when she arrived. Michael sat on the couch sullenly, the television blaring. She suspected that Charles had attempted a brief conversation. She also suspected he'd failed.

Then the peripheral concerns faded. Her attention was riveted on Charles. In a well-cut suit and tie, he looked rather magnificent. Up to now, she'd only seen him in his clerical collar, coat and slacks. Tonight, he could have modeled for an ad in *Gentleman's Quarterly.* If Lynn's party produced its usual quota of predatory females, Charles would have to fight them off with a stick.

Her gaze finally made it to his. The smile she saw lurking there told her he was aware of the intensity of her inspection. He let his own gaze wander over her lingeringly, appreciatively, sending her a silent message that made her flush. She started guiltily, her look darted around, and she found two pairs of eyes staring at them in astonishment.

Surprise, surprise! Mother's a female! Capable of stirring desire in the male of the species.

"Shall we?" Charles said smoothly, taking her elbow.

She sorted through a million comebacks and settled on the lamest. "Yes."

Not daring to look back, she let him lead her out the door, adding over her shoulder, "Uh . . . I'll see you guys later. Don't wait up."

As Charles led her to the car, she heard him chuckle.

"What's so funny?"

He helped her into the seat, went around and slid behind the wheel. Turning to her, he said, "I think Clark and Michael are in shock."

Kate smothered a giggle. "I can't say I blame them, the way we ogled each other."

"I couldn't help myself. You're such a pleasure to ogle."

Kate's cheeks stained. "I wasn't fishing for a compliment."

"But why shouldn't I tell you how lovely you are?" He ran his arm along the back of her seat and stroked the line of her cheekbone with a light finger. "You're beautiful. I think your children discovered that fact," he said as he checked his watch humorously, "about five minutes ago and were distinctly unnerved."

"Maybe," Kate said huskily, "that's because I only became beautiful five minutes ago when you looked at me the way you did."

"Then I'll never stop looking," Charles promised extravagantly.

"Stop looking and start driving. I think we're being watched."

His low chuckle sent tremors of mirth through her. Kate threw back her head and laughed out loud. Her nervousness melted. Suddenly, she felt incredibly alive and intoxicated with the moment.

She was beautiful. Charles had told her so. And he was the handsomest man in the world. And the cool night air around them was like wine to her senses.

Lynn and Hank's large two-story home was on the crest of a hill in one of the pricier enclaves west of Austin. When they arrived it was lit up like a fairy tale château.

Magic time.

Laughing, sipping champagne, with Charles by her side, Kate felt alluring, witty and seductive. She drew appreciative male stares that startled her at first. Then she glanced into Charles's eyes and saw the same appreciation, intensified and accompanied by humor, as though he could read her thoughts.

Kate flirted with him outrageously. And she was mildly shocked by her own behavior. He encouraged her when she might have stopped—with his look, his words, a certain possessive air. If there were any predatory females about, Charles ignored them.

Once, they were separated, and Kate felt lost. Her eyes searched until she found his, watching her over the heads of strangers. Across the crowded room.

It was an enchanted evening.

The first meeting with Lynn proved interesting. Their hostess had been cornered by one of the other guests when they'd first arrived, but she caught up with them over the hors d'oeuvres.

"You've been hiding from me," Lynn accused her accurately.

Kate thought it best to fight fire with fire. "Can you blame me? It wouldn't do any good to ask you to behave, would it?"

Lynn's eyes widened. "Behave? Why should I? It's my party, I'll do what I want to." She dismissed Kate and stared at Charles, pausing to study him intently.

"Well, I certainly hope you're who I think you are," Lynn spoke fervently.

"I'm Charles Sheffield." He introduced himself and smiled. "And you're Lynn."

"I'm not sure right now. You've stunned me. Damn, Kate. He's everything you said he was and more. We don't have anything like this in the Methodist Church. I think I'm missing something."

Kate closed her eyes in mute resignation. She opened them to find Lynn's scrutiny directed at her.

"Why, Katharine Amanda Byers Hennessey," Lynn breathed softly, "you look absolutely smashing. Being a seductress becomes you. How's it progressing? The seduction, I mean."

Kate was goaded into retorting, "I haven't started yet."

"Haven't you?"

"No. But when I do, I'll be sure and sell tickets."

"That won't be necessary." Lynn waved a graceful hand. "Just keep me informed. Charles," Lynn placed that same hand on Charles's sleeve and said confidingly, "be sure Kate takes you out on the second-floor deck later. The view's marvelous, even if I do say so myself."

Later, Charles reminded Kate of Lynn's words. Wondering what motive lay behind his suggestion, she guided him up the stairs into the family's private quarters, through the master bedroom and out on to the large wooden deck that hung precipitously over the swimming pool. Stairs led down to the patio area and to the hot tub nearby.

They could hear the murmur of the party below them, but for all intents and purposes Kate and Charles were alone. The two of them leaned against the railing, drinking in the view.

Out beyond the yard, the ground sloped dramatically downward. The outlines of craggy hills lay across from them, dotted with the lights of homes nestled among the cedar and oak. The road they'd driven on earlier was a narrow ribbon far below defined by street lamps and bejeweled by the headlights of the miniature cars speeding by.

On the horizon, the city lights glowed in the night sky, sending out a halo of false moonbeams. The real moon hung low near the opposite horizon, pristine in its beauty. The night air was mild and clear, and a wanton breeze ruffled their hair.

Kate turned to face Charles. "Are you impressed?"

"Oh, yes. Before I came, I had no idea Texas could be this verdant."

"You pictured desert and sagebrush?"

"Something like that."

"Most people make the same assumption. It's like that farther west. But for me, the Hill Country of central Texas is special. I wouldn't live anywhere else."

"The perfect setting."

She glanced at him, questioningly.

"The perfect time. The right place. The right two people."

"Yes?"

"What Lynn said was true," he continued. "Being a seductress does become you."

"Oh. That." Kate's hands came together, her fingers fidgeting.

It was one thing to smile at Charles tantalizingly, promising him untold pleasures, in a room safely filled with people. It was quite another matter to meet his eyes, alone like this.

Kate's heart beat frantically. Staring out into the darkness again, she said flippantly, "Actually, I've sent off for instructions—*How to Be a Seductress in Ten Easy Lessons*. Techniques and methods guaranteed to bring results. I expect it in the mail any day now."

"Only ten easy lessons," Charles marveled.

"It's a correspondence course."

"I shouldn't think a person could learn that sort of thing by correspondence."

"Don't you?"

"No. I should think it'd take first-hand experience. Besides, you don't need lessons."

She expected Charles to expand his last statement. When he didn't, the waiting silence between them compelled her to study his face. As soon as she did, he moved closer until they were inches apart, their gazes locked.

"Kate, all you have to do is follow your instincts."

For a timeless moment the man and woman stood motionless.

Follow your instincts...

As if in a dream, Kate's hand left the railing and settled on the sleeve of Charles's suit. The fine material felt smooth to her after the rough cedar boarding. She watched as her palm began to wander up his sleeve, feeling the hard musculature of his upper arm through two layers of clothing.

Slowly, that same hand inched across one broad shoulder. For a moment her fingers became tangled between the suit lapel and the intricacies of his tie and collar. Then they slid over the warm satiny skin of his neck and up into his springy hair.

Kate sighed shakily.

Her other hand snagged on the buttons of his jacket and slipped inside to feel the sheer linen beneath. Heat from Charles's body scorched her, and she skittered up the broad expanse of chest, sensing the mat of hair that curled just under the smoothness of sheer material. One finger traced his jawline tentatively, then discovered the angularity of his cheek.

She lifted her face and touched his lips with hers. As she did so, Kate caught hold of his shoulder for support and murmured his name faintly against the dizzying invitation of his mouth.

"Oh, Kate," he answered, his lips brushing her skin like butterfly wings. "That was a lovely beginning. Let's go on to Lesson Two."

He ran his hands slowly over the silky sheen of Kate's dress, molding her shoulders and defining the line of her backbone, drawing her closer.

Charles's mouth met hers again and his lips began a first delicate exploration. A first taste, the first sweet mingling of breaths. The first tentative parting as he nibbled the corner of her lower lip.

Kate felt a sharp aching need and gasped with its intensity. His arms tightened, pressed her further into him, and she melted with the heat radiating from his body.

Tentativeness went up in smoke. There was a tangle of limbs and seeking tongues. Moist kisses traced her throat and discovered a sensitive earlobe.

Every breath she took was filled with the clean, male scent of him. She was drugged with it. With him. With the taste and texture of him.

Urgency washed over Kate like a flood, making her feel as though she were drowning.

She twisted away and grabbed hold of the railing. Then she scooted back three...four...five steps—a safe distance.

"I thought I was supposed to do the seducing," Kate managed to say finally.

She noticed that Charles had taken hold of the handrail also, and he was breathing raggedly.

"Hadn't I made it clear I planned to participate?" he asked lightly. "It's more fun with two."

"And more dangerous," she muttered. "I'm not sure we have the—" she searched for the exact phrase "—the *savoir faire* to keep this on a proper level."

Charles's laugh drifted out into the night. Kate wasn't sure if it was in answer to her dire prediction, her mournful tone, or the irony of the situation.

His laughter settled into a sweet smile, utterly beguiling to Kate. "Live dangerously, Katharine. It's good for your soul."

CHAPTER SEVEN

"I'M PHOEBE REINECKE, the secretary here at Emmanuel. You must be Mrs. Hennessey, my temporary replacement. I've heard a great deal about you."

So much, Kate guessed, that Phoebe had no longer been able to contain her curiosity.

It was November first. Kate had been working for Charles almost six weeks, and not once during that time had this woman called or offered any assistance. Not that Kate was unhappy with the turn of events. She'd decided, early on, that the less she had to do with Phoebe Reineke the better. With Dan, Millicent and the others' help she'd managed nicely.

Which was probably why Phoebe was in the office now, looming before her, making the impermanence of Kate's position plain from her very first words.

Phoebe was exactly as Kate had pictured her. In her early fifties, she was holding age at bay with a shield of heavy makeup, each hair at stiff attention in a rather unlikely flip. She was wearing a cascade of bracelets and a chunky necklace that was too much for the tightly belted shirtwaist dress it adorned.

Kate could see how Charles might find any replacement to this woman a major improvement. The memory of his relieved expression when he'd first seen her enabled Kate to smile pleasantly and say, "How do you do. Yes, I'm Mrs. Hennessey. Won't you have a seat?"

Phoebe remained standing. "I'd expected you to call. Father Sheffield did give you the message that I'd be of assistance in any way I could?"

"Yes, he did."

"I'm surprised." Phoebe smiled a brittle smile that threatened to crack her layer of lipstick. "I sometimes found Father Sheffield as disorganized as his office."

Kate bristled, but her expression remained pleasant.

Phoebe continued, "Of course, I *was* concerned. There's so much to be done. Without experience, it would be easy for you to forget an important task. And of course, I don't expect you to have the understanding *I* have of how Emmanuel operates."

"I can appreciate your concern," Kate said evenly. "But as a temporary I've been trained to move into a job and organize it so no major mistakes occur. Then, too, everyone's been very helpful. We've completed the Every Member Census, which I'm sure troubled you. I understand you have enough to worry about with your mother's illness."

Phoebe could barely hide her baleful glare at Kate's unwelcome report. Kate was glad to be rescued by Millicent's entrance.

"Phoebe!" Millicent greeted the woman cheerfully. "We haven't seen you for a while. Have you come for the All Saints Day service?"

"Yes. I was sorry to miss church the past two weeks," Phoebe explained stiffly. "Mother took a turn for the worse."

Kate rose to help Millicent into a chair. The latter was pale and winded, but the light of battle gleamed in her eyes.

"I'm sorry to hear that," Millicent consoled Phoebe, once she'd caught her breath. "Tell your mother I'll visit her soon. With so many demands on your time, you must be glad to know that Kate's filled in so well. We've barely missed you.''

Kate gave Millicent a meaningful look. She didn't need Phoebe for an enemy. Then, again, she'd probably been Phoebe's enemy sight unseen. Probably nothing Millicent said could make matters worse.

Kate underestimated Millicent.

"In fact," Millicent said, beaming, "knowing how your dear mother might linger for years, it must comfort you to know Kate could take over permanently, if that were necessary."

Phoebe went rigid with shock. A bleak expression drained all the color from under her heavy coating of foundation and face powder.

Kate felt pity stir in her breast. Phoebe seemed to be as awful as the rumors had foretold. She'd probably sown a fair amount of contention and strife in the closely knit parish. But her whole life was Emmanuel.

"I hope that won't be necessary," Kate murmured. "I've only been here a short time, but I'm sure this office couldn't get along without you, not in the long run."

Phoebe stared daggers at Kate. *So much for conciliatory gestures.*

Holding her head high, Phoebe announced to the room at large, "Emmanuel could certainly do without certain *other* members who shall remain nameless."

She marched out and Millicent cackled loudly. She choked and fought for breath, as Kate rushed over to assist her.

After a moment the attack ended, leaving Millicent feeling shaky, but still triumphant.

"That was a wicked thing to do," Kate admonished.

"Pshaw. You're too soft. And you haven't had to listen to her poisonous tongue for fifteen years. It'd be wicked of me not to dislodge Phoebe Reinecke from her sanctimonious perch. I will before I die, the good Lord willing. I don't have much time.'' Millicent's words faded into a doleful silence. She looked pitifully at the younger woman.

"Millicent...are you angling for sympathy? Well, I apologize for scolding you. It wasn't my place. But don't expect me to feel sorry for you. You're too formidable an opponent. And don't give me any 'dying routines.' You remind me of my grandmother. She was feisty as hell, had a definite mean streak, and lived to be a hundred and three.''

Millicent preened herself as though Kate had bestowed a rare compliment. Then a strange look flitted across her face.

She studied Kate pensively and patted her cheek. "You're a sweet child. Let's talk about a pleasant subject. How are Charles and you progressing?''

An interesting question. One Kate found impossible to answer. She decided to play dumb. "Charles is excellent to work for as I've mentioned before. You and Phoebe can both put your fears to rest.''

Millicent's expression turned sour. Kate knew she'd scored a hit with that particular juxtaposition of names. Recovering quickly, Millicent shrugged. "Okay, don't tell me. I'll find out soon enough.''

She made one of her now familiar conversational turns. "Help me over to the church. I'm feeling weak, and I don't want to be late for the service. We're having a baptism. You must come.''

"Oh, I don't know, if it's a private christening.''

"Not at all, it's part of the feast day. A joyous event. You've met David and Linda. It's their new baby.''

Kate had met the couple. They were two of the friendliest people in the congregation.

Still...

Millicent sensed Kate's lingering hesitation. She placed a hand on Kate's arm. "You must come share with us. This is a new beginning. An unexpected new life. David and Linda have wanted children for years, but they'd given up hope. Then, just as Linda turned forty, she found out she was pregnant. Of course, they were anxious, her having the baby this late. But the child is perfectly beautiful. Everyone is ecstatic for them, so there should be a crowd. Have you ever seen Charles lead a service?" Millicent asked, in a casual tone.

Kate shook her head. She'd been avoiding that side of him. Charles didn't wear his religion on his sleeve, and Kate had fallen into the comfortable habit of thinking of him as a particularly effective social worker rather than as an actual priest of the church. Now she knew she couldn't avoid Charles in his priestly role any longer.

Without verbalizing her capitulation, Kate helped Millicent to her feet, and together they made their way across the lawn to the sanctuary. Kate had only been inside once before, to relay a phone message to Phil, who'd been practicing at the organ.

Now, as she shepherded Millicent to her seat, she took time to survey her surroundings. The interior was unpretentious. There was a timbered roof, a simple altar and railing, and the organ and choir loft were located in the back of the nave. There was accommodation for about three hundred people. At least a hundred members of the congregation had gathered for the All Saints' Day service and baptism.

Kate would have settled into a back pew. Millicent, however, set a direct course for the second pew from the front, carrying Kate along in her wake. Kate couldn't know it was Millicent's customary territory, and she felt conspicuous as she inched in beside Millicent, tripping awkwardly over the prayer bench.

Several people greeted the two women as they went by. Dan, who was robed and sitting in one of the high-backed chairs near the altar, smiled at Kate warmly, a surprised look on his face.

Then the organ began a triumphant processional and down the center aisle came Charles, preceded by three youthful acolytes bearing a silver cross and lighted tapers. Charles was wearing a simple long white robe tied at the waist like a monk's garment. Hanging round his neck was a wide tasseled band of embroidered silk.

Kate's breath caught and held for a moment.

Millicent had been right.

Kate glanced down at her feet furtively and was relieved to find her high heels were still in place. Charles's appearance hadn't knocked her socks off—quite.

Kate looked around anxiously. Didn't anyone else feel this internal earthquake?

All she saw were varying signs of devotion or tranquility. And then she came face to face with Millicent's knowing grin.

Kate immediately turned to the front, certain she'd been discovered.

The organ changed tempo. The congregation rose, singing. The service began.

As a rule, Kate darkened a church door once a year—on Christmas Eve. It was one of her family's yuletide customs. Because Kate and the boys celebrated Christmas with her mother, she felt it was the least she could do. Christmas was, after all, a religious holiday.

Kate thought of her family as a warm and loving one. The denomination she'd been raised in wasn't, however. From her earliest memories, religion had consisted of a litany of

"Thou Shalt Nots." All doubts were met with dogmatic answers, until Kate realized one day that none of the questions that troubled her had been given answers that made any sense.

From that point on, Kate shied away from the church, unsure of what she believed. She still considered herself a moral, ethical person, and because of her own experience, she'd never pressed religious training on Clark and Michael. Much to her mother's genuine distress.

Kate was uneasy here in Emmanuel's sanctuary, doubting Thomas that she was, in the midst of an unfamiliar rite, with lecherous thoughts about the presiding minister skittering through her mind. She blushed guiltily, trying to remember when she'd felt so fraudulent.

Charles sensed her presence, found her eyes with his and gave her a reassuring look.

Was that what she'd needed? His permission to come? Somehow, his acknowledgment made a difference in Kate's mood. Her nerves stopped jumping, and she found herself relaxing as the service continued.

The ritual unfolding held a richness Kate had not expected. The ancient words Charles spoke and the congregation's responses, were filled with a poetry that appealed to her writer's instincts. Dan's reading from the Psalms touched a happy chord in her memory. And when the baptism began, Kate was truly thankful that Millicent had persuaded her to come.

Charles called the family members together around the font. There were uncles, aunts, the proud grandparents and the honored godparents. Young cousins peered through their parents' legs for an unobstructed view. And at the center were David and Linda, their faces luminous with joy.

It was another beginning, as Millicent had said. A festive celebration. A new life being initiated into the eternal mysteries. For two thousand years, the church had presided over the drama of human existence. Birth, marriage, death. It came to Kate that only the church illuminated the magnitude and wonder of these events.

Charles cradled the infant in his arms for the rite of baptism and spoke the holy words. Kate blinked back tears, moved profoundly by the scene before her.

Moments later, the rite complete, David, Linda, and the other family members settled into the front pews. Charles donned an elaborately decorated mantle, moved to the altar, accompanied by Dan, and the celebration of the Eucharist began.

Kate's discomfort returned in full measure. Charles's invitation to participate was ecumenical, and yet Kate thought it would be the height of hypocrisy to participate. She remained in her seat, feeling like an outsider, as the rest of the congregation filed by.

Charles spoke the Prayer of Peace as he dismissed the congregation. The organ chimed out a recessional for his exit, and people around her began to stir.

Kate stood to offer Millicent her assistance. A hand touched her shoulder. She turned to find David and Linda in the aisle, words of welcome on their lips.

Kate admired the baby dutifully. Dan joined the group to add his welcome to theirs. Several other church members whom she'd come to know chatted with her cheerfully, before waving goodbye.

Kate no longer felt out of place. She'd been welcomed just as she was. It was an oddly pleasurable feeling. One she had trouble guarding against.

THAT AFTERNOON Charles sat in his office allowing himself some moments of idleness, his pen doodling over a scratch sheet of paper which was already covered with cryptic scribblings.

A head appeared under his hand, with arrogant nose, granite mouth, and receding hairline. A caricature. The author's private rendering of Burton Jeffries, crime solver extraordinaire. Women readers might swoon over the taciturn, rapier-witted detective hero. Charles had a more jaundiced view of his popular creation.

Inspector Jeffries was in some difficulty, his creator was satisfied to note. He'd lost his objectivity. Quite a comedown for the good inspector. But then, the good inspector was in a strange land, and never before had he wanted to bed a leading suspect.

Yet Jeffries felt she was being set up. Did he dare to trust his renowned instincts? Could he save the woman he was falling in love with from a murder charge?

Charles leaned back, a whimsical expression on his face. He was keenly aware the inspector's problems had parallels to his own. Charles had yet to sort out the dilemma Kate and he presented.

Not that Charles shied away from the challenge. He'd just come to recognize the enormity of the stakes. The kiss Kate and he had shared only confirmed his suspicions. Kate stirred him profoundly.

He remembered his marriage to Sarah. Theirs had been a placid relationship. Her gentle serenity had brought a balance to his firebrand youth. Curiously, her death tempered both his beliefs and his attitudes. His acceptance of the loss had brought him a measure of inner peace.

Kate was anything but serene, in spite of the lid she kept on her emotions. Vulnerable, repressed, sublimating her desires through writing, Kate masked a sense of inadequacy with the pragmatic, ironic facade she'd constructed. Those feelings of inadequacy spilled over, however, into anxiety for her children and apprehensiveness about life in general.

Kate was too hard on herself—that was Charles's opinion. As a parent. As a woman. Charles wasn't surprised.

She'd escaped from a long-term alcoholic marriage, where years of scapegoating had taken their toll. She was touchingly unconscious of her sensuality. Or more likely, if what Charles knew about alcoholism held true, her sensuality had been chronically stifled.

Kate hadn't been able to ignore her sensuality after the kiss they'd shared. For the past week she'd been a nervous wreck, her emotional state obvious. Still, he'd yet to break through the barriers she'd erected. As if there weren't enough real barriers for them to hurdle.

Charles recalled the look on Kate's face this morning during the service. Her eyes had held a mixture of guilt and yearning and surprised desire. Had he been wrong to set her up that way through Millicent? He thought not. Kate must come to terms with that part of him eventually, if there was to be any future for them. There *would* be a future, Charles was determined about that, because he'd already determined Kate's place in his life.

Women had been drawn to Charles before, because of his public persona or out of their neurotic needs and fantasies. Kate was the first to be attracted to him in spite of the collar he wore.

God alone knew how she'd react if she discovered his writing. But Charles had a pretty fair notion, and the notion filled him with unease. Kate wouldn't find out, he'd see to it she didn't, not until she was safely in his arms.

Charles let all troubling thoughts drain out of his head, picturing Kate, savoring details of her appearance. The winged line of her brow. The classic high cheekbones. The expressive mouth that curved into laughter at the absurdities of life.

Long legs, full breasts. A trim waist flaring to a fetching derriere, with an unconsciously seductive sway.

Charles had to practice great restraint to resist fondling it on occasion. Kate Hennessey was wreaking havoc on his libido, but the torture was divine.

She was in the next room. Dare he hope she was thinking of him? Was he crowding into *her* thoughts, disrupting every facet of *her* existence? Charles heard the sounds of paper rustling. The typewriter began to tap out an efficient, syncopated rhythm. Not likely, Charles thought, with self-deprecating humor.

Kate had the ability to compartmentalize her life. Charles found this capacity admirable but frustrating. He refused to be relegated to a corner of her mind!

The sound of muffled voices disturbed his reverie. In a moment, the door opened and Kate slipped through, a look of excitement transforming her face, highlighting the fine-boned beauty of it.

Charles's response was instinctive and primitive. It was all he could do to keep from sweeping down on her and dragging her into his arms.

"Greg Arnold's here," she confided in a low voice, oblivious to his piratical urges. "He asked to see you. Jill told me this morning when she dropped off the twins that he might come by."

Foolish man. You thought it was you who had evoked her pleasure.

"Good. Send him in," Charles said with commendable calm. He stood and gestured to a chair when Greg entered the room. Greg came forward and sat down stiffly. Charles wondered who or what had prompted this visit. Was he possibly here on his own?

"Jill said you wanted to talk to me." Greg answered Charles's unspoken question with an edge of hostility in his voice.

Charles paused before he spoke. "I explained to Jill, I'd like to talk with you . . . if that's what you want. I'd hoped to meet with you and Jill together. Have the two of you had a chance to talk?"

"She explained everything you'd done for her and the kids. We won't need any charity once I find a new job."

"How's the job hunt going?" Charles asked pleasantly. "Any luck?"

"All bad."

Charles heard the note of self-pity in the other man's voice and waited quietly for Greg to continue.

"No one's hiring with the economy down. They don't seem to care that I'm damned good at my job. My manager'll be sorry he fired me one of these days."

"Why did he fire you, Greg?"

Greg looked at Charles warily. "Didn't Jill tell you?"

"She told me what she believed was the reason, but I'd like to hear it from you."

"A loan. All I wanted was a lousy loan. You'd have thought I was trying to rob them."

"Why did you need the loan?"

"Didn't Jill tell you?"

Charles remained silent. He was interested in seeing how Greg chose to respond.

Greg shrugged. "I made a few bets. Got in hock to some gambling types. I needed cash quick, till I could make it up."

"How were you going to make it up?"

"With a line on this week's Dallas game. I can make a killing. I've got inside dope on the point spread."

"Is that why you were assaulted? Because you owed gambling debts?"

"You know the answer to that already." Greg sounded belligerent. "You don't need to ask me. Jill admitted she'd told you everything."

"I know some of the answers," Charles responded calmly. "But I'd like to hear them from you. Jill's very frightened for you. That's why she came to me. But I suspected the truth even before she talked to me. Lieutenant Eccles suspects the reason, too. He believes you're in a fair amount of danger, and you'll continue to be, unless you cooperate with him."

"Yeah, that's all I need. To go to the police. I'd be dead within the week."

"So, what are you going to do instead?"

"I...I haven't decided. If I could get my hands on some money..."

"Greg," Charles's voice cut through the wistful words, "Jill believes you're a compulsive gambler. What's your opinion?"

"I...don't know." Greg shrugged again. He avoided Charles's eyes. "I could quit if I wanted to."

"How do you feel when you try to stop?"

Greg's belligerent veneer cracked. His face twisted with emotion. After a moment he spoke. "I feel empty inside. Like there's nothing left of me. Like I don't know who Greg Arnold is anymore."

"How do you feel while you're gambling?"

"Like there's nothing I can't do. I have all the answers. I just need luck to come my way."

"And how do you feel when you lose?"

Greg didn't answer for a minute. Then the words trickled out. "Like taking a gun to my head and pulling the trigger."

"Is that how you feel now?"

"Yes. No. I'm not sure..." Greg's voice broke. He ran his hands through his hair. "God, I hate what's happening! Don't you think I know what I've put Jill through? How my kids would feel about me if they understood? Jill having to come here to put food on the table! We've never taken charity before in our lives."

"Greg, we all need help sooner or later. Help is available for you, I've checked. There's a Gambler's Anonymous chapter here in town, and a residential treatment center set up to handle addictions."

"You think I'm addicted to gambling?"

"All the signs are there."

"I'm going to lose Jill because of it unless I change." Greg's voice held anguish.

"You may. You're losing yourself, which is more important. You're throwing your life away, Greg. Is that what you want?"

"I don't know what I want! If I just had money..."

"How many times have you uttered that phrase? How many times in the past year? The past five years? How many times when you've had money has it made any difference? When you shave in the morning, Greg, can you look at yourself? Go to Lieutenant Eccles," Charles urged. "He'll make you a deal. If you turned state's evidence you could help shut down the Austin gambling rackets."

"And save my soul? Is that what you're trying to do? Is this a sermon?"

Charles shook his head. "I save that for Sunday. I'm not here to judge."

"Everyone else has. Jill's parents hate me."

"What hurts most is that you hate yourself."

Greg absorbed Charles's observation. "Have you talked to Eccles about me?" he asked harshly.

"Only generally. I didn't break Jill's confidences. Eccles already knew you were in deeply, I didn't have to tell him that. He knows his job. But do you realize, Greg, those debts are illegal? You can't be forced to pay. That's why those goons worked you over, it's the only leverage they have."

"Yeah. And they'd kill me if I went to Eccles."

"Ask for police protection. Once you testified to the Grand Jury, you'd be safe."

"I don't know. I can't think...!" Greg sprang to his feet and began to pace. "I need more time. They've given me an ultimatum."

"When do you have to come up with the money?"

"By the end of the week."

The futility of Greg's plight was like a wall between them.

"Listen." Greg's voice grew urgent. "I have to get away."

"Running won't help. You can't hide from yourself."

"I'm not running! I just need a little space. Will you keep an eye on Jill? See that she's all right?"

"You won't go without telling her?"

"I can't face her. Just...just tell her I'm safe. And not to worry."

"She loves you, Greg. How can she not worry?"

"You tell her not to worry, I can take care of myself!"

"I don't think so, Greg. You're in a great deal of danger from yourself."

"Shut up, damn you! I didn't ask for your help!" Greg lurched for the door.

"I'm here when you want it. Remember that."

The door slammed.

In a second, Kate came in, her eyes wide. "It didn't go well, did it?"

Charles shook his head, sighed and went to stand by the window. "Greg's in bad shape." He sounded tired. "He's running away. When Jill comes by for the boys, bring her in here first. Will you do that, please?"

Kate nodded.

"I have some things to say to her and they won't be easy."

"I'm here if she needs me," Kate offered spontaneously. She and Jill had become friends over the past two weeks. Kate didn't know anyone who was in more need of friendship.

Charles turned so that they faced each other. His gaze locked with hers. "What if I told you I needed you?"

Kate's expression clouded. She searched for words. "You? I don't think so. You have your beliefs. This morning you seemed so strong, I didn't know you."

"That man today," Charles's voice was leashed, "is no different from the man who kissed you. I need you, Kate." He turned back to the window. "But I can wait."

CHAPTER EIGHT

"Henri! Don't go, please! It's a trap! They'll kill you! I may never see you again!"

"Mon Cheri...I must go. There is no choice if I am to prove I am a man. Don't cry. I'll be back. You will always be able to find me. After a summer shower. At the small café where we first met. Along the Seine where lovers whisper. I will always be there for you..."

Kate wiped away a tear.

The shadowy figures on the twenty-one inch screen embraced each other, sharing a wild, desperate kiss.

A loud ring interrupted the moment.

Damn. Just as I was getting set for a good cry.

Kate went reluctantly to the kitchen to answer the summons, flicking off the VCR as she walked by. The only phone call for her today had been one from Lynn earlier. Since Lynn had persisted in dwelling on the stately pace of Charles's and Kate's developing relationship, Kate was reluctant to resume the conversation.

More likely it was a member of her sons' vast and talkative public. The boys were out of town spending Thanksgiving weekend with Kevin's parents, and Kate begrudged the frequent treks to the phone.

But instead of a youthful voice requesting Michael or Clark, it was Charles and he wanted her. "What are you doing? I've missed you."

It was the Saturday after Thanksgiving Thursday. They hadn't seen each other in three days. And truth to tell, Kate had missed him, too, rather badly, along with the rest of her normally noisy household. She'd just this moment realized how much loneliness had set in.

"I should be writing," Kate hedged, ignoring his last statement. "But I'm not."

"Did the boys arrive at their grandparents' safely?"

"Yes. They're probably supine right now in front of the television watching a football game and suffering from acute overnourishment, having just polished off the remains of the turkey and dressing. Kevin's mother makes the best cornbread dressing this side of Georgia."

"Cornbread dressing? That's something I haven't sampled. Is it a Thanksgiving tradition?"

"In the South. Be sure and ask for the credentials of the cook before you try it, however. It can be a disaster in the hands of a Yankee. How was your first taste of our American holiday?"

"Delightful. I spent it with Linda, David and their family. And yours?"

"The usual. Mother doesn't get many chances to fatten us up. She makes the most of them. I think I've gained five pounds. I'll have to starve myself for a week."

"Don't. I want to feed you. Have you had dinner yet?"

"Well . . . no." She'd defrosted a frozen dinner in the microwave oven thirty minutes ago and then forgotten it.

"Good. I'll be there in fifteen minutes."

"Wait—Charles!" Kate stared down at herself aghast. She was wearing a faded pair of jeans, a sweatshirt and no bra. Her face was shiny from its daily moisturizing treatment, and she suspected her hair had developed curious spikes from that morning's washing and subsequent neglect. "I'm not dressed. I look awful."

A pause. "That's not possible, Kate. The two are mutually exclusive."

There was another pause while she discerned his meaning. "Charles . . ."

"Twenty minutes. That's my final offer." Charles hung up before Kate could protest further.

She achieved respectability of a sort with only seconds to spare. Which was miraculous, Kate decided, considering she'd spent the first few moments rushing around like a decapitated chicken.

The jeans she hadn't bothered with. Don't sweat the small stuff, she'd told herself. Come to think of it, they did fit her somewhat snugly—around the rump. The extra portion of pecan pie was the probable explanation.

Kate had groaned silently as she dug hurriedly among her lingerie for a necessary item. After finding it and struggling with the straps, she'd pulled on a thick cable knit sweater, which was old, but a flattering shade of peach nonetheless. She'd seen to it that her face no longer looked like an advertisement for axle grease. And her hair had been brushed vigorously, with a command to behave.

Charles was three minutes early—on purpose, Kate suspected. He did have an expectant air when he strolled in, dressed casually in jeans, loafers, and a light blue wool pullover that was an exact match for his blue eyes. Eyes that were drawn like a magnet to her jeans and the territory they covered.

"I like the five pounds."

Kate threw up her hands. How could she keep her balance with a preacher who doled out sexy compliments?

"It hasn't been twenty minutes," she observed darkly.

"I know. Part of my new tactics. Called catching you off guard." He showed her another example of his strategy, successfully pulling her to him for a short but very effective kiss. At its finish, Kate clung to him, winded and limp. Charles was having a little trouble breathing himself.

Remembering Lynn's earlier complaint, Kate decided she would have approved the new tactics. Kate wasn't sure how she felt about them. In fact, right now, she wasn't sure of anything at all!

"Mmm." Charles nuzzled her throat, heaving a sigh of pleasure. "Not bad for no practice."

So who was doing the seducing around here?

He must have seen the panicked question in her face.

"I can't help it." He leaned his forehead against hers. "This is what you do to me. You plus weeks of frustration. Do you realize how long its been since we've been alone? Every time I get near you, you hide behind the typewriter."

Or the boys or anyone else who was handy, which Lynn had pointed out at length.

"I don't think your flock would approve of a passionate clinch beside the copier," Kate protested, just as she had to Lynn.

"You're right. This is much better. We have privacy for a change."

A dangerous privacy, Kate mused, all thoughts of Lynn fleeing her mind. She was still struggling to catch her breath and finding it very difficult with his body pressed so close. All around, the empty house enveloped them, whispering their solitude, charging the moment with expectancy.

Reluctantly Charles broke away and held Kate's face between his palms so he could gauge her emotions as he whispered seductively, "There is a moment of truth, you know. At the beginning of any affair. When time and place and circumstance conspire to lay bare the infinite possibilities. I believe, dear Kate, this could be ours. Will we struggle to suppress our wild animal passions?" Did she sense a ghost of a smile beneath the provocative words? "Or will we succumb to them, throwing caution to the winds, living only for the eternal moment we shall find in each other's arms?''

Actually, it wasn't a bad offer. Kate was loathe to refuse him, but refuse him she must. At least for now.

''The only wild animal passion I intend to succumb to is my passion for food,'' Kate informed him. ''You did offer to feed me.''

''Alas, so I did. Why do I have the feeling I'm expending all the effort around here? I don't think you're entering into the spirit of this.''

''I'm weak from hunger.''

''Do those words hold promise for later in the evening?'' Charles asked suggestively.

Kate smiled an enigmatic smile, finding it impossible not to play up to his extravagant teasing.

He returned her smile with one so charming that Kate felt breathless again, and she wasn't even in his arms.

Charles must know the effect he had on her. She could see the knowledge lurking behind the laughter in his eyes.

Why didn't that knowing bother her more?

Oh, Kate, you're a fool to ask questions! Why can't you just enjoy yourself? And hang the consequences...as Lynn would say.

Kate slipped her hand into Charles's, answering him just as suggestively, ''We'll let later in the evening take care of itself.''

Her words and look were blatantly sultry. But the gesture that accompanied them was curiously innocent.

Charles realized that Kate was placing herself in his safekeeping whether she realized it or not. The trust that fact implied released a flood of emotions in him. He fought to keep his tone light as he asked suspiciously, ''Have you gone on to lesson three behind my back? A look like that could get you into trouble.''

She shrugged daintily. "I've been picking up pointers from an old movie starring Charles Boyer and Simone Simone."

She tried out another look that set his pulse racing, then her vampish expression dissolved into a shy, self-conscious grin. Charles's pulse throbbed. He'd found out long ago that Kate was her most desirable when she was unaware of her own loveliness.

"It seems to me that I should watch some of this movie," he commented, drifting toward the couch. "I have a notion I'm lagging behind."

Kate went over and literally dragged him out of the house. "You don't need pointers. You're already far advanced of my amateur efforts. Any more expertise and I'll have to paste a warning across your chest: Danger: High Explosives."

"Only dangerous to you, sweet Kate."

And she could make what she liked of that statement, Charles decided, watching a flushed confusion wash over her face. If she didn't realize by now that what was growing between them was very special and not entirely manageable, he wasn't wasting any more opportunities offering evidence to that effect. The difficulties they faced, both real and imagined, could be dealt with once she admitted the fact of their mutual attraction.

Tonight was indeed the beginning of a new strategy, as he'd told her earlier. Kate had mistaken his honesty for a joke. It was just as well. Charles knew Kate was going to take a lot of persuading, which was one reason he'd been moving slowly. When she discovered his ultimate intentions she'd probably run for the hills. He'd need all his powers of persuasion. Perhaps, even, some divine intervention.

Kate noted the bemused expression that came over his face.

"What are you thinking?" she asked, as they walked to the car.

He took her hand in his and swung it playfully. "That tonight was made for us. Texas in November has to be seen to be believed."

The evening was marvelous. Crisp and clear and still. Late fall had brought with it a hint of frost, and just that week the trees had begun celebrating their autumn plumage. The scent of wood smoke hanging in the air signaled that someone nearby was enjoying his fireplace.

Another magical moment.

Or perhaps Kate was being fanciful. Perhaps it was just being with Charles that seemed to sharpen her senses and open her to all the wonders of the world.

"Did you order this night especially?" she asked, irreverently. "I mean, you two are, I presume, on a first-name basis."

"Perhaps." He turned to her as they stood by the car. "Maybe it was given to me, gratis. In the knowledge that I need all the help I can get."

"I'm not sure I approve," Kate remarked austerely. "That's like praying to win a baseball game. Where does that leave the other team?"

"But Kate, the night was given to both of us. No one's going to lose between you and me."

She wanted to believe him. Charles sounded so sincere. Resolutely, Kate swept away the kernels of doubt from her mind and gave herself to the night that had been bestowed upon them.

As the evening wore on, it occurred to Kate that she couldn't remember when she'd had such genuine fun. It was as if Charles had set out deliberately to coax the carefree girl she'd once been from hiding.

They kept the mood informal, as befitted their attire. Dinner was at a cosy Mexican café Charles had recently discovered. Kate hadn't even known of its existence.

The old adage held true. It took an outsider to teach you about your own hometown. "I should have you conduct me on a city tour, Charles. I think you know more about Austin than I do."

"I'll take you up on that. I'm preparing for a stint as a tour guide. I expect my family in the spring."

"Family?" Kate asked curiously. "Who does that consist of?"

"The usual. A mother, father, one older brother and a sister-in-law, plus a niece and nephew."

"They're all coming?"

"Probably. You know, we English really do have a thing for Texas. My letters have only piqued their interest."

"Spare me," she groaned. "You think we all behave like the characters in *Dallas*. I shudder to think what misinformation you've been feeding them."

"I've told them the land is vast, the people friendly and the women beautiful."

She opted to change the subject. "Tell me about this family of yours."

He obliged. "William Sheffield, my father, is a barrister. Stuffy, until you get to know him, yet witty and ribald when the occasion permits. My mother, Marian, is a certified eccentric. She champions obscure causes, writes poetry, keeps a journal and contributes stories to the local rag. Being minor gentry gives her a certain cachet. The Sheffields are tradesmen upstarts with a dash of Irish thrown in, but the Longworths, my mother's family, are of good yeomen stock and trace their lineage back to the fourteenth century."

"And your brother?"

"Henry? A barrister with the family firm. Fortunately, he was there to carry on the Sheffield tradition."

Which had left the younger son to follow another time-honored custom and enter the church. Except Kate knew by now Charles had joined the clergy for very personal and private reasons. Still, the whole family sounded almost too British to be believed. Kate had a feeling they would utterly entrance her.

She said as much, and finally confessed, "I have a thing for Englishmen. You're one of a list. When you thought it was your fatal charm, it was merely your BBC accent. Alistair Cook, Albert Finney, Sherlock Holmes. I love them all. Inspector Jeffries! Now there's a man!" She swooned elaborately.

"Inspector Jeffries?" Charles asked quizzically.

"Inspector Burton Jeffries—in the detective series by William Fitzgerald, one of the best-selling mystery writers in the world today, at least, the English-speaking world. And one of my favorites."

"Oh. *That* Inspector Jeffries. For a moment you had me worried."

"Jealous?' she asked with sudden boldness.

A distinctly odd glint came into Charles's eyes. "Perhaps. How can I hope to compete with a fictional hero, sans flesh and blood?"

"But that's the beauty of Jeffries. He's human, with all the sins that flesh is heir to. Fitzgerald's characterizations are excellent—one of his strengths as a writer. That and the authentic details he provides. He must be a cop. Either that or he's done an incredible amount of research."

Charles was watching her with an enigmatic expression, and Kate continued. "Actually, the author's the one I have a crush on. I've sat down with his books, you know, and analyzed them. Studied how he developed the plot line, inserted the clues. He's been my teacher, in absentia. What I wouldn't give to just talk with him for an hour and pick his brain.''

Charles started to speak, paused for a second and asked, ''What would you ask him if you had the chance?''

''Probably nothing,'' Kate decided, a wry note in her voice. ''I'd be too awestruck to ask questions. I'd just sit there with a stupid grin on my face, feeling like an idiot, and he'd know in five minutes I am what I am—a small-time, would-be writer who doesn't know what the hell she's doing.''

''Not would-be,'' Charles contradicted her sharply. ''If you write, you're a writer. Don't forget that. And don't put yourself down.''

A great well of tenderness rose up in Kate at Charles's chivalrous defense of her uncertain talent.

She patted his hand. ''Down, Sir Galahad. I'm not as timid as I seem. I've just come to realize that I have to look inside myself to discover my own creative strengths. No one, not even Fitzgerald, can give me a recipe for success. One of these days, when I *have* figured out what I'm doing—when that day comes, William Fitzgerald, watch out!''

This time the look he gave her was easy to read. It held satisfaction. She basked in the glow of his approval, a little unclear as to what she'd said that had pleased him so.

''How do you feel about your current effort?''

''I'm not terribly happy with it,'' she confided. ''Which is why the words are coming slowly. I don't like my characters. They're not fully realized. And I'm getting tired of them, which is a fatal sign. But I'm going to finish the manuscript and sail it into the mail to the publishers, like a boomerang, because I think the process toughens me up.''

''Any plans for a next one?''

"Yes. I'm going to write about a poor, hapless temporary who goes into the office the first day of her new job and finds a corpse for a boss, literally. Her new boss, the one who takes over, is tall, dark and handsome and she falls madly in love with him, in spite of the fact that he may be the murderer. And she knows who did it, because of something that happened when she first arrived. Only she doesn't know she knows. And before it's over she almost gets killed." Kate held up one hand. "And that's all I'm telling. If you want to know the rest, you'll have to read the story."

"I'll do that. I like the sound of it already."

Other than that neatly turned compliment, he didn't press her. They finished dinner discussing other topics.

At one point, Kate brought up the Arnolds. "I'm worried about Jill. She looks terrible, and Greg hasn't contacted her. I think only the boys and her job are keeping her going. Have you heard any word from him?"

Charles shook his head.

"Do you think—" Kate worked up her courage to express a private fear "—is he coming back to Jill and the boys? Or has he run away for good?"

"I believe he'll be back." Charles's voice held assurance. "He loves his family and feels responsible for them. If nothing else, his pride will come to his rescue."

"If that's true, then why did Greg run away at all?"

"Because he didn't understand the price of running...how dearly a person pays. But he'll learn."

"You seem so sure."

"No, but I have faith." Charles smiled at her faintly and brushed her cheek with the back of his hand. "Enough. Tonight, I'm feeling selfish. I only want to concentrate on you."

Kate was intrigued, in light of his words, when, moments later, he brought up the subject of Lynn. "I enjoyed meeting her, she's charming."

"She approves of you, too—as you well know. So don't expect me to feed your ego." Charles just grinned in response, as Kate continued. "This afternoon when we talked, she said to say hello." Kate didn't plan to pass on Lynn's more choice comments.

"How long have the two of you been friends?"

"She and I met in graduate school years ago. We've weathered many a crisis together. I like to think I played a small role in her marrying Hank."

Charles looked quizzical.

"Lynn wasn't sure Hank was the right man for her."

"But you were."

"Yes. Besides, Lynn needs a male in her life."

"She obviously thinks the same of you, so she's returning the favor."

"Yes, well..." For a moment, Kate had a hard time meeting Charles's gaze. She remembered one of the remarks Lynn had tossed out during their conversation, and the impulsiveness Charles brought out in her led Kate into danger.

She met his look once more with a certain bravado. "Actually, I think Lynn's convinced you're a dawdling lover."

"Oh?"

"She called you Speedy Gonzales. But it was definitely said in an ironic tone."

If Kate was trying to disconcert Charles, she failed in her purpose, because he leaned back in his chair and dissolved into laughter.

After several moments, he managed to compose himself enough to lean over and speak in a confidential tone. "You tell Lynn she should have more confidence in me. Courting you is an intricate task.''

Task? He made her sound like the object of a job description. "I think," Kate muttered, "I'll let you and Lynn discuss that yourselves."

Charles leaned back lazily. "It wouldn't be a bad idea."

Kate grabbed her purse and rose from the remains of their dinner, suddenly feeling a little hemmed in.

After leaving the café, they drove downtown to the state capitol and strolled through its softly lit grounds. By this time Kate had regained her equanimity.

"I haven't done this in years," she marveled, wondering now why she hadn't.

"When was the last time you toured Congress Avenue?"

"I can't remember."

The admission was enough. They exited the capitol grounds and trekked the main thoroughfare down to the shores of Town Lake, ogling, as they went, the high rises the boom of the early eighties had brought. Coming back, they ventured into one of the night spots on Sixth Street for a brief sampling of a local Western band.

Their ears were ringing when they made it back to the street.

"Have you ever been to Mt. Bonnell?" Kate asked, wondering if there was anything new she could show him.

"Mt. Bonnell?"

"Well, it's really Hill Bonnell. But it's the highest spot in the city. You can look out over Austin and it's *quiet*."

"Lead the way."

They went back to Charles's car and she directed him to the landmark. When they arrived, there were other cars parked along the roadside. Kate remembered too late that the tree-covered cliff was a traditional trysting spot for lovers.

"There's a park at the top," Kate commented brightly, as she started toward the stone stairs, trying to ignore the subtle change in atmosphere.

By the time they'd negotiated the hundred odd steps, romance was far from Kate's mind. She was panting. Charles, she recognized with faint bitterness, could have taken the stairs in a sprint. But then he usually did this sort of thing with ropes. For fun!

Still, the climb was worth it. The lights of the city lay all around. They went to the sheer western edge to find Lake Austin far below, the homes along its shore sending pools of light onto the water.

"Tom Miller Dam is just around the bend." Kate pointed to its identifying lights. "That's the dividing line between Lake Austin and Town Lake."

Kate went to sit at one of the picnic tables that presented the best view, meaning to catch her breath and drink in her surroundings. After a moment, Charles came and settled across from her.

It was dark at the summit. The city sounds were only a murmur in the distance. They could hear the voices of another couple faintly. For a time, they didn't speak.

Charles was the first to break the silence. "Have you lived in Austin all your life?"

"Yes. It's my home. There's been no reason to leave."

"And your family?"

"My mother's here, and my younger brother. My two sisters are married and moved away."

"Your father?"

"He died over twenty years ago of a heart attack. Mother never remarried."

Charles did some quick addition. Kate had been in her teens at the time of her father's death. Another bit of information fell into place.

"Don't misunderstand," Kate hastened to explain. "Mother's not still grieving him. But her children and grandchildren have kept her busy. And it was too much to expect a man to raise someone else's brats. When Dad died there were still three of us at home." Kate grimaced. "Teenagers are trouble enough when they're your own. By the time we were grown, Mom had settled into widowhood. She has always been the type to put her children first. Now, of course, she has grandkids to dote on."

Kate stopped abruptly, uneasy with the suspicion she'd said too much. When the breeze stirred, she shivered a little.

"You're cold," Charles said. "We'll go back down."

"I'm not sure I'm ready," Kate protested. "It's so beautiful here."

"Then I'll keep you warm."

He rose, came around to straddle the bench behind her and enveloped her in his arms. She settled back into his warmth luxuriantly, resting her head against his chest, covering his arms with hers, feeling secure and peaceful.

Two other sightseers emerged from the stairs, glanced at the couple and politely gave them a wide berth.

They probably think the obvious, Kate realized.

Peace fled. A feeling of anticipation replaced it. Charles's warm breath tickled the side of her throat. She murmured randomly.

"What?" Charles's question was a low rumble near her ear.

"I was just remembering. When I was in high school, this was the place to neck."

"Neck?"

"Canoodle, pet. Mess around a little."

"Sounds like an excellent suggestion to me. After all we have Lynn to answer to."

She felt Charles's lips wander down the plane of her throat and up again slowly. He rediscovered the sensitive spot just behind her earlobe. Something warm and moist explored the shell of her ear. She realized with a sharp pang of pleasure what Charles was doing.

Kate shivered again. It wasn't from the cold.

Charles's embrace tightened, drawing her back into the curve of his body. The band of his arms fit snugly under her breasts, so that when she breathed, it created an erotic friction.

Kate let out a shallow sigh. One of her hands reached up to touch his face, and her fingers lost their way in the springy texture of his hair.

Another sigh sharpened into a faint gasp of desire when she felt an unmistakable warmth caressing her uplifted breast. Fingers brushed her nipple lightly and it hardened instantly.

"Let's go home and watch that movie and neck on the couch." Even as Charles whispered the words, his lips explored, provoking shivers of excitement.

"Sounds..." It was hard to get the words out, but Kate managed faintly, "sounds like an excellent suggestion to me."

CHAPTER NINE

CHARLES STOOD, pulled Kate to her feet, and permitted himself one lingering kiss that promised a wealth of future pleasure. Then he took her hand again as he had so often that evening and swung it boyishly.

"Has anyone told you, Katharine Hennessey, that you're a fun date?"

No. Not for a very long time . . .

Kate's lashes swept over her cheeks, and she murmured coyly, "You're only saying that because I'm easy."

He laughed. "That, dear Kate, is a blatant lie. But I don't mind. You're worth it."

Am I? Kate's eyes darted over his face, trying to understand.

"Am I?"

She was feeling giddy and unsure. Nothing seemed real anymore. Ever since Charles had arrived at her doorstep at the beginning of the evening, she'd felt as if she were living in a dream world.

Charles's words, his every touch were meant for her alone. No woman had ever felt as special as she did at this moment. Or more appreciated or cherished.

Cherished. That was the word. Kate had never been cherished before. She wasn't at all sure she merited such an emotion.

Charles must have sensed something of what she was thinking, the doubts that lay behind her question.

"Don't you think you're worth it, Kate?" he asked in a quiet voice.

"I've never really thought in those terms before. I know I'm needed. Necessary. That people love and like me just as I do them. I think I have a realistic sense of my own value."

"I can see I have my work cut out for me." Charles's tone was light, but Kate picked up a hint of suppressed anger.

A horrible suspicion struck her. She stepped back awkwardly. "I . . . I'm not one of your charity cases, am I? Just another member of the flock who needs ministering to?"

This time when Charles spoke, the anger in his voice was evident. In fact, he barely held it under control. "It's a good thing I'm nonviolent, Kate. Because for that, I'd like to take you over my knees and spank you. I'm not sure who you insulted more just now—yourself or me."

What a curious creature she was, Kate thought, whimsically. That a man's threats should strike her so perversely. Because suddenly, she felt as if she'd just imbibed a magnum of champagne and all the bubbles were whirling around inside her.

She stepped forward, leaned to press her body against his, and felt the tension gripping him.

Placing her arms around his neck, she stood on tiptoe and whispered in his ear. "You didn't tell me we were going to get kinky."

His body registered her words and he reached for her shoulders to shake her with a mock menacing air. "See what I mean? You're not easy. You're very difficult. Has anyone ever been murdered on Mt. Bonnell? Because I've decided to wring your neck instead of spanking you."

She slipped away from him, content with her handiwork, and headed for the stairs. "No. But legend has it an Indian maiden flung herself into the river. Her lover was from another tribe and they were forbidden to wed."

"Sounds like a terrible waste of Indian maidens," Charles commented as he followed her.

"I think the story's beautiful. Have you no romance in your soul?"

"Yes. But this lady I know keeps plucking it from me."

Kate decided, wisely, to ignore the remark.

TWENTY MINUTES LATER they were back in Kate's living room. Charles plopped himself down on the sofa, stretched his long legs in front of him and instructed her, "Roll 'em."

"Are you sure you want to watch this picture?" Kate asked hesitantly. "It's a five-hanky tearjerker. I look awful when I cry."

"I told you I was a romantic. I may cry, too."

"You won't. You'll be like Clark and Michael. They giggle and make faces while I weep copiously. This is a woman's movie. I'm not sure a man has the sensitivity to appreciate it."

"You're being unfair. I positively ooze sensitivity."

Yes, that was part of the problem. Charles was all too sensitive where she was concerned. Kate wasn't sure this joint viewing was such a good idea. Still, she obediently rewound the tape.

As the credits rolled by, Charles turned off the lamp on the end table, settled back amongst the throw pillows on the couch, found her in the darkness and hauled her against him so that her head was just under his chin. Within minutes he'd become absorbed in the unfolding story.

Kate found it more difficult to relax. She was very aware of Charles's body pressed against her back, of the hand that absently stroked her knuckles, the stir of his breath in her hair.

And yet, gradually, as war-torn Paris was recreated before them, Kate was once more drawn into the poignant drama. Her vivid imagination took over, and the couple on the screen became Charles and Kate.

The sudden meeting of two strangers, from separate worlds. The initial reluctance to become involved. The dawning of desire. The first brief, shattering kiss. The stunned realization that theirs was a love that broke the bounds of time and custom.

The foreshadowing of disaster. The inevitable parting. The awful knowledge they would never see each other again.

When the shattering sounds of gunfire rang out, Kate flinched and tears began to fall.

In her mind's eye the hero was Charles, bleeding on the cold pavement. While she, Kate, was far away, condemned to the hell of not knowing her lover lay mortally wounded.

But Kate did know. Just as did the woman on the screen.

The last fade-out was of the woman's face, filled with sudden shock, then drained of all expression except mute resignation. One tear trickled down a luminous cheek.

Kate buried her face in Charles's chest, moved beyond words. He shifted her weight, then went to turn off the VCR. When he came back, he gathered her into his arms.

Kate reached for him blindly, with a kind of helpless seeking. Charles's embrace tightened. His lips found hers, and she pressed herself against him, opening her mouth to his, demanding his intrusion. She was giving in to a crazy, mindless need that swept over them both.

He groaned and shifted under her weight until they lay together, and she felt for the first time the urgency of his desire.

She fed on that desire with a deep hunger. Their kisses were hot and searching. Their hands moved, greedy for tactile knowledge.

Her sweater twisted and he discovered the exposed band of flesh above her waist. She felt a touch that lingered, then slipped along her skin like liquid fire, finding the soft mound of her breast. His fingers began a delicate torment.

Kate arched beneath his touch. Her own hand did a dance of discovery over the line of his torso.

The male body. His male body. Iron covered with velvet. Perfection, fulfillment within her grasp.

The scent and taste and feel of him exploded deep inside her.

Kate's fingers clutched his thigh, beyond any conscious control. Her consuming desire for him had become a passionate tyrant, sapping her will and thought.

At the intimate touch, Charles shuddered convulsively and for an instant he ground himself into her palm. Then he clutched her wrist and held it to the sofa beneath them as he buried his face in her throat and fought for sanity with long gasping breaths, while Kate shook helplessly.

After a strained moment she was able to say with commendable calm, "You're right, of course. I'd have hated myself in the morning. Thank you for saving me from my baser instincts."

Charles made a strangled noise that was halfway between a moan and a curse. He hauled himself up, pulled her to her feet and without a word led her into the kitchen, pushing her firmly into a chair.

When he flipped on the overhead light, Kate blinked. She brought a hand up to cover her eyes. Her hair was tangled, her lips felt swollen, and passion had left its mark on her face. She felt naked and vulnerable. And confused.

Charles ran a restless hand through his own tangled hair. Then he started to pace. After a while he seemed to think better of it and took a seat across from her.

When he spoke it was with a controlled intensity. "I'm saving you for me." He let the import of his words sink in and went on plainly. "I heartily approve of your baser instincts."

"Then why...?"

"It's not time."

"I know," Kate acknowledged mournfully. then her voice broke into a plaintive, "Oh, I *don't* know! This is awful. I'm in over my head. I told you I couldn't handle this with finesse. My—" she searched for a word "—my needs keep getting in the way. I...uh..." her eyes fell and she turned her face away from his intent regard. "It's been...a long time since a man's made love to me. My husband lost the knack of it toward the end."

She spread her hands helplessly before her on the table. "What I'm trying to say is, I just don't think I'm capable of a nice, friendly affair." Her voice became a whisper. "At least not with you."

"I don't think you are, either," Charles echoed her words thoughtfully.

Kate wondered why the truth seemed so bleak coming from him. Smiling politely, she gathered her tattered dignity about her.

That dignity disappeared when he said, "That's not what we contracted for, as I remember." Charles searched her eyes. "Mad and passionate were, I believe, the terms you used."

"But I don't want that!" Kate exclaimed. "Don't you understand? I don't want to need you!"

"I understand," Charles said matter-of-factly.

Kate caught a glimpse of quiet pain. Her chest tightened with a stabbing sensation.

"Damn it to hell!" She sprang to her feet. "Why do you have to be so understanding! Even when I hurt you. You accept your feelings as well as mine. Don't you see? I don't want to los—" she bit back the fatal words.

Kate was trembling. Her cheeks felt wet. She wiped at a tear.

"Shhh. It's okay." Somehow Charles had pulled her down into his lap. Now he enfolded her in his arms. "Nothing's going to happen that you don't want."

"But that's the trouble," Kate wailed, allowing herself to lean against him, nestling her body into the warmth of his solid frame. "I don't know what I want."

"I know." He stroked her hair. "But I do. And that's enough for now."

KATE'S NIGHT was very restless. She dreamed about Charles. The dream was immediate, sensual and vividly graphic. She woke with a start, replayed a certain scene in her mind as she regained consciousness and lay aching with need. At 6:30 a.m., resigned to sleeplessness, Kate threw off the covers, shrugged into her robe and stumbled into the kitchen to plug in the coffeepot.

As soon as it started brewing, she went out to fetch the Sunday paper, determined to lose herself in the details of yesterday's news. But the only news she could concentrate on was of the personal variety.

Giving up on the paper, she folded it carefully, took her coffee cup in her hands and stared into space, resigning herself to the inevitable discussion. The one she must have with herself.

"You're in love with him, Kate," she admitted at last. "The Reverend Charles Sheffield. Blue eyes, clerical collar, BBC accent and all. This isn't a crush. It's the real McCoy."

She glanced at the wall clock above the refrigerator. Soon he'd be leading the Sunday service. It was one of the many ironies of their relationship. For here she was, lounging in her gown and robe.

They were the original odd couple. And Kate knew it was too late to back away from Charles now. Her gaze fell on the telephone. She was drawn to it, picked up the receiver, dialed a number.

"Lynn?"

"Kate, you just caught us. Hank's gone to bring the car around and we were headed out the door for church. What do you need?"

"Lynn, I'm in love with him."

"Well, of course you are, darling." Lynn's voice became muffled. "Emma, tell Hank I'll be there in a minute. I'm on the phone..." Lynn turned her attention back to Kate. "I never expected you to be anything else. I gather the pace has picked up. Have you slept with him yet?"

"Lynn, this is serious. He's leaving in June."

"Kate, you're a worrier. Details like that will work themselves out."

"You call that a detail? Besides, there's nothing to work out."

"Whose fault is that?"

"Not mine," Kate confessed with sudden candor.

"That's an interesting statement. Why don't you come over this afternoon and we'll discuss it?"

"I can't. The boys'll be home."

The boys.

"Lynn, Michael doesn't like Charles."

"Of course not. He still harbors hopes for you and Kevin."

"Surely he doesn't, not after all this time."

"Don't be too sure. Michael's worried sick about his father. You've told me so yourself. Maybe he thinks you can somehow save him."

"Oh, Lynn, we both know better than that."

"But Michael may not. Besides, he's had you to himself for these past few years. Don't expect him to welcome another male into your life."

"You make him sound selfish. Michael's not that kind of kid."

"He's been through a lot. You're his only security. Charles represents a threat."

"No." Kate shook her head dumbly. "I won't let him be." She admitted the validity of Lynn's assessment, but the truth wasn't something she was ready to hear.

"Listen," Kate said, brushing aside Lynn's words, "now's not a good time for you. I'll phone later when you're free."

Lynn knew she'd pushed too hard, and she backed off with a warning. "You'd better, dear, or I'll cheerfully strangle you."

"Funny. That's the second time in less than twenty-four hours that I've been threatened that way." Kate gently replaced the receiver.

Let Lynn make of those words what she liked. Kate had called wanting a new perspective. All Lynn had done was compound her confusion.

Later that afternoon, when her sons arrived home, Kate found herself studying Michael. He seemed a little quiet but in genial spirits. Sometimes a long stretch with Kevin proved difficult for him. Apparently this time the holiday with the Hennesseys had gone smoothly enough.

The only thing out of the ordinary was his unlikely curiosity about Kate's holiday.

She tried to be open as she answered his questions. "I spent Thanksgiving Day at your grandmother's house with the rest of the family. Everybody made it into town this year." Kate launched into news of his various cousins, but Michael wasn't interested.

"What did you do the rest of the time?"

"I got a little writing done."

"A little? You told me you were going to finish twenty pages."

Kate's eyes narrowed at his belligerent tone. The role of interrogator didn't become Michael, and it was wrong of her to permit him to play it.

She folded her arms and answered the question he was afraid to ask. "I goofed off yesterday. In fact I didn't go near the computer. Last night Charles came by and took me to dinner." She offered Michael a friendly smile. "We had a lot of fun. Perhaps if we go out again, you'll come with us."

"No, thanks." Michael closed the conversation abruptly by leaving the room.

She started to call him back, then thought better of it. What, after all, was there to say?

"I love you, Michael. Nothing can change that. What's the harm in my having a man in my life?"

Each one of those statements had hidden nuances that were as dangerous as land mines.

And, in fact, Kate was already beginning to feel as if she were in the middle of a mine field with no idea about which way to step. She still had to face Charles the next day, knowing the depth of her wayward feelings.

As it turned out, facing Charles was the easiest part of Monday. Before he came in, she'd received the call.

"Yes. Oh no! How bad is it? Yes, I'll send Father Sheffield as soon as he arrives."

Minutes later, Charles walked into the office. He knew immediately that something was wrong.

"David had a heart attack this morning," Kate said without preamble. "He's in critical condition. They don't know if he'll survive. Linda's sister just called from the hospital. They paged you there, but you'd already left. The family would like you to come as soon as possible."

Charles absorbed the news. His expression tightened harshly with involuntary emotion, before composing itself into a minister's face, shaped by caring and compassion.

But who, Kate wondered, comforts the comforter?

"I'll leave right away. Take my calls and explain the situation. Nolan and I were going on patrol tonight. Please, ring his office and tell him I won't be able to make it.

"The other church members will be phoning as soon as they hear the bad news, so I'll keep you informed of any changes."

"Charles..." Kate touched his sleeve, feeling the rigid muscles of his upper arm. "If there's anything I can do? If you need me...?"

He covered her hand with his. His grasp was steady, but she was shocked to feel how cold it was.

"Just be here. Okay? And if I don't see you before you leave this afternoon, be somewhere later where I can reach you."

Kate nodded. "I will."

But there had to be more she could do. Reaching around his waist, Kate drew him into a hug. Then she raised her lips to brush them along his newly shaven cheek. "I'll hope for good news."

"We'll all be praying for that." Charles gazed down at her and smiled faintly. "I think one of my prayers has already been answered."

Kate saw him only briefly for the next two days.

She heard from him often, as he'd promised. They spoke about David's condition, about how the family was holding up and what could be done to help them. When anxious phone calls began to pour in from other members of the congregation, she was able to relay the necessary information. Within hours, a support system had been established. The church community was rallying around its own.

David's condition didn't change. He remained in intensive care, constantly monitored and kept alive with all the devices of modern medicine. One piece of good news did arrive. Despite the cardiac arrests, his brain waves remained normal, which suggested that there was no permanent brain damage.

During this time, Kate battled a constant feeling of helplessness. She knew Charles's attention was focused entirely on the family. But how was he holding up under the strain? Was he eating enough? Was he getting any sleep? she wondered.

Kate took to asking him such questions whenever he called, and she recognized, from his surprised reassurances, that he was finding her anxiety about him an inadvertent source of amusement. That was okay. She didn't mind. Someone had to look after him.

Both nights she almost drove to the hospital on her way home. But knowing there was a constant stream of visitors keeping vigil, she didn't feel she knew the family well enough to intrude. And so, she'd forced herself to her computer, turning to her writing to relieve the strain.

At work, Kate concentrated on keeping the office running. She canceled and rescheduled Charles's appointments. She made sure the various church meetings went off without a hitch. And the weekly newsletter, with Millicent's help, was mailed out on schedule.

When Jill came in Tuesday afternoon with a frantic expression on her face, Kate knew there had been a new crisis in the Arnold family. She fortified herself to deal with it in Charles's absence.

"Have you heard from Greg?" she asked Jill quickly.

Jill shook her head. "No. In spite of everything I've tried. I've called his friends, his family. No one knows where he is. I just hope the other people haven't found him. I don't think they have . . . because Kate . . . I'm getting phone calls late at night when I'm in bed. At first when I answered they hung up. But last night, there was a man. He asked where Greg was. I said I didn't know. He said . . . I'd better find out, or something might happen to the kids and me. Twice, I've seen someone in a car across the street from our house. I think they're waiting for Greg to contact me." Jill stopped, caught her breath and swallowed hard. "I'm frightened, Kate. Do you think those people would really hurt Lance and Dane?"

"No," Kate responded quickly. "They're trying to get to Greg through you. Still, I think you ought to call the police."

"I can't! Not with Greg in the trouble he's in. But we can't stay in the apartment, I've already decided that. We're moving back in with my parents. I've talked to them, explained the move is temporary. And that it doesn't necessarily mean that Greg and I . . ."

Jill paused and continued, "But with Greg gone like this, not knowing when he'll be back—I don't know what else to do. . . . He *will* be back! I know he will, when he can. I know he loves us. I think he's just trying to sort through everything in his mind. Anyway," Jill said more calmly, "it'll save money on rent. Although I've insisted on paying for my share of the groceries."

Jill paused to ask Kate anxiously, "Do you think I'm doing the right thing? Mom and Dad are furious with Greg already. This will only add to their anger. I've made them promise not to say anything against him in front of the children."

"You're doing the best you can under the circumstances," Kate reassured her. "It's never easy to move back home. But as you say, this is only temporary. We'll see what we can do about finding you another place later." When they knew what they were facing.

Jill brightened, then her expression grew anxious again. "Do you think there's any possibility that Greg's contacted Father Sheffield?"

"No. Charles would tell you if he had. I promise we'll contact you with any word."

"Perhaps, if Greg comes back and can't find me, he'll call here, and you can tell him where I've gone."

"Right. I'll fill Charles in just as soon as he has a moment free."

"Is he here? I'd like to talk to him."

Kate explained the situation at the hospital.

"Oh, how horrible!" Jill exclaimed after she heard. "And with a new baby." She shook her head, saying, "It's easy to get wrapped up in your own troubles and forget that everyone has them."

Which was exactly why Kate had shared the story. "Yes. The fact is, we're all in this together. So if you get to feeling down and want to talk, remember I'm here."

"Thanks, I will. And I'll come by tomorrow when I pick up the kids. I want to find out . . . well, if there's been any change."

Kate nodded and waved a goodbye.

After Jill's exit she glanced at her watch. It was after four. She'd be late for Michael.

But she was reluctant to leave. All afternoon a sense of unease had gripped her. She'd only pushed it aside during her talk with Jill. Charles hadn't called since late that morning. What if there'd been a turn for the worse?

Finally, realizing she couldn't linger any longer, Kate locked up the office and went to her car.

When Michael saw her, his eyes widened. He knew about David's condition and how anxious everyone was. Now, he must have sensed her distraction.

"Did he die?" Michael asked baldly.

"Not that I've heard. There's just been no word, and I'm worried."

The ride home was silent for them both. Supper was subdued. Only Clark ventured a bit of humor.

"Say, Mom. You think the next job you take could be with a tax accountant? That way the worst thing that could happen would be someone landing in jail."

"It'd be Mom's luck that some poor dude would keel over right in front of her when he saw how much he owed the government."

Kate frowned disapprovingly but let them joke. It relieved the tension.

By tacit agreement the television stayed silent that evening. Clark and Michael did their homework early and retired to bed. Kate went to her computer, coffee in hand. But all she could do was read and reread words she'd already written. Finally, giving up on the session, she took a bath and prepared for bed.

For a moment, Kate thought of trying to locate Charles. She reached for the telephone to call his number then she put down the receiver. If he was at home, he'd be catching up on sleep. She couldn't disturb him.

Just then, the telephone rang.

"Kate? Did I wake you?"

"No," she laughed shakily. "I was just thinking of calling the parsonage. You must have read my mind. Any news?"

"The doctors think David's going to make it. The family's just heard. He's breathing on his own now and fully conscious. He'll need bypass surgery, but he's young and in fair condition. It should be a success."

Kate breathed a huge sigh of relief and murmured inconsequentially, "Thank God."

"Yes."

Kate realized what she'd said and felt a little foolish.

Charles had already gone on. "Kate? May I come by? Is it too late? I won't if you feel the boys would object."

Hang the boys.

"Come. Clark and Michael are asleep. I'll brew you a cup of decaffeinated coffee."

He managed to laugh. "I've had so much coffee, I slosh when I walk."

"Then I'll make you an omelette. My cooking's basic, but I can manage that."

"I'm not hungry. Linda's brother-in-law insisted on taking me out to eat."

"Oh. Well..."

Charles laughed again. "What I need from you, Kate, is emotional nourishment."

Kate smiled. "In that case, I'll see what I can do about scrambling up some TLC."

"TLC?"

"Tender loving care. I keep a supply in the cupboard for just this sort of occasion."

"I'll be right over."

CHAPTER TEN

CHARLES WAS as good as his word.

Kate was faintly shocked when she saw him. The residue of strain had cut grooves in his face. He looked every bit of his forty-two years. Fatigue made him sag a little as he walked through her door and straight into her arms.

"Mmm. You smell good."

"I smell like soap. I'd just taken a bath when you called." Kate pulled away slightly. "You want to talk about it?"

"In a minute. Right now I just want to hold you and be quietly thankful."

They stood embracing for a long moment before Kate asked, "Are you sure David's going to make it?"

"Reasonably sure. We're over the worst."

"I know your being there meant a lot to them."

"It's never easy," he confessed. "It shouldn't be. When I stop feeling the family's pain, I've lost my purpose in being there. Fear's a very isolating emotion, as is grief. That's why there's a need for community when there are crises."

Reluctantly, he broke away from her and dropped to the couch. For a second he held his face in his hands, rubbing the stubble of a beard absently.

"I don't have any easy answers when something like this happens. No facile words of comfort to dole out. Only my frail human faith. What I can do is be near, let them talk, and show them I'm not afraid to share what they're feeling."

He glanced up at Kate. "Linda held up beautifully. At first she was in shock, not wanting to face what had happened. She was completely stunned that life should treat her this way. It's a common reaction. But as soon as there was the least bit of hope, she pulled herself together. Hope's the necessary ingredient. Thankfully, this time it was rewarded."

"With David so young, does it remind you of. . ."

"Sarah?" Charles's look confirmed Kate's guess. "She was young and filled with hope and promise, too, like David. We were on the verge of adopting a child when she became ill." Kate could tell Charles was remembering. "Two years before, she'd discovered she couldn't have children. Sarah took the news badly. It was hard on us both. But she'd worked through her feelings and decided there was a reason for everything."

Charles looked at Kate. "Sarah was an accepting person. In that way she reminds me of you."

Kate found the comparison disturbing. His wife sounded like a saint. She herself was anything but.

"We were working with a Vietnamese relief agency at the time, but once we realized Sarah was dying there was no question of bringing a child into our lives."

No wonder Charles saw the parallels between the two couples.

As if he'd read Kate's thoughts, he went on to say, "One of the hardest aspects of David's collapse was Linda's fear that he might not live to see his son grow up."

Charles fell silent. He seemed to be reliving the past forty-eight hours. His hand went up to rub the base of his neck, wincing as though his muscles ached.

Kate brushed his fingers aside and began to knead his shoulders slowly. They were tensed and knotted. But as she continued her massage, he let out a small sound of pleasure and little by little she felt him relax.

They made a domestic scene. Husband home at last from caring for his flock. Wife waiting patiently to minister to the minister.

Kate's movements stopped. She pulled away carefully, shaken by the direction of her thoughts.

Charles picked up the change in her mood. He took her hand and brought it to his lips.

"Thank you for the TLC," he murmured into her palm. "It was just what I needed. Even if you did decide to ration me."

"If I did, it's because I'm not sure the supply is adequate." Kate made the admission haltingly.

"Could it be you're selling yourself short? You can't have it both ways, Kate. First you say I don't need you at all. Then you're afraid you can't give me all I need. Neither is true."

He hauled her up before she could respond and took her face between his hands. "You're a beautiful, kind, giving woman, Kate. You were here for me tonight. Bless you for that."

Charles kissed her very tenderly and was gone before she could utter another word.

"Mother?"

Kate turned with a jerk. Michael was standing at the entrance to the hall, his face in shadow.

"Who was that just now?" he asked.

"Charles. He came by to tell me David's going to make it."

"Why didn't he phone?"

"He did. I invited him to come. He needed to unwind."

"With you?"

"Yes. I'm removed enough from the situation, so that he could relax."

"Oh." Never had one word conveyed so much.

"Michael," Kate began, trying to explain her motives. "Charles holds a special place in peoples' lives. He's there at the best and worst of times. Sometimes it's hard for him. He needed me tonight."

"You like him a lot."

She acknowledged the accusation with a nod. "And I'm going to keep seeing him."

"Why?"

"Because I don't know what's going to happen. And I can't leave before the ending."

Michael turned and walked from the room, leaving her standing there.

The men in her life kept doing that, Kate thought with exasperation. Later, when she climbed into bed for the second time that night, it was hard to sleep.

LYNN DROPPED BY Kate's house the next afternoon. They often walked together evenings for exercise, but Kate knew there was more to this particular visit than met the eye. She detected the faintest hesitancy beneath Lynn's breezy manner. The reason for it soon became clear.

"You didn't get back in touch with me Sunday. I worried."

"That you'd pushed too hard?" Kate teased. She felt Lynn relax.

"That was part of it, although you always forgive me." They shared an understanding look. "But I was also concerned."

"I know. I meant to telephone. There just wasn't time. Work's been crazy this week—one of the members of the church had a heart attack. But he's pulled through."

It was a feeble excuse and a tacit admission of Kate's reluctance to confide in Lynn. But it wasn't Lynn's fault Kate had been avoiding her. Right now she'd just as soon avoid everyone.

Okay, okay, especially Lynn.

Kate knew it was because the relationship with Charles was stirring up a wealth of conflicting emotions and she wasn't ready to face them. Not with a person who knew her as well as anyone in the world.

Right now Lynn was performing her managing act. "Well, I'm here now, ready to render aid and comfort. So lace up your Reeboks for a 'walk and talk.'"

Kate followed orders, and they set out on their accustomed course.

"Any time you're ready..." Lynn prompted after the first brisk block.

Another stretch of road went by. Their breaths were misting as they panted slightly.

"Kate...I'm listening. It's not good to hold things in."

"Sure...that's easy enough for you to say," Kate huffed as they trudged up the first steep hill. "You won't be doing the talking."

By this time, they were approaching the neighborhood elementary school and Lynn, bidding Kate to follow, detoured toward the swings on the playground. She settled in one of them, then turned to Kate sweetly.

"This is better. Now you have no excuse."

The two women swung back and forth a few minutes in silence as Lynn waited patiently, gauging Kate's mood.

When the latter spoke, her tone was sober. "Lynn...I want you to know that Charles is a very special man."

"I can see that," Lynn agreed quietly. "You two were made for each other."

"You don't understand. It's not that simple. Charles cares deeply. He gives of himself. When David had his heart attack, Charles was with the family constantly until the worst was past. He came over last night, totally drained." Kate looked into the distance, remembering his face, lined and drawn.

"At first I thought his religion made him self-sufficient. But now I realize he does have needs. He needs someone strong and selfless enough to replenish the caring he dispenses."

"Do you begrudge him that need?" Lynn asked probingly.

"Oh, no! It's not that I begrudge him. It's just that I want him to have more than I can possibly give."

Lynn harrumphed. Kate turned to her and saw a look of exasperation that took her aback.

"Dear Kate," Lynn said deliberately, "that is one of the stupidest statements I've ever heard you utter."

At Kate's bewildered expression, Lynn continued impatiently. "More than you can possibly give, my hind leg! That's all you know how to *do*, is give. You've been in training most of your life, certainly during your marriage—to a man who took and took and *took*. And in the end he left you with all the guilt, and feelings of inadequacy to boot. What you haven't learned to do, my friend, is to receive."

"I let you and Hank give to me," Kate protested.

"The operative word is 'let.' As though we were on a rationing system. Two favors to me, two in return."

"That's not true, Lynn. We've never kept score."

"Lord, don't I know it! No telling what mine would be by now if we had. I remember after my divorce when I was crazy, and you kept me out of that insane affair with the biology professor who had a wife and four kids."

"You've helped me, too, Lynn, so many times."

"And I'm not through helping," Lynn promised firmly. "Look, Kate, for the first time in your life, you've met a man who has the capacity to give to you, who would care for you and cherish you. Am I wrong?" Kate looked away. "I didn't think I was. You've blossomed these past few weeks under Charles's tending."

"You make me sound like a wilting petunia."

Lynn gave a short burst of laughter. "When instead you can act as thorny as a prickly pear." Her tone changed abruptly. "You don't realize it, Kate, but you're being selfish."

Once more Lynn had startled her. "What do you mean?"

"To give and give and never receive. To deny Charles the pleasures of his tender mercies."

Kate blinked back sudden tears and tried to respond to Lynn's accusation. "It's not selfishness, not really. I feel awkward taking. It doesn't come easily."

"No. For you it'll be very difficult. You're more comfortable giving, because then you feel safe."

Kate stared down at the ground and scuffed her tennis shoes in the dust beneath the swing. "You're right. I'm no prickly pear or petunia either, Lynn. I'm a scared rabbit. Loving Charles has thrown me. I don't know what to do with the feelings—" her voice faltered "—or the needs he's stirred up in me."

"What are you thinking of doing?"

"I told Michael last night I was going to continue seeing him. But I don't think that's such a good idea."

"Wrong! It's an excellent idea."

"But Lynn . . ."

"No buts. Listen to one who loves you. You are going to lean back, relax and let Charles do all the work."

"But Lynn . . ."

"You are not going to worry about Michael, next spring or tomorrow."

"But Lynn . . . !"

"You are going to open yourself to each new experience," Lynn gave her friend an arch look, pausing for effect, "including . . . the throes of passion."

Silence fell between the two women.

Kate's eyes left Lynn to gaze around, noticing for the first time the winter dusk that had colored the sky aquamarine and cast the bare-limbed trees of the school grounds into a bold relief of absolute stillness. Only a neighborhood couple out for their evening constitutional disturbed the quiet air. They waved.

Kate acknowledged them absently, completed her visual tour and returned her attention to Lynn. "You're saying I should stop running, throw off my inhibitions and go to bed with Charles."

"Every chance you get."

It was the week of Christmas, and Kate was met with the sweet scent of fir and votive candles as she entered Emmanuel's sanctuary. The church was being decorated for the twelve feasting days.

Activity flowed around her. Friendly faces said hello. Voices called out a welcome. She spied the person she hoped to see and headed toward him.

"David, I heard you were home. How are you feeling?"

"Glad to be alive." David made the statement with a smile that lightened the intense emotion. Bypass surgery had been successful. The hospital stay had ended. David looked pale and thin, but serene.

"It's not a bad life." He grinned. "All I have to do is sit in a pew and issue orders."

Linda, who was perched on a ladder arranging a garland of holly along one wall, waved a branch at him threateningly before she went back to her work.

Kate threaded her way across to a ladder where Charles was poised on the next-to-top rung. He stretched to his full height while he hung a banner of an angel, which had been drawn, Kate guessed looking at the uncertain line of its profile, by one of the children's Sunday School classes.

Charles dropped his hands to balance himself and greeted her with an easy smile.

"Lieutenant Nolan just phoned," Kate called up to him. "I told him you were knee-deep in pine boughs. But he said he'd like to talk to you the first minute you have."

Charles nodded and started down the steps. The ladder wobbled precariously. Kate reached up anxiously to catch him and he slid through her grasp as he landed on the floor. For a moment, his arm hugged her waist.

Kate glanced around warily. Certain smiles told her the observers read the significance of his gesture.

It was typical of Charles, discreet yet open. He seemed to have no qualms about the congregation knowing of his and Kate's relationship, even if Kate doubted his prudence.

She was following Lynn's advice in her own fumbling way. She and Charles were dating each other but not as often as Charles would have liked. The church calendar was full this time of year, and Kate was leery of too many outings. Still, they'd been together enough to establish themselves as a couple.

Clark and Charles now had a standing handball match on Saturday mornings. And Kate, in a moment of courage, had invited Charles over to participate in an American tradition, the decoration of the family Christmas tree.

The occasion had been only a qualified success.

Clark's attitude to the burgeoning romance was easy enough for Kate to deal with—if a little lowering, since it included thinly disguised surprise that "dear old Mom" should attract a man for whom Clark had more than a pinch of hero worship.

Michael, more troublingly, had disappeared behind a wall of silent censure. He was finding it hard to actually dislike Charles. Charles's respect for his ambivalence had already earned him a measure of Michael's grudging regard.

Kate had, however, seen a look of distinct dislike directed her way. Michael wasn't at all happy with the Kate who was emerging outside his old frame of reference. He must have felt that his whole world had turned upside down.

More than once Kate had started to approach him. Then Lynn's words would come back to her: *"Don't worry about Michael...lean back, relax, and let Charles do the work..."*

Heaven knew Kate was making the effort. She'd worked up her courage to embrace each new experience, just as Lynn had instructed, including the throes of passion.

Only the throes of passion never came. Charles's wooing was frustratingly circumspect, and the erotic episode on the couch had not been repeated.

Yet, his smile held promises. His touch whispered tantalizing awareness. His kisses at her door at night made her dizzy with desire. She was a creature ruled by her emotions, in a continuous turmoil of delight.

Kate had never felt more alive, more vulnerable or expectant. She looked back on the years past and saw how gray and featureless they'd been. Her new perspective made each new day, each new moment precious to her.

Only the Arnold situation cast a pall on the season. There was still no trace of Greg. It was the first Christmas Lance and Dane had experienced without their father, and his continued disappearance seemed ominously permanent. Jill was on holiday vacation with time to brood. So Kate had whisked her out one day to lunch and to the mall for budget shopping. They'd had fun over their respective Christmas lists, comparing little boy toys with big boy toys, noting the difference in price tags. By the end of the afternoon Jill's spirits had improved. Kate was pleased.

On December 22nd, she called her mother, Connie. "We won't be going to church with you Christmas Eve, Mom. The three of us are going to the midnight service at Emmanuel."

"That's nice, dear." Kate could sense the older woman thinking. "You must enjoy working there. Have you gotten to know the people?"

"Yes. It's a small parish."

"Perhaps you're thinking of joining them?"

Connie's hopeful suggestion was met with silence. After a resigned sigh she announced, "We'll expect you over around three, Christmas afternoon, for dinner. That'll give you and the boys time in the morning to enjoy your presents."

"I might be bringing a guest with me—if that's all right with you. Father Sheffield."

Connie's hope sprang anew. She responded brightly, "I think that's a delightful idea. We'd love to meet him and his wife."

"I don't guess I mentioned," Kate ventured cautiously, "he isn't married."

"Oh?" Kate heard the note of speculation.

"I thought we'd show him an American Christmas," she explained quickly.

"I see."

Kate suspected she did. "Charles and I are friends, Mother. We've gone out a few times. Don't make more of it than there is."

"What do the boys think of this?" Connie asked shrewdly.

"There's no 'this' to think about. I told you, we're just friends. The boys like him," she went on defensively, casting doubt on her denial. "And if I bring him Christmas Day, you have to promise you'll behave."

"Of course I will, dearest. He'll feel right at home."

Which was exactly what Kate was afraid of. She'd been deviously maneuvered into this invitation by Clark and Charles. Clark had also been in favor of attending the Christmas Eve Eucharist. Michael had seemed reluctant, but he was as curious to see Charles in action as Clark.

Kate privately admitted her own curiosity. This would be only the second time she'd seen Charles lead a service. She hoped her reaction wouldn't be as volatile as before.

Most of the parish attended the midnight service. The sanctuary was filled to the rafters, and Michael, Clark and she crowded into the pew where Millicent had saved them space.

In the muted light, Millicent looked frail, her expression pensive. When she saw Kate, the two boys in tow, however, Millicent smiled with twinkling satisfaction. Kate made the introductions and forgot her previous unease.

The sanctuary on Christmas Eve was a special place, bedecked in its holiday finery, filled with symbols of the nativity, the still, cold, peaceful night just outside the stained glass windows. Inside was warmth and joy and celebration. And glorious music.

Phil and the choir were outdoing themselves. Kate had heard them practicing for days. Now she lost herself in familiar carols.

When Charles appeared in the processional Kate felt a small shock. It wasn't the earthquake she'd experienced before, although he was still shatteringly attractive.

But somehow, it felt natural to be watching him leading the congregation in the holy rites of the season. She'd grown more comfortable with his priestly role. And on this most Christian of nights, the words and rubric of the liturgy had, for Kate, a poignant beauty.

When Charles read from the Gospel, retelling the ancient story, she let the words flow over her. The sermon that followed was simple and filled with the celebration of communion. The rich texture of Charles's voice carried into the corners of the church.

Suddenly, Kate knew it was right and good for her to be here. A deep peace settled in her heart.

At the end of the service, she turned to Clark and Michael. They both wore bug-eyed expressions.

Kate laughed. "I know. It's hard to believe that's the same man who helped decorate our tree."

"He's good," Clark observed matter-of-factly.

"Yeah," Michael muttered. "But I'm not sure I believe all this stuff."

"I'm not sure I do either, Michael. It's not necessary to be sure. You can still be moved by the spiritual truth of it. Come on." Kate started to make her way through the throng of people. "We've got to get home. Santa has unfinished business."

In Kate's household, belief in Santa Claus assured his annual visit. She'd probably have the only thirty-year-old sons who still expected their stockings to be filled.

Charles greeted them at the rear of the church. "Leaving already?"

"I have to go home and play Santa."

"I'll be over as soon as I've finished here."

Kate spied Phoebe a few feet away, watching the interchange with tightened lips, waves of disapproval emanating from her.

Phoebe's presence didn't seem to bother Charles. He noted Kate's hesitation and said coaxingly, "I have your Christmas present."

"Can't it wait until tomorrow?"

"No."

Millicent touched Kate on the sleeve, as she spotted Phoebe and gave the woman a look of pleased triumph. "I'll get Charles away from here in a minute. He's promised to drive me to Linda and David's, where I'm spending Christmas. After that, he'll be right over."

Charles smiled down at her warmly. Kate's heart melted in spite of the chilly night air. She nodded agreement, and fighting to mask a rising excitement, began mentally making plans for the evening to come.

CHAPTER ELEVEN

KATE HAD JUST TOPPED OFF Michael's and Clark's stockings when Charles arrived. Hers lay mysteriously lumpy on the fireplace mantel, stuffed by the boys who were now snug in bed, visions of compact disc players dancing in their heads.

The lights of the Christmas tree twinkled brightly. Despite the kids' raised eyebrows, Kate had put a log on the fireplace. A fire blazed cheerily and a late-night radio station softly played a collection of carols.

"I still have two presents to wrap for tomorrow afternoon," Kate explained as she sat cross-legged in the middle of the rug and began to cut through gaily decorated paper.

"Can I help? I'm an excellent wrapper."

"No. It's my fault I waited this long. You can provide the entertainment."

"Delighted to." He stooped to bestow a kiss on the nape of Kate's bent neck. An excited tremor went through her.

"You're distracting me," she murmured.

"Am I?" Charles asked innocently, lowering himself to the floor beside her. He unbuttoned his jacket, stretched out and turned on his side, propping his head on a palm.

"You're beautiful in the firelight," he said without preamble.

"Firelight makes every woman beautiful," Kate said, glad the flickering flames hid her embarrassment. She glanced at him from under her lashes. "Why do you think I lit it?"

"To seduce me, I hope."

Kate's lashes fell. Charles raised himself and with sure fingers taped the package that was coming unwrapped beneath her fumbling hands.

"Maybe I do need some help," she said under her breath.

"Maybe you do at that."

Charles taped up the other package, finished it off with ribbon and placed both presents carefully under the tree.

Which left nothing for Kate to do with her hands. She twisted them nervously.

"Do you want your present now?" Charles asked as he settled back down beside her.

"Yes." Kate shrugged helplessly. "I never could wait."

Charles handed her a small neatly wrapped box. She tore the paper off clumsily, recognizing the logo of a local craftsman who was famous for his unique jewelry.

Inside, Kate found a delicate gold chain that seemed to have been made to fit around her neck. At the end of the chain dangled a dove of peace.

It was exquisite. She'd seen the design once and wanted one. But even the artist's silver pieces lay outside the range of her pocketbook.

"Oh, Charles...it's beautiful," Kate breathed softly. "You shouldn't have."

"Shouldn't have?" he asked in mock affrontery. "Is that any way to accept a gift?"

"I'm sorry. It's just that..." She felt guilty. It was far too much money for him to spend on her, living as he did on a minister's pay.

"Here. Let me put it on."

As Charles took the necklace from her, the simply wrought golden figure caught the reflection of the flames and shimmered. Kate felt his fingers fixing the clasp, then the soft pressure of his lips once again on the curve of her neck.

She glanced down to see the dove settling between the vee of the Christmasy hostess gown she'd slipped into when she'd arrived home earlier.

She put her hand over the hollow where it nestled.

"Thank you very much. It's lovely."

"Merry Christmas."

He smiled at her tenderly and accepted the light kiss she offered.

"Would you like your present?" Kate asked, moving away from him slightly.

"Didn't I just get mine?"

Kate made a disapproving face. "I may be broke, but I can afford more than a kiss."

"Your kiss is precious to me," Charles swore, his hand over his heart. "I value your lips above rubies."

She patted the side of his face. "You're being extravagant in more ways than one."

"You bring out the poet in me." He leaned toward her, his gaze intense.

Kate ducked her head away and crawled over to rummage under the tree.

"Here." She held out her gift to him.

As Charles began to unwrap it, she said shyly, "I hope you like it." The gift was a book of photographed Texas landscapes, from the sand dunes of Padre Island Seashore to the Chisos Mountains of the Big Bend. Even on the bargain rack at the book store it had cost her a pretty penny. But when Kate had seen it, she couldn't resist.

"I thought . . . once you returned to England, you'd have something to remember us by. Merry Christmas."

Kate accepted his kiss of thanks.

Charles moved away reluctantly to flip through the book's pages. "I can see I have some serious traveling ahead of me."

She shook her head, laughing. "You forget how big Texas is. You'll never see all that in six months."

Charles closed the book and focused on Kate again. There was a mysterious gleam in his eye. "I may not be returning to England. At least not to live. I have an appointment in Houston with the bishop. We'll be discussing my taking over Emmanuel permanently. Father Palmer is toying with the idea of another year in Great Britain. Then he'll return to a Dallas parish where he's from originally."

"N-not going back?" Kate said the words slowly, her heartbeat accelerating into triple time.

"Not for a long time, except to visit."

"But why? England's your home."

"My home is where I make it. Haven't you noticed? I've fallen in love. With this land." He brushed a finger lightly down her nose. "And with its people. I don't think I can go back in six months."

All Kate could do was stare at him wordlessly, confusion and happiness transforming her features.

"Oh, Kate," his voice was like velvet, "you should see your face."

"W-what's wrong?"

"You're absolutely lovely."

Charles cupped her chin with his hand, leaned over and touched her lips with his. Kate swayed toward him. He whispered something as he drew her close.

Her arms went around his neck. She made a small murmuring sound as his lips met hers once more. Their kiss deepened as they spoke to each other, communicating the beginning of desire in a thousand ways.

Desire quickened, then flared into passion. Kate's murmurs turned into a moan. For Kate, it was a mindless moment, filled with Charles's nearness. When he lowered her head back against one of the pillows scattered on the floor, she pulled him down until he lay against her, his hard body pressing her into the rug. Kate sighed with delight, arching herself closer.

Yet she sensed Charles's restraint. It drove her to wantonness. Nibbling on his lower lip, she let her fingers slide over the bunched muscles of his back and down his side, until she found the curve of his buttocks and pressed him against her, her own body offering itself suggestively.

Charles chuckled huskily and pulled away. He ran his fingers over her hair so that it splayed across the pillow. He stared down at her.

"Kate...I want you..."

"I want you, too," she breathed, her vision blurred with pleasure.

"...to marry me."

Kate blinked.

"Marry you?"

Her eyesight improved.

"Marry you?"

She tried to scuttle out from under him. "I...I thought you wanted to go to bed with me."

"I do. Madly and passionately. I also want us to live together. Don't you think both could be arranged?"

"I don't know." She shook her head, looking vaguely shocked. "I...I don't think so. Charles..." Kate's voice stiffened with reproach. By this time she'd extricated herself from his embrace, and she rose to her knees, facing him. "You can't propose marriage out of the blue without asking certain questions. You have a duty to yourself and your calling."

Charles had watched the expressions scuttling across Kate's face. When he saw the hint of censure, he seemed keenly amused. "What questions do I have a duty to ask you, Kate?"

"Well, for one thing, about my religious beliefs. We can't get married."

"Why not?"

"It would be a mixed marriage."

He raised one eyebrow.

"Haven't you guessed? I don't know what I believe. *If* I believe in . . . Don't you see? I don't have any answers, only questions. And I'm not sure what good it does to ask them anymore."

"Most people have more questions than answers."

"But you have your faith."

"Each person's faith is a private matter. It takes many forms."

"But mine has no form." She sighed at his obtuseness. "Charles, what I'm trying to say is, I can't be a minister's wife."

"I don't want you to be a minister's wife. Whatever that is. I want you to be my wife. I would never try to make you believe as I did."

"But wouldn't my doubts bother you?"

"Why?"

"Well, because the God you believe in . . ."

"The God I believe in, Kate, accepts you, doubts and all. How can I do less? What would bother me—" Charles shook his head at the inadequacy of his words "—is if I had to do without you."

The phrase swam in Kate's head, but she wouldn't be deterred.

"Okay, so you two accept me. What about your congregation? Could they accept me, too? I wouldn't know what my duties were or how to behave. I have no experience in this line of work."

"Just be yourself. That's more than sufficient."

His answer wasn't.

"Charles—" she protested.

"Kate," he interrupted. "Listen to me. The church has joined the rest of the world in the twentieth century. It doesn't expect ministers' wives to be accessories or handmaidens, and I couldn't minister to a congregation that had that kind of antiquated notion. As my wife, you'll be viewed as a person in your own right with a separate life to lead. Many spouses have demanding careers of their own." His mouth quirked. "I know one minister's mate who's a lapsed Hindu neurosurgeon."

"And her husband accepts that?" Kate asked, startled.

"She's a he. His wife's the priest."

His twitching lips invited her to see the irony of the conversation as well as the reversal of roles Kate and Charles were playing.

Kate tried to keep her expression sober, but a bubble of mirth escaped her lips. Then another. Finally, she broke into laughter even as she accused him, "You don't play fair, Charles Sheffield."

"You know what they say about love and war." He paused. "I love you, Kate."

The sudden intensity of his tone reduced her to silence.

"And I believe you love me, too."

He waited for confirmation.

Kate refused to give it.

A new suspicion stirred in her mind. Slowly she voiced it. "Is that where this 'seduction' was leading? To a proposal?"

"Yes."

"You tricked me."

"Did I?"

"We never mentioned marriage."

"No. But if we had, I'd have been honest about my intentions."

"You can say that now! A woman doesn't go around asking a man if he intends to marry her."

"Especially if she's afraid of the answer." His astute observation cut too close to the bone.

He said the next words with a gentle ruthlessness. "Kate, we've known each other for months. Did you really believe either one of us could enter into a sexual relationship without a commitment? Love? The need to care for each other? Those feelings spell marriage in my book."

"Yes," Kate answered with a trace of bitterness. "But we don't operate from the same book. We've already established that."

He shook his head. "Don't try to fool me, Kate. You're one of the most moral persons I know. That's why you were shocked just now that I hadn't vetted you, because you thought I hadn't fulfilled an obligation. You give too much, Kate, and take too little. You're a mass of guilts and shouldn'ts. My dutiful, puritan agnostic."

Charles's voice became a soft wooing, causing all thoughts of their discussion to flee Kate's mind. "I want to change that. I want to cherish you. I want to make you feel more alive than you've ever felt before."

He ran a gentle hand over her brow, down the side of her face and over the line of her throat until he cupped her neck, making her tremble. "I want to make love to you, to love you and give to you all the days of my life. I can only do that if we marry. I admit, I'm being very selfish about it all."

"And...and you won't have an affair with me?"

"Not without love."

"But—" she objected and her voice wobbled "—I do love you."

"I know. And I can't tell you how happy that makes me."

Their eyes met and locked together as he continued quietly. "But I'm not sure you love me enough to allow yourself to need me. I'm really being greedy. I want it all. Because you see, I need you. Not just anyone. You. Katharine Amanda Byers Hennessey. Will you marry me?"

Kate tore her eyes away from his. She yearned to say yes. In her haste to suppress that longing, Kate scrambled to her feet and turned her back to Charles so that she didn't have to face him.

"I . . . I can't give you an answer tonight." Kate stumbled over the words. "At least, not the answer you want. There are too many factors to consider."

"The children?"

"Michael." Kate turned to face him again. "Charles, are you staying in this country because of me? I couldn't live with that. Especially not knowing what will happen between us."

"I'm staying because I want to. And yes, you're a part of it. I'm sorry." Charles's tone was gentle but determined. "You don't have any choice in the matter." He came to where she stood and held her so that she couldn't turn away. "Kate . . . don't look so grim, love. Nothing terrible's happened."

"Hasn't it?" she asked woefully.

The smile Charles gave her as an answer was so tender it tore at her heart.

"Look," he said patiently, "I . . . love . . . you." He punctuated each pause with a kiss. "And you love me. We'll start from there. And let the tomorrows take care of themselves."

"Tomorrow!" she yelped, remembering. "I'm taking you over to my mother's. It's all arranged!"

"Yes?"

"But she'll know! She has an extra sense about this sort of thing."

"You mean about the fact I'm in love with you. Kate...the whole world knows. Everyone who sees us together realizes I'm absolutely besotted. I can't keep my hands off you. I'm randy as hell."

"Charles, you've got to promise to behave yourself tomorrow. My mother thinks you're a priest."

"I am a priest," he objected mildly.

"Yes, but she's very conservative. At first she hoped you might save my soul. Now she'll know..."

"...I'm after your body. I'm after them both, Kate. I want you, body and soul."

"Will you be serious?"

"You're serious enough for both of us. Can't you just let dinner with your family take care of itself?"

SHE DIDN'T HAVE ANY CHOICE, Kate realized the next afternoon. When they arrived at Connie's, the atmosphere was thick with unspoken questions. Both of her sisters were in town with their families. Her brother was there with his long-time girlfriend. The entire mob had gathered. Everyone was noisy, convivial and astir at the appearance of Kate's escort. She could sense the avid speculation beneath the holiday chatter and knew once Charles and she were gone, they'd be the main topic of conversation.

Kate remained in a perpetual state of nerves during dinner and afterward. Charles, on the other hand, carried off the visit with panache, complimenting Connie's cornbread stuffing lavishly, answering questions about England, giving his impressions of Austin, and generally falling in with everyone's suggestion that he make himself at home.

By the time they left, Connie was starry-eyed, Kate was limp, the boys were blessedly preoccupied with their various treasures and Charles seemed quite satisfied with the day's events.

When Kate went to bed that night, her last exhausted thought was that this Christmas season had been like no other she'd ever known. Heaven alone knew what the new year had in store. Because Charles's proposal changed everything between them. It was as if Kate were looking through a kaleidoscope at her life and with a single twist, he'd changed the familiar patterns.

Charles wasn't leaving Austin in the foreseeable future. And he envisioned a permanent commitment between them. The grand six-month passion Kate had accepted as her fate had become an illusion, a convenient fiction in her mind.

Maybe a six-month passion had been all she'd wanted. A temporary ill-fated love that she could look back on with a twinge of pain and nostalgia while she settled into the same old grooves, living out a four-hanky tearjerker of her own creation.

Instead, Charles was challenging her with very real choices. Asking her to create a whole new life with him. And she had a million doubts and questions. The problems she saw before them seemed insurmountable. When she'd tried to confront Charles with some of them, he'd brushed them aside.

Now, she wanted to see Lynn in the worst way. But Lynn was in San Antonio visiting family. After that she'd be in Colorado skiing. It might be two weeks or more before they'd have a chance for a heart-to-heart talk.

Help came to Kate, as it turned out, from a different source.

IT WAS THE MONDAY after New Year's Day and Millicent was assisting Kate with the bulletin as she did every week. Kate was used to the older woman dropping in at odd moments to volunteer her time. Sometimes Millicent would stop by the office for a chat after a meeting of the altar guild. Kate realized early on that Millicent had not been such a constant visitor to the church office when Phoebe was in charge, for the two women had cordially despised each other.

Millicent and Kate had become fast friends. Both enjoyed matching wits. Millicent would slyly probe the state of Kate's heart and Kate would usually parry with some benign comment that frustrated Millicent. Then the older woman would make an unexpected ribald remark that could render Kate speechless. Kate didn't know what she'd have done without her.

Today, as Millicent folded and stapled the newsletters so that Kate could paste on the address labels, she asked her standard question. "So... how are you and Charles progressing?"

The query had become a joke between them. Yet, now, it brought a blush to Kate's face that she couldn't control.

"Ahhh, I detect a fresh development." Millicent stopped her folding to scrutinize Kate. "You're such a shy child, I'm not sure how to phrase my next question."

"You won't phrase it at all," Kate retorted and continued blushing. Millicent detected more than embarrassment in Kate's face.

"Come dear," she said, putting an end to her teasing. "What's bothering you? You can talk to me."

Suddenly Kate realized she could do just that. Perhaps Millicent was the perfect person to confide in.

The words rushed out before Kate lost her nerve. "Charles asked me to marry him."

As happened so often, Millicent's response confounded her. "That's very nice, Kate. What do you get out of the deal?"

Kate went into a fit of choking laughter. "I... Well, I...I hadn't really thought before. Charles, I suppose."

"I guess it's a fair trade. You get a sexy husband. He gets the perfect wife."

"That's just it," Kate protested, Millicent's words sobering her. "I'm far from perfect. In fact, just the opposite."

"And that's what's troubling you about accepting his proposal."

Kate looked at Millicent sharply. "You're a fox," she murmured.

Millicent shrugged daintily and began to probe. "Have you talked to Charles about this at all?"

"I tried to. But he refused to discuss it. He said I should just be myself, and that would be sufficient."

"Men," Millicent snorted. "They can be so stupid."

At that particular moment Kate had to agree.

"You see," Millicent explained to Kate, as though she were in a classroom, "Charles is afraid you'll feel hemmed in. He's determined for you to have your freedom. What he doesn't understand are the practicalities of life."

"That's right! That's exactly right. As Charles's wife people will expect certain things of me. I'm not sure if I can meet those expectations."

"You do every day."

"What do you mean? Are you telling me being Charles's wife is like being his secretary?"

"With a few extra perks thrown in. Listen, Kate, I've been in the church all my life. I've seen every variety of pastor's wife, good, bad and indifferent. I know the qualities it takes."

"And they are?"

"Discretion, for one thing. It doesn't pay to gossip. Which you never do." She cast an impish glance Kate's way. "More's the pity."

Kate smiled. "And?"

"Compassion. An ability to think the best of people and not to condemn them when they're at their worst. Also a generosity of spirit. There's pettiness in the church just as any place else. You can't stoop to that, but I have no fears that you will. And luckily for Charles you have a giving nature. To fill him up when he's drained himself dry."

She paused to gaze at Kate sympathetically. "Most of all, you can't be possessive. You'll share Charles with every member of the flock. If you recognize that now, you'll be a happier woman."

Her tone was matter-of-fact. "As you can see, Kate, you fit the bill perfectly. Charles couldn't have picked better if he'd ordered from a Sears catalogue."

"Oh, Millicent..." Kate was half way between tears and laughter. "I'm not all that."

"You're that and more." Millicent defied contradiction.

"But what if—" Kate's voice was still troubled "—there's something lacking in me?"

"And what would that be?"

"An orthodox belief system. Millicent, I don't want to be hypocritical."

"You don't have to be. Is that all that's bothering you?"

"Is that all?"

"You know, child. Billy, my husband, used to say I was a terrible Christian. Never crossed my *T*s or dotted my *I*s. I used to, though, when I was young, before Bill Jr. died."

"Your husband?" Kate asked, confused.

"Our only child. He was killed in the Korean War when he was twenty-two years old."

"I-I didn't know."

"I don't talk about him much. There's nothing worse than an old lady who cries over the cards she's been dealt. At this stage of life acceptance is a necessary virtue."

Sure enough, there was moisture in Millicent's eyes, but her voice remained steady. "When Bill Jr. died, my tidy structure of beliefs came tumbling down. I've never felt so lost and alone. Then faith came to my rescue, a conscious leap of faith beyond the boundaries of belief." Millicent smiled at Kate gently. "And my faith has sustained me. Even when I lost my Billy after forty years of marriage."

"Oh, Millicent," Kate said, with heartfelt sincerity. "I wish I could feel as you do."

"I suspect you will, dear, when you need to. When the time is right."

CHAPTER TWELVE

"EMMANUEL CHURCH. This is Kate Hennessey speaking." There was a moment of silence at the other end of the line. Kate could hear the sounds of traffic in the background.

"I'd like to speak to Father Sheffield." The familiar voice tugged at Kate's memory.

"Certainly," she said. "May I ask who's calling?"

There was another pause. "Tell him Greg Arnold. It's urgent."

Kate relayed the message, then she sat staring at the red light on her telephone until it blinked out. She jumped to her feet and met Charles as he came out of his study, shrugging into his overcoat.

He had an air of purpose that fed her apprehension.

"Well?"

"It's Greg all right. He's at the bus station. Just came into town. He called Jill at work to find she'd phoned in sick. Tried the old number. When he heard it was disconnected, he became frantic to know where she and the kids could be. Since he doesn't have any money for taxi fare, I'm going to pick him up and bring him back here. Will you call Jill at her parents? See if she's ready to see him."

Kate nodded and asked, "Where's he been?"

"I don't know yet. But I think...he's stopped running."

As soon as Charles was gone, Kate found the number Jill had given her and dialed it.

Jill's mother answered.

"This is Kate Hennessey. I'd like to speak to Jill, please."

"Hello, Kate. Jill's not feeling well. May I take a message?"

"I really need to speak to her. It's important."

When Jill came on the line her voice was thick and a little weak. "Kate? What's wrong? Is it one of the kids?"

"No..." Kate hesitated.

"You've heard something, haven't you? About Greg."

"Yes, it's Greg. He's just called from the bus station. Charles's gone to bring him here to the office."

"I'll be right over."

"Jill, wait. Are you sure?"

"Kate, I have to see him."

Kate could hear Jill's mother's protest in the background. "Mom, I'm going," Jill said faintly. "Don't try to stop me! Kate, I'll be over as soon as I dress."

Ten minutes later, Charles reappeared, Greg Arnold by his side.

The weeks of running had taken its toll on the younger man. Kate remembered his blond, clean-cut good looks. When he'd come to see Charles before, he'd worn a stylish suit with a swaggering air.

Now Greg looked beaten down as he hovered near Charles, drawing strength from him. His hair was longer and lank and he looked as if he needed a shave. His frayed jeans and wrinkled shirt looked none too clean.

"Did you get hold of Jill?" he asked Kate hesitantly.

"Yes. She's sick with the flu, but she's coming right over."

A wave of relief washed over his face, followed immediately by a look of apprehension. "I don't know how I'm going to face her."

"Some food would help." Charles glanced over at Kate and asked with a creditable drawl, "Do you think you can rustle up some lunch?"

"Are hamburgers okay? I'll phone out for them."

Charles nodded. "I think," he said, for Kate's benefit, "we'll go into the library away from the telephone."

Greg followed Charles mutely. Jill arrived minutes after the hamburgers, which Kate had taken into the two men. The woman looked worse than she'd sounded. Kate urged her to sit a moment before facing Greg.

"How does he seem?" Jill croaked.

"Haggard. He doesn't look as if he's eaten right." Kate sat down beside Jill and covered her twisting hands. "But other than that, he's in one piece."

Jill's spidery fingers turned upward to clutch at Kate's. Jill had lost weight, too. Her clothes hung on her. She and Greg were a matched pair.

"Will you come with me when I see him? I'd like you to be there."

"Of course."

The two women stood. Jill swayed and grabbed Kate's arm.

"I'm all right," she assured Kate unconvincingly.

"I know you are." Kate knew nothing of the kind and she was determined to stay by Jill's side. When they entered the study, the two men shot out of their chairs, alarmed. Kate guided Jill to a chair and perched nearby.

"Jill...honey," Greg said tentatively as he approached his wife.

The look Jill gave him stopped him in his tracks. "It's a little late to be worried, Greg. Where were you when I was sick out of my mind, because I didn't know where you were or even if you were alive? Where were you for Lance and Dane's Christmas? We had to move back in with my parents, because of the phone calls and people watching the house. Where were you when they threatened me?"

Jill's anger faded from her voice leaving only anguish. "Where were you, Greg? I looked everywhere I could think of."

As Greg repeated, "Threatened? They threatened you?"

"Before I moved. The last time they called. They said if I didn't tell them where you were, something might happen to me and the kids. That's when I knew I had to leave."

"Did you call the police?"

"I couldn't do that, Greg. You know why."

Greg's jaws worked. "I'm sorry, if I'd only known. You have every right to hate me. I acted like a fool when I ran away. I've spent the last month trying to work up the courage to come back and face you. I had no idea they'd try to get to me through you."

"Where were you, Greg?" Jill asked for the third time.

Greg closed his eyes tightly, his shoulders hunched over. "I was in hell."

Greg looked over at Charles. He smiled twistedly. "Hell covers a lot of territory. I hitched a ride to El Paso. After that, New Mexico. Eventually I ended up in L.A. Took odd jobs to feed myself, but most of what I made went to the horses. Christmas Day I was at the track losing my last week's wages." His hands clenched into fists. "It was the worst day of my life. And the funny thing is," Greg said in a humorless voice, "no matter how hard I ran, I couldn't stay ahead of myself. For the first time I had to take a hard look at what I'd become, the people I'd hurt. How fast I was falling."

Greg's voice began to shake. "When I looked into the pit, it didn't have a bottom. That's when I knew I had to come back and get help. And straighten things out with you, Jill. I can't expect you to come back to me after all I've done.

But I want to do what's right and responsible by you and the kids."

"Does that mean," asked Charles, "you're ready to talk to Lieutenant Eccles?"

There was a strained silence before Greg answered. "If I have to. If that's what it takes to get those goons off my back and away from my family. A lot of other guys in this town are in the same fix I am. The scene here is rotten. Maybe what I know will save some other fool who's in over his head."

"Good." Charles cupped Greg's shoulder for a moment. "I'll call Nolan now."

After Charles left, no one spoke. The silence was broken at last by a wrenching sigh, then a faint sob.

Greg sprang from his chair and knelt beside Jill, whose shoulders had begun to shake.

"It's all right, honey. Everything's going to be okay."

One of Jill's hands reached out blindly to touch his face. "I was so scared of what you might do to yourself."

"Don't be scared," Greg pleaded in an agonized voice. "I won't do anything to hurt you like that, I swear. I won't give up. And I won't fight it alone anymore. Father Sheffield has already looked into professional help."

"I want to help," Jill said urgently. "I won't run away either, Greg. I love you."

"Don't say anything you'll regret later." Greg's tone was harsh.

"No. We'll just take one day at a time."

Kate blinked back tears.

Charles reentered the room and took in the evidence of reconciliation between the Arnolds. Kate felt his touch along her back. She reached up, grasped his hand and squeezed it.

"Nolan'll be here shortly," Charles announced to the room at large. "Are you sure Jill shouldn't lie down?" he asked Kate.

"An excellent suggestion," she replied, smiling.

Greg helped his wife to her feet. They all moved back into Kate's office and propped Jill up amongst the cushions of the couch.

Jill giggled. "This couch and I are getting to be old friends."

Her feeble joke helped lighten the mood. Greg asked about the twins, and Jill proudly listed their accomplishments. When Nolan arrived, he found a surprisingly peaceful group.

Everyone became tense as he entered, however. A policeman's lot in life, Charles thought. The badge inspired fear. Jill looked haunted, Greg's face was a study in conflicting emotions and even Kate seemed a little wary.

Nolan assessed the situation. "Greg. Mrs. Arnold."

"This is Kate Hennessey, my assistant." Charles made the only necessary introduction. Nolan turned to Kate with obvious interest.

Kate held out her hand. "We've talked on the phone. I feel as if I know you."

"I feel as if I know you, too," Nolan said, "especially after everything Charles has told me."

Kate's eyebrows shot up. She saw the teasing glint in the lieutenant's eyes and cast a suspicious glance at Charles who studiously ignored it. If Kate didn't know better, she'd have sworn Charles looked guilty. Charles guilty? What on earth for?

Her musings stopped with Nolan's next words.

"Is there somewhere we can talk without being disturbed?"

Charles motioned the way into his study. When the women followed, Nolan halted abruptly.

Jill read his expression. "You're not keeping me out, Lieutenant. Greg's my husband. I have a right to know what's going to happen to him."

"Jill..." Greg protested.

"No, Greg. We're in this together. You can't keep me in the dark."

Kate, who'd elected herself the younger woman's protector, was determined to take a stand of her own if necessary. But Nolan Eccles voiced no objections to Kate's presence. She realized why when she caught his eye on her supporting arm around Jill's waist. Lieutenant Eccles was a perceptive man, Kate realized. But then if Charles respected him, he'd have to be.

The foursome had become a quintet. This time as everyone settled around the table in the library, Nolan took charge. He did so firmly, yet with a sensitivity that pleased Kate. Without realizing it, she felt better about his presence.

"Charles told me you'd left town," Nolan said to Greg. "Been doing some thinking?"

"Yes."

"And what did you decide?"

"I decided to come home and try to straighten out this mess I'm in. Lieutenant, they've threatened Jill and the boys. I want police protection."

"You'll get it for yourself as well as your family. But we need your cooperation."

Greg's expression was bitter. "Is that the only way we'll get protection?"

"No. The department will do all it can to ensure your family's safety. Mrs. Arnold—could you tell me about the threats?"

Jill told her story.

Afterward Nolan asked, "Have you had any phone calls since you moved in with your folks? Seen anything suspicious?"

"No. Kate said they were only trying to get to Greg through me. Maybe I convinced them I didn't know where he was."

"Kate was right. Let's hope you did convince them. But you realize, Greg, that until we have the evidence to put the men who assaulted you and their bosses behind bars, neither you nor your family can rest easy. I'm not trying to scare you. Those are just the facts."

"I'll do whatever I have to do."

"Good. But first I must warn you. By cooperating with us, you'll admit to illegal gambling. We'll plea bargain. You should get off with parole, but I can't promise anything until we know more." Nolan read Greg his rights and turned to Charles. "Have you checked with a lawyer?"

"He can be here in fifteen minutes."

"I don't need a lawyer." Greg's voice cut through Charles's. "I need...peace." He took a deep breath. "I agreed to talk and I will. Father Sheffield said I could trust you, I trust him.... So—" Greg hunched over "—let's get on with it."

"Greg," Nolan's tone conveyed his sincerity. "I can promise you this. If you can supply us the information we need, we'll use it to get further evidence. Evidence that will stand independent of your testimony. It's possible you won't be called to testify at all. If you do, we'll make it appear that you're an unwilling witness. If necessary, we'll get you and your family out of town. We'll do everything it takes for your safety. Do you understand what I'm saying?"

"Yes."

Everyone in the room understood. The ordeal was far from over. In a way, it was just beginning.

"Okay." Nolan seemed to switch gears. He looked at Kate. "I'm going to have to insist that you and Jill leave now."

Jill started to protest again, but Nolan was firm. "This is a major investigation that might lead anywhere. Greg's knowledge puts him in danger. I won't place you two in danger, as well."

Greg agreed. "Jill, please, the Lieutenant's right. Besides . . . I'd just as soon you didn't know all the sordid details. Charles is here. I'll be okay. You can stop protecting me."

Jill gave in grudgingly. "But I'm not leaving. I'll be just in the other room."

"There are logistics to be worked out," Nolan said. "This is only the beginning." His words echoed the thoughts of everyone in the room.

Kate and Jill exited and Kate closed the door behind them. Truth to tell, she was relieved for herself and Jill. Still, she found it very interesting that Nolan had wanted Charles to stay. He had no qualms about Charles being privy to the investigation. Didn't that spell danger for Charles just as it would have for Jill and her? For a moment, Kate felt an irrational fear. She banished it firmly and put her mind to tending the younger woman.

Jill's skin was flushed by now and hot to the touch. She displayed a weak docility. When Kate brought her two aspirin and a glass of cool water, Jill drank it thirstily, lay back on the couch, and stared at the ceiling.

They settled in to wait. Jill dozed occasionally. Kate went to her desk and shuffled papers. But both women's minds were on the room two doors down.

Fifteen minutes ticked by, thirty. An hour passed. At one point, Kate sensed movement, looked up and saw Jill fighting tears again. She went over and knelt down. "Is there anything I can do?"

"Make them hurry. I can't stand it much longer."

"I know. It's hard. But in some ways, don't you think the worst is past?"

"Please, keep reminding me of that. At least now I know where Greg is. Do you think Lieutenant Eccles can really be trusted?"

"I'm sure of it. Charles wouldn't have urged Greg to talk to him if he didn't feel he was placing him in good hands."

Jill seemed unconvinced.

Kate grinned encouragingly. "You know what our trouble is, don't you? We're not used to being placed in such a traditionally feminine role. I feel like I'm standing at the gate of the old plantation home waving a white handkerchief as my man marches off to war."

She'd given Jill something new to think about. "Is Charles your man?"

Now Kate's skin felt hot and flushed. "I was speaking metaphorically."

But Jill wasn't stupid. She grinned at Kate. "Sure you were. I've seen the looks you two exchange. I just didn't put two and two together. What's it like?" Jill asked curiously, "being attracted to a man like Charles?"

"Disconcerting," Kate answered wryly, after a minute. At least she'd gotten Jill's mind off the interrogation.

"I can see why you're attracted," Jill went on. "He's incredibly handsome. But he doesn't give off sexual vibes."

Only to Kate.

"Of course, I can see why he wouldn't," Jill remarked thoughtfully. "That could be risky in his line of work."

Kate decided she'd had enough of being Jill's diversion and she was relieved when the men chose that moment to enter the room.

Greg looked white as a sheet and drained. Charles was grim, and Nolan Eccles appeared grimly satisfied.

He surveyed the room and its anxious inhabitants. "The next question is, where do we put Greg so that no one can find him?"

Charles spoke up immediately. "The best place for him to stay is with me."

Nolan started to protest. Charles cut him short. "I'm the logical choice, Nolan. No one knows I'm involved except the people in this room. Would you like to come stay with me, Greg?"

"Not if it puts you in danger."

Kate looked at Charles, the word danger setting up a clamoring in her head.

"I'm in no danger," Charles said, dismissing her unvoiced protest. "Not if we take the necessary precautions. When you meet with Greg, Nolan, you can come out to the parsonage. Admit it. I have the perfect safe house."

Jill chose this moment to speak up. "Why can't we find a place and stay together? I don't want Greg to go through this alone."

This time Greg protested. "Don't kid yourself, Jill. They know where you are. It's what they're waiting for...our contacting each other. Stay with your parents. That way you and the kids will be safe."

"But what about Lance and Dane? They've missed their father."

Greg's look grew bleak. He shook his head.

Kate decided this was the proper time for a suggestion. "I can handle that. No one knows I'm involved, except with

Jill. No one would think anything of it if I were to take Jill and the children for a ride and drive by Charles's house.''

"No." Charles bit off the single word. Kate's eyes challenged him. Danger? Oh, yes, there was danger. She could read it in his face at the thought of her involvement.

But I'm in this, buster. Just as deep as you. And it's too late now to hustle me out.

Charles's eyes said, *"Kate, please, no. You don't know what you're doing."*

I know what I'm doing. Just like you.

Charles turned away, admitting defeat. Kate looked at Nolan, issuing another challenge. But she got no more silent arguments, just a stern caution to them all.

"All right. Everybody gets to play. But remember I'm in charge and don't make a move without my permission. Nobody does anything rash. I want Jill to go home and get back in bed." He pointed to her. "Get well. Those are your orders."

He turned to Charles. "I'm going to drive around and scout out the neighborhood, see if you and Greg picked up a tail from the bus station. When I give the okay you take Greg to your house. And you," this time he addressed Greg. "I don't want you to so much as show your face at a window. Stay put and out of sight. Remember you're the one they're after."

Greg nodded obediently, cowed a little by Nolan's tone.

"Any orders for me?" Kate asked pertly, trying to clear the air of the menace they were feeling.

"Yeah." Nolan grinned. "You stay here and man the phones so we don't look like ants clearing a nest. Tell anyone who calls that Charles is with a parishioner. And—if you can—see if you can keep this guy," he said, jerking a thumb at Charles, "out of trouble."

"That's a pretty tall order," Kate responded demurely. "But I'll do my best."

"Lieutenant Eccles," Jill said, interrupting the banter. "How...how long will we have to live like this? How long will it take to use Greg's information to build a case?"

Nolan sobered again. "I wish I could tell you. If we're lucky, we'll have enough evidence to present to the grand jury when it convenes in February."

"A month?" Jill asked, horrified.

"If we're lucky. So everybody might as well hunker down for the duration. Greg, Charles...I hope you can stand each other when this is all over."

By this time, it had finally dawned on Greg just what he'd done. He was no longer running. He'd faced Jill, Charles, Lieutenant Eccles. Himself. A relieved euphoria washed over him. Nolan's comment made him smile, and his charm returned. "Well, I can tell you, Charles isn't my first choice for a housemate." He grinned at Jill. "But I guess he'll do."

What happened next surprised everyone. Charles smiled and stared directly at Kate. "I have to confess, Greg, you're not my first choice for a housemate either. But we'll both have to make do for now."

Kate turned beet red. Nolan chuckled. Jill studied Charles and Kate with interest. Greg was pleased with himself that he'd injected a note of humor to the gathering and he was encouraged at Jill's reaction to his unspoken message.

After Jill picked up her purse and put her coat on, she reached her arms around Greg and cradled her face on his chest. "I'm glad you're back. I missed you. No, don't kiss me, you'll get germs."

"The hell with germs. I missed you, too. And I'll keep missing you until this is over. Jill," he whispered as his lips brushed her cheek. "I love you. And I'm going to do whatever it takes to get over this craziness. Don't give up on me."

"I won't. I love you, too."

"Be careful driving home. Kiss Dane and Lance for me."

"I will. And I'll call you." She looked over at Lieutenant Eccles beseechingly. "I can at least do that, can't I?"

Nolan nodded. "Until I say differently."

Kate walked Jill out to her car, glancing around warily. She saw nothing suspicious. She could tell, however, that the woman beside her was feeling better. It was amazing what a little hope did for aches and pains.

Jill showed her improved health with an aside as she slipped into her car. "I take back what I said, Kate. The man's very sexy. You bring out a whole other side to him."

Kate's only comment was an amused glance.

She watched Jill drive away and glanced around once more, walked back in and reported to Nolan. He left. Moments later, the telephone rang and Kate answered.

"Put Charles on the phone," Nolan instructed.

Charles took the receiver and had a brief conversation before he hung up. Then he nodded to Greg and put on his coat. Kate couldn't help herself. She rushed over to him, put her hand on his sleeve and pleaded earnestly. "Be careful."

Charles grinned. Kate sensed that he was in a playful mood and wondered uneasily how it would manifest itself. In spite of his sober clothing, there was very little of the priest about him at that moment. Instead, with his British good looks and blazing blue eyes, he reminded her of a dashing cavalier off to seek adventure.

He shattered her fantasy with a Bogart twang. "Listen, Doll Face, don't lose sleep over me. Careful's my middle name."

Without warning, he swept her into a wild embrace reminiscent of a forties tearjerker. The kiss he planted on her lips left her feeling dizzy.

"This isn't goodbye. It's merely *au revoir*," Charles announced dramatically.

All Kate could do was roll her eyes and push him through the door. After the two men left, it was several minutes before she regained a modicum of composure.

CHAPTER THIRTEEN

"FRIENDS, ROMANS, COUNTRYMEN, lend me your toes...
and fingers...and a kidney and a spleen...."

Kate shifted her gaze from the book she was holding and
glared at her younger son, whose face assumed an innocent
expression. "Very funny. You're not trying. We'll never get
the speech memorized at this rate."

"But Mom, I thought my version had a real ring to it.
After they hacked Caesar up, he probably needed spare
parts."

He coaxed her with a grin. Kate valiantly ignored it.

"You know what, Mom. You're a grouch." This time
Michael was aiming to punch one of her buttons.

He succeeded with a vengeance. "A worried grouch!" she
countered. "You've got to have this speech down by day
after tomorrow. It's thirty-five lines long, and we've just
begun. You asked for my help. Now take advantage of it."

"Oh, what's the use," Michael said. "I'll never get it
memorized in time. I hate this stuff."

Kate was indignant. "This 'stuff' is William Shakespeare."

Michael shrugged but stopped short of saying, "So
what?"

She changed tactics. "Okay, okay. Forget that he's the
greatest playwright of the English language. Forget the fact
that he has a love affair with words that would sizzle your
innards. Michael, Shakespeare's a showman. He's a thrill a

minute. *Julius Caesar* has as much blood and gore as a Mad Max movie. I thought he would appeal to you.''

"Oh, he's okay, I guess, when I understand him. I'm just no good at memorization. We have to recite this in front of the class. It'll be my luck to go blank like a bozo.''

Kate felt a tug of sympathy. Her son was resentful and defeated before they'd even begun. She remembered how some of their past study sessions had gone. By the end of the evening, the air would probably be thick with mutual panic.

Kate tried to stay cool. "We have plenty of time, so let's take it slow. I'll read the speech aloud, then we'll discuss what it means, and Antony's purpose in giving it.''

Michael didn't look excited about her proposal. Still, he didn't object.

Kate forged ahead. "Friends, Romans, countrymen, lend me your *ears*. I come to *bury* Caesar not to *praise* him.''

As the stirring words tripped off her tongue, Kate tried to infuse them with a sense of high drama. The crowds, the noise, Antony's persuasiveness. Her free hand began to slice the air flamboyantly. She was really getting into the spirit of the speech, her voice reverberating around the walls of the kitchen. Then she made the mistake of looking up.

Michael was fighting giggles.

Kate had to fight back a giggle herself. "All right,'' she admitted, "so I don't make a good Marc Antony. You think Richard Burton could have done it better?''

Michael's amusement broke its bounds and he began to whoop. Kate joined him helplessly.

Charles found them like that. He answered their surprised looks at his appearance. "Clark let me in. He told me you were in the kitchen, struggling with *Julius Caesar*. I thought maybe I could help.''

Michael's expression changed from mirth to alarm. Kate glanced at Charles warily. He'd known her agenda for the evening, for she'd mentioned it in passing at work that day. And he'd never said a word about coming over.

Now her look switched to Michael. How was he taking Charles's offer? She crossed her fingers silently, hoping Michael's manners would triumph.

They did ... just. "How can you help?" he asked baldly.

Charles settled comfortably at the table. "I had to memorize this speech when I was about your age. As it turned out, I had to memorize the whole bloody part. I fancied myself quite an actor at the time." He drew himself up at Kate's raised eyebrows and looked at her down the regal line of his nose. "I'll have you know, I was considering a career on the boards. I took the role of Antony when we performed this play one term."

His haughty look vanished, replaced by a boyish grin. "I was a disaster." Kate's eyebrows rose again. "Oh, I was very effective—when my voice didn't crack, which it did at every dramatic moment. I kept getting laughs on my best lines."

By now he had both Michael and Kate smiling. "The experience nipped my acting career in the bud, for which the London stage should be very thankful. The only vestige of my stint as an actor is that every line of this play is etched indelibly in my mind."

Charles's look grew whimsical as he remembered. "Friends, Romans, countrymen..." he began absently as though testing his recall. "Lend me your ears. I come to bury Caesar not to praise him." Charles's voice grew stronger. "The evil that men do lives after them, the good is oft interred with their bones." A pause. "So let it be with Caesar."

The words continued to roll out in that rich English voice. His tone was sometimes quiet, sometimes reasonable and finally, urgently pleading.

Kate and Michael sat enthralled. Charles was wrong—the stage had missed a rare talent. The two of them were being magically seduced by it and by the sheepish grin Charles bestowed upon them when he finished, as if he was admitting he knew he'd put on a show.

"Oh, that I could have spoken the Bard's words like that twenty-five years ago."

Before either one of them could respond, Charles turned to Michael. "I had real trouble with this speech. Perhaps I could give you a few pointers on how I finally learned it."

"Yeah," Michael agreed, slightly stunned. "Maybe you could."

Kate got up from the table hastily, taking her diet drink with her. "You don't need two coaches. I'll leave you in peace and go back to the computer."

Michael looked at her imploringly. Kate ignored him. As she exited the room, Charles had already moved over a chair so that he and Michael shared the book between them.

Kate kept an eye on the clock as she made herself write, determined to stay away an hour. But she wondered how long it would take Michael to search her out with a feeble excuse to escape Charles's clutches.

The police detective studied each of the persons gathered in the lawyer's study for the reading of the will. All of them were relatives of the dear, departed Randolph.

Lovely lacquered Rebecca, his wife. His envious sister and greedy brother-in-law. The simpering aunt. The laconic second cousin. Everyone had a motive for killing the unlamented Randolph. But which one—or more of them—had had the opportunity?

The detective stood up to speak. "Of course you realize that we have to find the murderer—or murderers—before any of you can profit from this will."

"Murderers?" The speaker was the second cousin, the brightest of the lot.

"Yes. This is a very interesting case. I have only one body, but there were three killings." A faint sigh drifted across the room. The detective glanced around sharply, but it was impossible to say where the sound had originated. He continued his calculated explanation. "First, Randolph was stabbed, a wound that would have proved more than fatal. Then he was bashed over the head causing a massive hemorrhage. Finally, he was dragged out into the driveway and run over by a car." The detective waited for the words to sink in.

"Now, I ask myself," he continued finally, "am I hunting for one killer who was particularly versatile. Or am I faced with a group effort?"

Kate looked at her watch and was surprised to see two hours had passed. Not a soul had been in to disturb her. Suddenly overcome with curiosity, Kate wandered back into the kitchen on the pretext of refilling her glass.

Michael and Charles didn't notice her entrance. The latter was leaning back casually in his chair, his expression offering encouragement, while Michael negotiated an unfamiliar line.

Michael stumbled over a phrase and scowled. Then he made a rude remark. Charles grinned and twisted the garbled words even further, causing them both to break into laughter. Michael was as relaxed as Kate could ever remember seeing him in Charles's company. He was a hell of a lot more relaxed than earlier, when she and he had had a go at it.

Smiling vaguely to herself, Kate strolled back to her computer.

LATER THAT WEEK, Kate wore that same vague smile. She was daydreaming, the thoughts drifting through her mind filtering out the sounds of a Thursday morning. Charles and Phil were in Charles's study discussing future music selections. The preschoolers had trooped through the reception area minutes ago from a morning recess, on their way to their classroom. The procession had swept in the crisp air of the January day that still clung to their cheeks and hair and coats.

Earlier in the week a cold front had pushed through Austin, plunging the temperatures into the thirties and chilling bones with a freezing drizzle. This morning, however, the sun had risen into a milky blue sky to reclaim and warm its dominion. The temperature had climbed to fifty degrees, and the clear winter light outside her window beckoned to Kate as she sat at her desk, struggling with the filing. She had a sudden urge to fling open the outer doors and run onto the lawn to test the playground equipment. She controlled that urge but let her thoughts continue to wander as she sorted papers.

The Trials of Rebecca. Not a bad title. Not good, but not bad. And not terribly descriptive of the nearly completed manuscript. Or how about—The R and R Murders. Catchy? Gimmicky.

Kate discarded her idea and sighed. She'd do well to finish the book before she named it.

The Marriage of Kate and Charles. Now that was an interesting title. Of a fairy tale.

Kate wondered if she had the nerve to write that one.

She remembered Lynn's words on the phone before her friend had dashed off to the mountains, in response to Kate's confession of a proposal.

"And what were your objections?" Lynn had asked.

"I had several," Kate had said a little stiffly. "And they're valid." She'd searched for an excuse that Lynn would buy. "For one thing, I'm not sure it's the ethical thing to do."

Her words had elicited a hoot of laughter. "It's nice to have a friend," Lynn had finally managed to say, "with refined scruples."

"I try my best," Kate had muttered sourly.

"Well, try a little harder. Think about it, dear. You're saying you consider it right to sleep with Charles, but wrong to marry him."

"Put like that, I admit—"

"That's just what you're not doing, admitting..."

A gentle voice intruded on Kate's recollections.

"Millicent hasn't arrived yet, Kate. Should we check on her?"

"Oh, hello, Mrs. Marsh. Is it that close to eleven?" It was almost time for the weekly Bible class of which Mrs. Marsh and Millicent were members. Kate glanced down at her watch and saw it was nearly twenty after the hour. She felt a prickling of anxiety. Millicent was never, never late. Tardiness, she was wont to say, was a sure sign of encroaching senility.

"If you'll watch the telephone for a minute," Kate said to Mrs. Marsh as she rose from her desk, "I'll drive over and pick her up. I've been meaning to do that beginning this week. I was working up my courage."

Kate was glad for the excuse to get outside, and once there she took a minute to breathe in the fresh air that nipped at her senses. Peering down the street through the naked branches of a tree, she saw Millicent's figure leaning heavily on her cane as she made her way slowly up the gentle slope.

Kate shook her head wryly. How like the lady. Willing to sacrifice her vaunted punctuality to maintain her fierce independence. Millicent knew Kate or Charles would have gone for her. She had only to ask.

The older woman looked up. Kate waved and started toward her. Millicent made a vague gesture. She seemed to halt for a moment as though catching her breath, then clutched the front of her dress and crumpled slowly to the road.

From Kate's vantage point, it looked as if a bundle of used clothing had been discarded on the pavement, bathed in the clear white light of the day.

No!

But Kate knew instantly what had happened.

"Charles!" she yelled his name as she banged on his window. "Call 911! Millicent's collapsed on the street."

Running across the church yard, Kate's high heels dug into the rain-soaked ground, then skittered over the hard surface of the asphalt, impeding her progress. The sound of her own breathing rasped in her ears.

As she drew closer, Kate heard Millicent moan softly.

Kate breathed a silent plea of hope as she crouched down beside her.

Pain. It gripped Millicent's body, contorting her face. The force of it flooded over Kate, squeezing her own heart. Millicent's breathing was shallow and labored, but she was conscious. She knew that Kate was there. And one fragile hand waved feebly in the air until Kate captured it, murmuring assurances.

Although she hadn't heard his footsteps, Kate felt Charles's presence immediately. He knelt down and took Millicent into his arms, loosening her clothing.

A travesty of her wicked grin appeared on Millicent's face. "Took a heart attack...to get a man...to do that. Why...didn't I think of it before."

Charles smiled down at her tenderly. "You are a brazen woman, Millicent Greer."

Kate's throat constricted as she choked back tears.

A wailing siren pierced the deceptive quiet. As it grew louder, Kate looked up to see a huddled crowd of spectators standing in a semicircle, absolutely silent, their faces blank.

The ladies from the Bible class and an assortment of neighbors had gathered. Their stillness struck Kate as strange, until she realized that Millicent was a friend to each and every one of these people. This was no anonymous tragedy, bringing out the curious. It was as if a collective breath had been drawn in the immediate vicinity. Everyone was waiting, not daring to comprehend the moment.

The ambulance's arrival seemed to break the spell. The crowd made way for the medics. People began to whisper anxiously as Millicent was examined. Within minutes, she'd been lifted into the emergency vehicle, Charles by her side. The siren renewed its awful howling, the sound fading slowly.

"I'll meet you at the hospital," Kate had called to Charles before she hurried to her car. Fifteen minutes later, she brushed through the hospital doors where she found Charles answering questions for the admitting clerk.

Kate rushed over to them. "She's still alive, isn't she?"

Charles turned to Kate and nodded, but his expression was bleak. One arm went around her as Millicent's personal history was detailed and the forms completed.

"She's a widow," Charles answered, when asked about next of kin. "No living children. No family here in town. There's only one niece, I believe, who lives in Houston. I'm her minister. She was walking to the church when it happened.''

The rest of the information was gathered from the documents in Millicent's purse. As Kate riffled through the handbag, which was neat and scrupulously organized, a coldness came over her. She sank down into a nearby chair to heap the few possessions in her lap. These were so few items to represent so rich a life.

Kate wasn't ready for it to end. She wasn't ready for the clear, crisp, daydreaming morning to turn into a nightmare.

The hospital clerk had left them. Charles now sat beside her in the waiting room and the two of them were isolated by the empty chairs on either side. Kate looked around dazedly and noticed other clusters of people waiting restlessly, each group's boundaries marked by separate fears.

"I was on my way to get her," Kate fretted.

"Kate..."

"This shouldn't have happened."

"Kate, she's had a heart condition for years."

"But why today? It shouldn't have happened today." Not while Kate watched, feeling helpless, unable to halt the unfolding scene. It replayed endlessly in her mind. A small frail figure, falling silently into a heap in the bright sunshine.

"No day is exempt. For everything there is a season—a time to live, a time to die. Death, Kate, shares each and every moment with the living."

Kate turned to face him. "She won't make it, will she?"

"I don't think so." Charles closed his eyes and took a sharp breath.

For a moment his grief was naked. It wrenched her as much as did her own.

"I'm sorry." Kate laid a hand over his. "I know how much you care for her."

"How the whole church cares." His eyes met hers. "I said she has no family. That's not true. We're her family. Losing her is going to be hard for everyone to bear. She led by her example." Charles's voice caught for a second. "Despite all that had happened to her, Millicent never gave up on life."

"Maybe she won't give up now, either."

"Maybe..." Charles tried to prepare Kate. "But maybe she recognizes when it's time to let go."

By this time, Phil had appeared carrying the communion kit, which Charles took, thanking him. A member of the staff approached the three of them. "Father Sheffield? I'm Doctor Travis."

"Yes?"

"Mrs. Greer's asked to see you."

"What's her condition?" Charles asked.

"She's conscious, but deteriorating. She's asked us not to perform heroic measures. I'd hoped to talk to her family."

"There's none nearby. I'm her minister."

The doctor seemed faced with a hard decision. "Do you consider her rational? Does she know her own mind?"

Charles smiled wryly. "I've never met anyone who knew it better."

"I had that feeling myself." Dr. Travis sighed. "We're doing all we can to make her comfortable, administering oxygen to ease the stress. But it's only a matter of time. Come with me."

"Please, may I go, too?" Kate pleaded.

Dr. Travis turned to her.

"I'm just a friend. But...I want to be there."

He studied Kate for a moment and came to a conclusion. "It's normally against the rules. Only one visitor allowed at a time. But I think, in light of the circumstances, we'll bend them. There's also a fifteen-minute time limit." This time his words included them both. "I'll write up permission for you to stay as long as you need to."

They left Phil in the waiting room to fill in the other people as they arrived.

There was noise and purpose in the Intensive Care Unit when Dr. Travis led Kate and Charles into it. Only the curtained cubicle where Millicent lay held a curious peace. A heart monitor registered her ragged heart beat. An I.V. dripped slowly by her bedside. Oxygen tubing led to a connection in the wall. A nurse stood by Millicent, one hand on her shrunken shoulder. She nodded to them and stepped back so that Charles could approach the bed. Kate went around to the other side.

The pain was gone. That was Kate's first relieved thought. Then she noted how small Millicent looked as life slipped away. How frail and porcelain white.

"Millicent..." Charles spoke her name as he took her hand. "This is Charles. I've come to give you communion. Can you hear me?"

Millicent slowly opened her eyes. "Charles? Of course...I can hear you. Just because I'm dying...doesn't mean I'm deaf."

Charles smiled down at her. "Irascible to the end."

There was a ghost of a grin on Millicent's face as her fingers struggled to wrap around his. "Don't believe in maudlin scenes. Glad you're here though. Dying's...a lonely business."

Charles spoke the ancient words slowly and simply as he administered the sacrament. After they were finished, he said, "Kate's here, too."

"Right here," Kate said as she took Millicent's other hand.

When Millicent turned her head, Kate sensed she was pleased. "Good. I like seeing you two together. I wish...I could stay for the wedding. I hate unfinished business.'' An old twinkle animated her eyes for a moment. "I don't suppose . . . you'd grant me . . . a death-bed request?''

Kate leaned over to kiss her cheek. "Millicent, you're a stinker.''

Kate heard the faint rustle of laughter that turned into a sigh.

"Charles . . . don't let her get away from you.''

"I'll do my best.''

There was a period of silence, and Kate thought Millicent had drifted off to sleep, or into a coma. Her next words proved she was still aware they were there. "I wish you could have met Billy, my husband. He was a stinker, too.''

"I'm sure he must have been,'' Charles said with gentle teasing. "To stay married to you.''

He was rewarded with a smile that faded to be replaced by a haunted look. "I've missed him. I'm glad that's over.''

She seemed to drift into a serene sleep as they stood over her. Charles drew up a chair, holding on to her hand. Kate did the same. He bowed his head. The moments went by, measured by the bleep of the monitor. Kate wasn't sure how long they sat, waiting, watching, trying to accept.

The nurse came in and left again quietly.

Millicent spoke in a wisp of a voice. "Charles . . . ?''

"I'm here.''

"Tell Win Palmer . . . I'm sorry . . . I broke my promise. I won't be here when he returns. Don't let him know . . . I'm glad it was you. Win never did have the stomach for death.''

Charles brushed away a strand of hair that had fallen over her parchment cheek and leaned closer. "Millicent, thank you for letting me be here.''

There was another faint rustle of laughter. "I couldn't . . . have done it without you, boy. Are you praying for me?''

"Yes."

"Good. You do the praying. I'll do the dying...."

This time her eyes stayed open, locked on his face. He moved so that she was cradled against him. They remained like that for a time.

There was a wheezing sound and the line of the monitor went flat.

Charles looked drained. He seemed to sag a little. With careful fingers, he closed Millicent's eyelids, then laid her body back against the pillows and bowed his head once more.

Kate rested her cheek against the small bundle of bones and skin she held between her hands, unaware that she was crying, not wanting to let go and accept what had happened.

It was only when she felt Charles's touch and stared up into his weary face that she moved. She rose into his arms. They held one another tightly, seeking the warmth of physical contact as the hospital staff went about their grim tasks.

There was a small circle of friends waiting for them outside the doors of the ICU—Dan, Phil, several ladies from the Bible class. One of them broke into tears when Charles and Kate came out, the couple's expression making words unnecessary. Friends went into each other's arms. There were murmurs of disbelief and regret. A kernel of anger.

Kate herself was angry. She knew it was unreasonable and selfish and belittled Millicent's courage and acceptance.

But Kate felt cheated. She'd only known Millicent a little while. She wasn't ready to let go. She'd come to depend on her friend's frequent visits. The mock skirmishes. The sage advice. The tart exterior and the generosity of spirit that lay beneath. The will and courage and independence.

As Charles and she walked out to her car to drive back to the church, Kate kept wiping away tears. She seemed to have an endless supply.

"Shall I drive?" he asked quietly.

Kate dug in her purse for her keys, glad he was with her, but feeling oddly resentful that in the midst of tragedy Charles had found a measure of peace.

It took her a while to realize that they weren't heading back to Emmanuel.

"Where are we going?"

"To your house. I think we could use a few moments alone. I'll have to get back to Emmanuel soon, but Dan's subbing for me now. He knows Millicent's niece, and he's calling her to make arrangements for the funeral. Apparently, Millicent had drawn up explicit instructions for the occasion some time ago." He smiled. "She would." As he spoke, he steered Kate's car into her driveway. He got out and went around to help Kate.

Charles's gentle smile and words tore the scab off Kate's grief. It took all her strength to control herself as they went inside.

"Okay. Let it out. Say what you need to say."

"Why . . . ?" Her voice was guttural.

"Why Millicent?"

"Why now? She was so full of life, of spunk. She was so necessary to all of us."

Charles started to speak. Kate interrupted him harshly. "No! I don't want to hear garbage about how she'd lived a long life. Or how she was old and her time had come. Millicent was young. I don't care what her birth date was. Millicent wasn't ready to die."

"She'd accepted it."

"But it wasn't time!"

"Thank God it wasn't."

His quiet words stopped her short.

"Would you rather mourn her life or her death, Kate?" Charles let that question sink in before he continued. "What if her time had come a year ago, two years? And yet she'd lived on. What if she'd become enfeebled, dependent on others, her will stripped away? Would you have wished that on her?"

"No."

"No. So instead we hurt. Because we've lost someone precious. But rather we lose, than that Millicent had."

"But we were friends such a short time. I feel cheated."

"Would you rather not have known her, or be grieving now?"

Charles led Kate to the couch and enfolded her in his arms, the gesture reminding Kate of how he'd cradled Millicent.

"That's the crux of the dilemma." His voice was husky. "No love...no grief. Yet without love, there's only desolation."

Kate felt Charles's chest heave. He laid his cheek against her hair and at last, with a wrenching sigh, he began to weep.

Kate's nurturing instincts welled up in her. She turned into Charles's embrace, her arms wrapping around him. Her lips moved over his face with small murmurs of comfort, his tears salty in her mouth.

"Oh, Kate," he whispered brokenly. "It's good to hold you. To feel life coursing through your body. I love you so."

He reached up to capture her face and sought her lips with his, greedy for her taste, his need spilling over them in shuddering waves. She ran her fingers into his hair and pressed his mouth closer, her need and greediness matching his.

His hands made their way over the supple definition of her body. Along her back, down over her hips, up to caress her breasts. His touch was more than sensual. He seemed to be satisfying a primal need for warmth and contact. Kate gave him that willingly, feeling no shock at the intimacy of his touch.

It was right and natural and necessary for them both. It was a way of giving comfort. A great wonder filled Kate that they could bring each other respite from pain.

At last, his seeking hands settled quietly over her. One lay over the soft mound of a breast, the other smoothed the curve of her buttocks in a stroking motion that slowed until she could feel the stationary heat against her skin.

He kissed her softly, with a moist tenderness. Her brows first, then her nose, her mouth. His lips rippled over her face, nestling against her temple.

"Millicent would have loved this. That we left the hospital to grieve and ended up making love." Charles gazed down at her. "That's what we're doing. Making love. Creating it. Out of death, life."

"Yes," Kate whispered, "I think Millicent would approve."

They sat for several long minutes, letting a sad calm settle over them.

"We have to go," Charles murmured finally. "We'll be needed."

"I know."

CHAPTER FOURTEEN

"GRA-A-AB YOUR PURSE and fetch a smile..." Charles sang the words in a lusty baritone, as he breezed into the office. "Leave your worries in the desk drawer..." He waltzed around Kate's desk and dragged her to her feet, grabbing her jacket from the back of her chair as he went by. "Just direct your shoes..."

"Charles!" Kate yelped, digging her heels in. "What's going on?"

"We're playing truant," he said as an aside, before he finished the song. "... To the sunny side of the mewwws."

Charles was dressed for playing hooky. He wore hiking boots, khaki pants and a lightweight parka. Kate, in a long-sleeved shirtwaist and high-heeled pumps, felt stodgy in comparison. But then she'd been under the impression when she got up this morning that she'd be working today. After all, it was Monday, just a week and a half since Millicent's death.

Apparently, Charles had other ideas for what the day should hold.

"What about the office?" Kate asked anxiously.

"Linda's volunteered her time for today and tomorrow. She says she needs to get out of the house, because she's beginning to think like a six-month-old."

"Tomorrow!" Kate latched on the operative word. "Just where are we going?"

"To Enchanted Rock for an overnight camping trip."

"But I can't...!"

"Of course, you can," he said reasonably. "There's no reason not to."

In fact, there were a million reasons. But none that Charles would accept. Clark was between semesters at the university and skiing on the cheap with friends at a youth hostel in New Mexico. Michael was staying at his father's for a few days boning up for the finals. Kate was free and Charles knew it.

"What about Greg?" Kate asked, thinking of Charles's houseguest.

"He's taken care of. Jill's staying over tonight."

"But Lieutenant Eccles..."

"I've already cleared it with him. In fact, he's in charge of transportation."

"I thought I was supposed to be her chauffeur." In fact, Kate had been on several occasions. But not today.

"I didn't want you in on the plan."

Kate knew why. If Charles'd given her time to think about this crazy scheme she'd never have agreed to it.

By this time they were outdoors, and Charles twirled her around briskly. "Just look at this day. It's perfect. Why didn't you tell me it could be like this in the dead of winter?"

"You never asked." she protested, but did as instructed.

The morning *was* gorgeous. There'd been a warming trend all week, and now the temperature hovered in the mid-sixties. The air was fresh, the wind soft, and puffy clouds dotted the sky.

"I've been waiting for a Monday like this to come along. It has, and we're taking advantage of it. Besides, Greg and Jill need time alone."

His tone brooked no opposition, and anyway, he was right.

After a moment's indecision, Kate gave in, trying not to dwell on the ramifications of a two-day jaunt.

"I have to change clothes and pack."

"Certainly," he agreed. "I'll follow you home and we'll go from there. But Kate..." By this time he'd marched them to her car, and he gazed down at her pleasantly as he opened the driver's door. "You're not allowed to change your mind. Consider yourself kidnapped."

"And you a man of the highest principles," she chided.

"I never said I couldn't be ruthless when the occasion demanded."

And single-minded, Kate decided, as she drove to her house. She had the sensation of having just been run over by a steam roller. Except that she suddenly felt as buoyant as the day.

Just as long as she didn't stop to consider what kind of statement they were making to the world, no matter how innocent the excursion.

What must Linda think? What if the entire church found out?

Ruthless was the way Charles described himself. It was an accurate term. She was being drawn inexorably into the circle of his love. Trying to keep her feet on the ground was like fighting a whirlwind. A wonderful, dizzying whirlwind. Maybe, when they landed, she'd find herself in the Land of Oz.

Kate was still bemused twenty minutes later when she came out of her bedroom dressed in jeans and a soft flannel shirt. She'd tossed a change of clothes, toilet articles and her pajamas into one of the kids' duffle bags. Speaking of pajamas, she was very curious about the sleeping arrangements.

When Kate walked into the kitchen, Charles looked ready to go.

"Should we pack some food?" Kate asked. She moved toward her refrigerator but Charles propped himself against it, blocking her way.

"It's taken care of," he assured her smugly.

"An ice chest?"

"Already filled with drinks and ice."

"Towels?"

"Trust me. I've thought of everything."

"Sleeping bags?"

"Two." He grinned at her and folded his arms. "Unless you come up with a better suggestion."

She knew exactly what suggestion he had in mind.

Almost a month had passed since the Christmas Eve proposal. Not once had he brought up the subject again, but Kate was sure the terms he'd laid down between them hadn't changed.

Charles was still holding out for commitment and marriage. And Kate had the sneaking suspicion he was using himself as bait. This trip could turn into a war of nerves.

She folded her arms as he had done and stared at him accusingly. "Has anyone ever told you, you're unscrupulous?"

Charles followed her train of thought and denied the charge, humor lurking in his eyes. "Not unscrupulous." His voice deepened, disturbing her breathing. "Just determined. And willing to use the weapons at hand."

He moved in closer, dangerously near. Before she could stop him, he ran his hand over her cheek and into her hair, so that he held her head when she would have backed away. "You could accuse me of arrogance because I feel I'm what you need. Because I'm sure we should be together. I've never denied my sins."

He covered her lips with his, stealing her breath away.

"You're a thief," she murmured, adding this charge to the list as she moved into his arms. "You rob me of my will."

"I take away your doubts," he whispered, his lips gliding over the planes of her face. "There's a big difference."

A difference of semantics at the rate they were going. And all of a sudden they were going very fast. Falling headlong into a well of mutual desire, as Charles's hands reacquainted themselves with the contours of Kate's body, discovering anew her various delights. As he opened her mouth with his and kissed her deeply. Urgently. Recklessly.

Kate broke away from him, panting. "I thought we were going on a camping trip, not an exploratory expedition."

His expression was blurred with desire. He was having as much trouble breathing as she was. His voice was thick and it had a rural lilt to it, "Ah, Kate, would you deny me so?"

"You're the one who drew up the agreement," she pointed out.

"So I did," Charles said dryly. He dropped his hands with a sigh. "At great personal sacrifice. You've a warm, soft, responsive body, Kate. Made for loving. I've had all I can do to keep from answering its invitation."

As Charles must have known, his words affected her, sparking desire as surely as his touch. She closed her eyes and swayed slightly.

What he said was true. When they'd kissed the first time at Lynn's party, and Kate had felt the unfamiliar male contact, the emotions that had surged through her had held as much ambivalence as desire.

Now, after months of his easy, arousing ministrations, when their lips and bodies met and caressed each other, she felt only a languid, heated need to open up to him. To take him into her.

Kate's eyes blinked open in shock. She stared directly into Charles's eyes, finding a response that indicated both speculation and sensual amusement. Her face must have mirrored her forbidden thoughts.

"A penny for them," he offered with gentle mockery. "I'd like to be included."

"I don't think so," Kate said shakily. "They were X-rated, and you weren't left out. I . . . uh . . . I say let's move on. The day's wasting."

"On the contrary, I've found it very profitable, with distinct possibilities in store." His look defied the dark one she sent him, but he followed her agreeably out the door.

ENCHANTED ROCK, their destination, was one of the more spectacular rock formations of the Texas Hill Country. It lay seventy-five miles to the west of Austin, and in the space of those miles Texas became the West of cactus, mesquite and limitless sky.

Charles and Kate leisurely drove the back route, sometimes talking, sometimes comfortably silent, enjoying the vistas at each bend of the road.

"How are you and Greg getting along?" Kate asked at one point, bringing up an earlier subject. "Every time I've seen Greg he looks better."

"I think the healing process has begun."

With Charles's help, Kate knew. Jill had told her of long conversations between the two men, during which Greg had bared his soul. Kate couldn't think of a more trustworthy person for him to confide in.

"And how's the investigation coming?" she probed tentatively.

"Nolan's satisfied with its progress," Charles answered noncommittally.

And that was all the news she'd be getting on that front, Kate realized. She started to protest, then changed her mind. Why bring troubles along on such a beautiful day? She leaned back to enjoy the ride.

When they reached Fredericksberg, they lingered for lunch. The picturesque town had been settled by German immigrants in the nineteenth century, and many buildings and homes bore the imprint of Old World architecture adapted to a frontier way of life.

Charles was eager to explore two of the churches with historical plaques. Kate, happy to tag along, decided his native enthusiasm would make him a fun traveling companion.

Still, Kate felt the need to apologize. "History is spread thin on the ground in this part of the world. Everything around you is little more than a hundred years old. Quite a change from England."

"But don't you see, Kate, what all this represents?" Charles asked rhetorically. "Men and women striking out, leaving a settled way of life to venture into the unknown. I find it a testament to the human spirit."

"You *are* a romantic," Kate teased him, enjoying his simple pleasure. She looped an arm through his and leaned her head against his shoulder.

He accepted the words and gesture with equanimity. "I told you I was a romantic. An incorrigible one, I'm afraid. Do you mind?"

"I find it very sweet."

He grimaced at her choice of words, but accepted the sentiment behind them. And felt general satisfaction at the turn of events.

Ten minutes out of Fredericksberg, the great rose granite dome where they were headed bulged over the horizon and began to dominate the landscape. As they drew closer, it dwarfed the surrounding terrain.

Charles pulled up beside the ranger station at the entrance to the state park, nestled at its base. While he paid the overnight camping fees, Kate studied the handouts they'd been given.

"It says here," Kate read eagerly as they drove through the campground, "that the formation is over six hundred million years old. It seems we're not so young after all. And listen to this. It's called Enchanted Rock because it was sacred to the local Indians. They believed the formation was a holy place and performed religious rituals on the summit. It's like a natural cathedral."

"That's why I keep returning."

"You've been here before?"

"Twice, last summer. I climbed the west face."

"Then why did you let me ramble on?"

"For the same reason you let me wax poetic about the pioneering spirit. For the sheer pleasure of watching your face and hearing the excitement in your voice."

"Oh." Kate reddened, suddenly inarticulate.

Charles had the knack of saying a lot with few words. He'd captured a facet of their relationship with a turn of the phrase.

"You should have thought about becoming a writer instead of an actor," Kate said half-seriously.

She'd startled him.

"Why do you say that?" he asked, an odd expression on his face.

"Because you have the ability to distill a thought. An emotion. You're very skilled with words."

"And you're a discerning woman."

"Why? Because I recognize another person's talent?" She thought over what he'd just said. "Discerning? That was a strange adjective to use. And after my pretty compliment."

Charles didn't back down. "You are discerning. And you have talent of your own." By this time he'd parked under a tree and cut the engine. "Listen, Kate, I believe in you. I think you can make it if you don't give up."

Sudden tears sprang to Kate's eyes. She reached over and hugged him in gratitude. "Oh, Charles, no one has ever said as much to me. As if they honestly felt my success were a realistic possibility. Thank you." She pulled back out of his arms to give him a misty smile.

It was one of those rare moments when Charles seemed embarrassed. "Kate..." His voice was strained.

She interrupted him gaily, not wanting his words of faith in her to be diluted with explanation. "Enough of my er-satz career. I thought we were here to get away from it all."

Charles relaxed and let her have her way. "We are, but there's work involved." He glanced around. "How does this campsite look to you?"

Kate followed the direction of his gaze. They were in a secluded location, abutting a trickling creek. She spotted the rest rooms and showers nearby.

"Perfect. You've thought of everything. Now I guess you expect me to earn my bed and board."

"Only if you expect to get it."

For the next twenty minutes they set up camp.

Kate was a novice at the rustic life, as she'd have been the first to admit. However, Charles was patient and amaz-ingly organized, especially in light of the chaos of his of-fice. She realized he was an experienced outdoorsman.

"Is this Father Palmer's gear?"

Charles shook his head. "Mine. I bought it soon after I arrived in the States. Camping's my form of recreation.

Seeing your country, relaxing in a spot like this, restores my peace." He smiled wryly. "Although, I don't know how much peace I'll have with you along."

"Why? I don't snore," she assured him sweetly.

He raised one eyebrow. "That's a relief."

Yes, she could see that it would be. Since they were sharing a tent, if not a bedroll. She watched him spread their sleeping bags over the pumped up air mattresses.

"There. That should do it."

They stepped out of the tent.

Kate looked around at their accomplishments. A tarp was stretched high over the picnic table giving them shelter in case of rain. There was a camp stove, a lantern, an ice chest and groceries. A nearby faucet sported "cold and cold" running water. All the comforts of home.

Except that there was this gigantic hunk of rock in their backyard that Charles expected her to climb.

Kate headed back toward the tent and the cushiony bed roll. "I'll take a nap. You go play on the mountain."

"Oh, no, you don't," Charles grabbed her hand and led her toward a path. "Come along. We'll take the easy route. I'll introduce you to the joys of rappelling later."

"Charles," Kate knew she needed to be firm about this, "you will *never* introduce me to the joys of rappelling. I will *not* hang off a precipice on the end of a rope. I have a confession to make." She laid her hands over his shoulders and spoke very distinctly. "I'm scared of heights."

"Ahhh, that's the problem."

Kate ignored the undercurrents of that remark. "I'll walk to the top of this monster to show you I'm game," she said reasonably. "But I want you to recognize my limits."

"I'll hold your hand every step of the way."

Charles was as good as his word. He even was careful to make frequent rest stops, due no doubt to the sound of her huffing and puffing.

"Has anyone ever told you, you're disgustingly healthy?" she wheezed at one point as he guided her to a perch on one of the outcroppings of rocks.

"No," he grinned indulgently, offering water from his canteen. "That's why I need you. To list my sins and keep me humble. Kate—look around."

She turned her attention from him to the location of his wave, and for a moment her heart stopped beating at the magnificent view, stretching out for miles below them.

They saw the gray green of the semidesert landscape. Other rugged granite formations jutted out from the earth and the gnarly trees far below looked like Japanese bonzais in the distance. Above them was the azure blue of the sky.

Kate felt a surge of adrenaline at the beauty around her. She jumped to her feet, no longer weary. "Let's get to the top."

The view there was even more spectacular, because at the summit the world lay below them in every direction. The vista was vast, almost limitless, with scant sign of human intrusion. No wonder the Indians had considered this sacred ground. With no one but themselves to disturb the enchantment, Kate fell under its spell.

Charles chose a boulder near the middle of the flattened summit and the couple stretched their legs in front of them, leaning their backs against the rock to shelter them from the constant breeze.

For a long time, they sat silently, content.

The heat of the sun-washed granite seeped through the material of Kate's jeans and shirt. The muffled roar of the wind cuffed her ears. The tangy smell of a wild fresh day was intoxicating. And everywhere she looked there was a feast for her eyes.

"Want an apple?" Charles asked, offering her a treasure from his back pack.

She bit into it greedily, the flavor deliciously tart.

"Aren't you glad you came?" he asked quietly.

"Oh, yes." Kate turned to face him as she answered. "Thank you for kidnapping me."

Charles's gaze locked with hers. "Now that we're here, are you afraid?"

It wasn't a simple question. And it didn't refer simply to the heights they'd scaled. Kate couldn't pretend she hadn't understood.

"I'm a little afraid."

"Why?"

"Because. I'm dangling off a precipice at the end of a rope," Kate said as she took a deep breath, "and you're the only one who can catch me."

"Haven't you learned to trust me yet?"

"I do. I think. But there are too many things that can happen."

"I love you, Kate." Charles stopped talking in riddles. "If we married, it would be for life. I'd never leave you for another woman. Or a bottle of whiskey. Outside of my faith, you'd be the most important part of my existence. And nothing in the vows of ordination I took diminish those of marriage."

"People change," Kate murmured, remembering her past. "Love dies. It's not immutable and everlasting."

"We'll change, too. Our relationship will shape us. And as we do, our love will grow. We'll keep creating it. Because we understand love must be nurtured to survive."

"Situations change," she said somewhat desperately. "Life can tear apart a relationship."

Charles remained patient. "Kate, we can't bend life to suit our will. But we can choose how we'll respond to it."

"I'm not the type of woman you need." Kate's eyes left his as she stared into the distance. "I'm not right for you."

"Haven't these last few months proven anything to you?" Charles asked, mildly exasperated. "You are exactly the woman I need." He turned her head so that she was forced to face him. "I wasn't aware I deserved a 'type.' And we've already established that my character is thoroughly despicable." That brought a ghost of a smile to Kate's lips as Charles had intended.

He went on quietly, "Kate, I'm just a man. Not a saint, nor a martyr. I've felt my share of failure and despair, just as you have. Don't condemn us both to a life of loneliness, because of the fear that loneliness brings."

"There are other people involved."

"Clark?"

"No. He'd accept you. Although he thinks you're feeble-minded for being attracted to me."

"Michael."

She nodded.

"Can't you trust me with Michael?"

"That's not the point. He's scared and insecure. I can't topple his world entirely."

"His world's already about as shaky as it can get, with an alcoholic father and a mother who's as scared as he is, her self-confidence precarious, her courage used up just making it from day to day. Your anxiety plays into Michael's, Kate, whether you admit it or not. That's why the two of you have a hard time dealing with each other. Have you ever thought I might be able to provide a stable compass point in his life?"

She stared at him, knowing what he said was true. Recognizing how accurately he'd diagnosed the situation. Seeing for the first time how he might help.

"Why don't you let Michael and me sort out our relationship? We could both fool you."

Kate's expression softened. She was giving ground.

Charles continued, pressing his advantage. "And even if Michael and I do have a rough time of it, you still have your own life to live. I'm not saying your mother's life was wrong, centered as it was on her children. But it would be wrong for you to follow her lead and refuse to marry me because of Michael. It'd only hurt the relationship between you and your son, I promise you. In years to come, he won't thank you for your sacrifice."

Slowly but surely he was delving into the recesses of her mind where her fears festered, taking them out, shaking them, exposing them to the purifying rays of logic.

"Of course," he reached for the last one and examined it carefully. "I can't promise not to die on you like your father. I might fall off a cliff or have a heart attack. Or be run over while crossing the road. I am, however, a reasonably prudent man, who values his life and doesn't feel the need to take unnecessary chances. I'm disgustingly healthy, as you pointed out. Longevity runs in the family. Both my grandmothers are alive, as well as my mother's father, who's a hopeless rake at ninety-five."

"What happened to your other grandfather?" Kate asked suspiciously.

"He died at eighty-eight in a fit of apoplexy," Charles confessed, a glint in his eye. "His temper was infamous. In case you're wondering, I remind my mother of Grandpa Longworth."

The glint faded, leaving Charles's emotions laid bare. "Kate...there are no guarantees in life. That's a cliché, but a true one. Neither one of us can promise the other immortality."

One of his hands reached out and he touched her face. "Do you think since I've met you, I haven't wrestled with that particular demon? Remembering Sarah? Do you think I haven't had to face the fact that something might happen to you?"

"Yes. I guess you have. But better—" Kate was remembering the lessons Millicent's death had taught her "—to love someone and grieve for the loss of them, than to deny love and grieve at the cost."

"Can you love me, Kate? Will you take the risk of it?"

She took a first faltering step. "I want to, Charles. If you're there to catch me."

He took her hand and kissed it. "I'm here. You won't fall. Will you marry me, Kate?"

She clung to his hand for dear life, finding security in his grip. Bringing his knuckles up, she rubbed her face against them, the blond hairs on the back of his hand tickling her cheek.

"Yes," she murmured against the warmth of his skin.

Charles caught her chin so he could see her face clearly.

"Say it again, Kate."

"Yes," she repeated, fighting a sinking sensation.

"I love you." Charles took her in his arms, breaking the fall.

He held her close for a long moment, a great swell of relief and joy rippling through him, blessing the enchanted ground that had sanctified their union.

CHAPTER FIFTEEN

KATE SHIFTED HER BODY with a sigh of contentment, settling in to Charles's embrace. She leaned her head back against his shoulder and wiggled her fanny closer, so that the length of her back was cushioned by his accommodating torso. Her soft breasts brushed along his forearm, heating his skin.

Awareness stirred, then desire. Charles smiled faintly at the inevitability of passion and glanced down at the woman he loved. From this vantage point Kate's face was all bones and angles and silky eyelashes. She was beautiful from any angle. He couldn't help feeling a primitive exultation. They'd taken a vow here, today, in one of nature's holy places.

The shadows were lengthening; the sun riding low in the west was giving way to the faint moon, high above. The azure sky was deepening to indigo blue. The wind blew colder. It nipped inside their clothing.

"It's late," he murmured.

She tilted her face so that their eyes met. "I've just promised you my hand in marriage, and all I hear is, 'It's late?' What an eloquent lover I have."

She stopped ensnared by the words she'd just uttered. They stared at each other silently, sharing a mutual awareness that intensified with each passing second. Then Kate's eyes flew from his. She glanced around nervously. "I guess it is getting late. We'd better go back down. I'd hate to be marooned up here all night."

"I can think of better ways to spend it."

Kate's lashes flickered, signaling she understood his words.

He held out his hand and after a last lingering look at the evening drifting over the landscape, they started down the well-marked path.

The descent held its own set of problems, and Kate's legs were wobbly by the time they reached level ground.

Searching for something to say, she pointed up the trail they'd just negotiated and predicted, "I guess you're going to tell me the best time to be up there is sunrise."

"The sunrise is spectacular," Charles agreed lazily. "But for tomorrow I had something else in mind—a warm sleeping bag on a cold morning."

His provocative words unnerved Kate, and she managed to land her sneaker in the small ribbon of water that called itself a creek.

She held up her dripping foot and lamented, "This is the only pair of shoes I brought."

He bent down, took her shoe and sock off and swung her up into his arms. "We'll start a fire and dry it. It'll be fine by tomorrow."

"Charles . . ." She flailed about, feeling ridiculous. "I'm perfectly capable of walking."

"It's getting dark," he said reasonably. "You could step on a scorpion or gash your foot on a rock. Besides," he added as he looked down at her, "I'm glad for the excuse to hold you. Now stop wiggling, or you'll miss dinner. You're giving me ideas."

Kate settled back meekly while he proceeded to their campsite. Once there he set her down at the picnic table and ducked inside their tent. He returned in a moment with her duffle bag.

"You have another pair of socks in here?"

"No," she admitted, chagrined. "I was in such a hurry, I forgot them."

"Not to worry. I packed a spare."

He went to dig them out from his belongings, took longer than expected, and Kate was beginning to think the hunt had proved futile. But he finally came out of the tent, the elusive socks in his hand.

When she would have slipped one on her bare foot, he insisted on doing the honors, taking the other sneaker off, stripping that foot of its dry sock and slipping on both of his.

"A matched set."

They were certainly warm and fuzzy, but Kate had to protest. "Charles, your socks are too big. I can't get my other sneaker on. You'll have to carry me everywhere."

He glanced up from his kneeling position. "I don't mind."

"I won't be able to help with supper," she cautioned him.

"You can peel potatoes, can't you?"

"But I'll need to go to the rest room. What are you going to do, haul me over there?"

"You're not heavy. Besides, you need someone with you to keep away the beasties."

"The beasties?" Kate asked in alarm, discovering the dark side of camping.

"Well," he said, relenting, "a deer or two and maybe an armadillo."

Kate tutted, shocked at his underhanded tactics. "You'd say anything to get your way. I'm uncovering a whole new facet of your personality."

Charles planted his palms to either side of her on the table so that she was caught between them. His face was disturbingly close as he growled, "You talk too much, woman."

Kate's eyes widened mockingly. "And a bully, besides. Just what have I gotten myself into? What other surprises do you have in store?"

Charles's eyes flickered. He suddenly looked like one of her boys caught with his hand in the cookie jar.

"You'd be surprised," he muttered.

She laughed at his sheepish expression. "Why, Charles, I believe you *do* have a skeleton or two in that closet. It's okay," she said, taking his wind-roughened cheeks between her palms. "I'll love you no matter what." She planted a kiss on the end of his aristocratic nose. "But I'll love you more after I'm fed. I'd like to remind you we just climbed a mountain."

"Is that a promise?" he asked softly.

"Merely a suggestion."

"I'll see what I can do about dinner."

Charles set to work while Kate drew up her knees and wrapped her arms about them, content with the role of observer.

She found herself studying Charles's movements, enjoying the lean fluidity of his body. He made an effective advertisement for the outdoor life as he went about domestic tasks.

Within moments, the kerosene lantern was pumped and glowing. In ten minutes more, a fire was blazing. He'd cleaned out the grill that the park provided, and when the charcoal he'd lighted had flamed down to embers, he retrieved two large steaks from the ice chest, seasoned them and threw them on the grill.

"Is this your usual camping fare?"

"On special occasions."

"Oh—" Kate suddenly remembered "—the potatoes. I forgot."

"We'll make do with steak, salad and hot bread." Charles had gotten out an uncut loaf and was wrapping it in foil. As soon as he'd finished, he placed the bread on one side of the grill to warm and observed, "You had your mind on other matters."

"I'm not sure I like having you read my thoughts," Kate complained, glad the lantern glow and firelight disguised her color.

"Why not? You can read mine."

Charles was right. Kate knew what he was thinking. Right now the message in his eyes created a hollow feeling deep inside.

Must be hunger pangs, she reasoned. Once her plate had been set before her, however, Kate found her appetite had vanished. When she looked over at Charles's plate, she saw his food half-eaten, also. Kate suddenly found it hard to swallow and took a sip from the orange juice she'd poured.

Silently, Charles cleared away the remains of the meal while Kate cleaned off the table and packed groceries away. When they were both finished, he went to their lantern which was hanging from a tree limb and tightened the air-flow valve. Slowly the mantel's glow faded until they were in near darkness, only the flames of the camp fire licking at the night.

"Is it that late?" Kate asked, irritated with the catch in her voice.

Charles threw another log on the flames, sending sparks flying, before he sat down beside her. "You can't watch a campfire by lantern light. It spoils the effect. This is, by the way," he said as he hauled her onto his lap, "an ancient and honorable camping tradition. Dates back to neolithic man.'' He ended his lecture with a kiss.

''Which tradition are you talking about?'' Kate asked as she settled into his arms. ''Watching the fire? Or smooching?''

''Both. Or we probably wouldn't be here.'' Charles began to plant sweet kisses along the delicate line of her neck.

Kate was breathless with the sensations his lips were stirring. ''You're . . . you're not watching the fire.''

''I'm too busy starting one.''

Charles skimmed his hand down her back and over the side of her hips, lingering there, before he slowly traveled up to cup one of her breasts, his thumb exploring her hardening nipple.

Kate's body quivered at the intimate touch and the heat it generated.

''You're cold,'' he whispered against her mouth. ''We'll go to bed.''

Kate's muffled chuckle told him she saw the irony in his statement.

She felt his lips curve against hers. Without further comment he stood, hoisting her with him, and headed toward the bathhouse.

''Wait—I need my overnight kit.''

He went back so she could rummage through her bag.

''And my pajamas.''

''You won't need pajamas,'' he assured her, resuming his intended journey.

''I really will get cold.''

''I'll keep you warm.''

''From a separate sleeping bag?'' Kate asked provocatively.

''I zipped them together,'' Charles informed her calmly, and lifted her into his arms for their trek to the washrooms.

Once back in camp Charles stood her up on the mat outside the entrance to their tent. "I need to bank the fire," he explained, moving away from her. Then he chuckled huskily, and added, "One of them at least."

Kate lifted the flap and went inside. Moments later he joined her, the flashlight he carried shooting a circle of light over the floor and walls of the canvas, orienting them. Kate heard a faint click, and there was total blackness.

Even the darkness seemed to quiver with expectation.

For a moment neither of them spoke.

In the darkness she heard Charles say softly, "A time to embrace, a time to love... Kate will you make love with me?"

"Haven't we already discussed this?" Kate hid behind her teasing question.

"Yes." Charles's low laughter sent fire through her veins. "But I'd like to hear you say it nonetheless."

"Charles," Kate said, taking her courage in hand, "I'd like very much to make love with you." Her voice faltered as she added, "If that's what you want."

Kate turned with a sigh and found herself in Charles's arms. His lips unerringly sought her mouth. And for a long piercingly sweet moment, they communicated with languorous kisses that robbed Kate of thought and any lingering doubts.

Her body melted into his. Desire quickened. Kate felt the heat and hardness of him through their layers of clothing. And she gave a small frustrated moan as she tried to move closer.

Charles answered her with a yearning murmur and moved just far enough away for his fingers to unbutton her shirt.

"We'll have to get into the sleeping bag once we're undressed," he whispered raggedly. "It's close to freezing."

"I hadn't noticed," she murmured, shivering, her hands as active as his.

"Ahhh." Charles made a sound of pure pleasure.

By this time, he'd slipped off her shirt, unhooked her bra and discovered the satin smoothness of her skin, the hardening tips of her naked breasts.

"That's not because of the cold," she explained, breathlessly, and gasped when his mouth went the way of his hands. His tongue and lips exploring her nipple shot a bolt of pleasure through her. All the while his hands stayed busy until she was completely naked.

"You're very good at this," she teased him, trying to control the need that threatened to sweep over her.

"It's like riding a bicycle," Charles murmured, stripping off his clothes. "You never lose the knack of it. Come here." He pulled her nude body against his and sighed. She arched her hips in mindless invitation.

"If you don't watch it," he warned her, "we won't make it into the sleeping bag."

"What sleeping bag?" Kate asked, opening her mouth to his. Together, they tumbled down onto the bedding, the air mattresses breaking their fall.

Charles's hands began to move over her in the darkness. Kate moved restlessly. His fingers and mouth trailed fire over her skin. Her hands ran down his back, pressing him closer, wanting, demanding. She was aching with desire and the swelling need to give herself completely.

And then they were one, in a shattering moment of love. Together they created a timeless bond of body and spirit as they gave and received in bounteous measure.

Darkness swept over them, filled with touch and taste and exquisite sensations. They sighed and whispered love words. They heard the pounding of heartbeats, rhythmed cadence of mounting passion that built and built into an agonized urgency, sweeping them over the edge of sanity, floating them down to earth at last.

They lay, their hearts and breathing slowly quieting. Charles kissed Kate tenderly. His loving hand smoothed over her, and he felt the sweat of their lovemaking evaporating in the cold dry air.

"Scoot over," he commanded and pulled at the sleeping bag's zipper. "Let's get inside this thing."

For the first time, Kate felt the biting chill and she crawled in hastily. Charles followed and pulled her close. He settled her so that she lay half on top of him. The heat of their bodies began to warm the confined, insulated space.

His breath stirred her hair when he spoke softly. "Ah, Katie, my love, you are magnificent."

Kate's fingers tightened over his furry chest. She rubbed her cheek against his shoulder slowly. "Do you find me desirable?"

Charles turned her on her back so that he could look down at her, his gaze trying to pierce the darkness.

"Damn. I wish I could see your face to get some clue why you asked that question. What do you think our lovemaking just proved?"

"That it's been too long for both of us?"

He laughed ruefully. "Well, I admit our first time went faster than I'd planned. But then you've been tempting me, lady, for months. With these saucy hips." He stroked the objects of his observation sleekly. "And these soft rounded breasts." he ducked down and sampled one of them.

"Why, Charles," Kate gasped, "I believe you're as bawdy as your grandfather."

"Mmm," was his only response.

"Charles?"

"Mmm?"

"Charles..."

A certain note in her voice made him stop his pleasureable endeavor. He propped his elbows to either side of her so that their faces almost met.

"What is it, love?"

She reached up to stroke his face. "I just wanted to say that I've never felt this exciting...this sensual...this female."

Charles laid his head on his bent arm so that his other hand was free, and he murmured in her ear.

"You feel very female to me. All the necessary ingredients." He elaborated this point with his wandering touch. "And very tidily put together. And so responsive," he breathed, his lips and tongue nuzzling the side of her face.

"I can't be anything else with you. Oh, Charles..."

"And so generous with your passion. Be generous with me."

"Yes..."

"Because I'm finding I want you again very badly. And this time I'd like to linger along the way."

Much, much later, they lay in the midst of the tumbled bedroll, the zipper of the joined sleeping bags half undone to cool their steamy bodies.

They were drowsy, momentarily sated.

"Are you convinced yet that I find you desirable?" Charles's voice was sleepy and still blurred from passion, as he scooted her body close to his side.

Kate smiled at the obvious understatement. He'd just taken great pains and much pleasure in showing her the strength of their mutual desire.

"For the moment," she temporized softly. "Of course, I may need showing again. In case I forget."

The low rumbling of Charles's laughter in her ear told Kate he hadn't fallen asleep just yet. "You take a lot of convincing, love. I'd say about forty years' worth. Luckily, I'm man enough for the job."

"Was that a macho note I just heard in your voice?" Kate asked in disbelief.

"Blame it on yourself. You bring out the male in me. Now go to sleep, woman. I plan on getting an early start."

"I thought you said we weren't..."

"There's work to be done right here in camp. I expect to refresh your memory."

Kate thought about his words for a second and snuggled closer. She was glad to know that Charles took pride in his work.

Within minutes they both were asleep.

THE NEXT MORNING Kate stirred and awakened slowly. It was so warm. Warm and soft. The flannel lining of the sleeping bags cradled her body, enveloping her in a cozy cocoon. The light of the early-morning sun filtered through the canvas tent, teasing her eyelids. She tried to ignore the invitation, until she realized suddenly where she was and whose leg covered hers.

There was a heavy weight over her belly, and soft breathing heated her cool cheek. The weight came alive and began to stroke her lingeringly.

"Good morning." Charles raised himself so that he could look at her face.

"Good morning." Kate gazed into the eyes of the man she'd made love to so urgently under the cover of nightfall. Although she tried not to, she blushed, remembering their abandoned passion.

"You're beautiful in the morning." Charles ran a finger over her flushed skin, intrigued by her shyness.

"I'm a mess. And my hair needs combing."

"You're beautiful," he insisted, tucking a lock of wanton hair behind her ear. "And very sexy. Especially when you blush that way. I can feel it all the way to your toes."

Since his body lay intimately over hers, Kate was sure he could.

Charles looked delighted as his fingers trailed down her skin experimentally. It was as if he were testing its temperature, raising her body heat by his rousing touch.

"You know, making love last night lacked only one ingredient. I couldn't see your expression when I touched you. Like this. And this."

Kate's lashes drifted shut and she began to move restlessly. She heard the random sounds of Charles's satisfaction.

With a single motion he unzipped the cocoon they were wrapped in, exposing their bodies to the filtered sunlight. "And last night I couldn't see your flesh responding to mine. I learned the sleek feel of you. Now I want to know you with my eyes."

He sat back on his haunches and let his gaze run over every inch of her. Kate felt the tips of her breast tightening. The deep tension inside her began to throb.

The laughing glint in his eyes clued her to his intentions. "Let's see. Those are there." He cupped her breasts, nibbling them gently.

His hands moved lower. "There's a curve here. And there. Around this way and...ah, yes, now I remember." Charles stroked her intimately. "Just as I suspected. You're every bit as delightful to look at as to touch."

His sexual maneuvering shot a knife of pleasure through Kate. Her shyness was forgotten in the heat of his teasing foreplay.

Just as he started to swoop down to kiss her, she pushed against his chest, saying, "Wait. Don't I get a look, too?"

Kate took her time, just as Charles had done.

She used her palms to guide the way over his broad shoulders, then down the firm musculature of his chest which was sprinkled with blond hairs. She fondled his nipples with her tongue, puckering them, and felt her own answering. But she refused to give in to their urging.

Instead, she trailed lazy fingers over his narrow waist. Then she touched his thighs and calves and ankles.

With a frustrated murmur, Charles pulled Kate down into the soft flannel bedding. He stared at her intently, shaken, for a moment, with the measure of his love.

His need was passionate to show her how much he cared, and so with slow deliberation, he cherished her with desire. Their bodies joined in a dance of love. Their mouths accompanied the dance. Their hands gave mutual pleasure.

They both felt need. Spiraling, throbbing need that urged them on to a dizzying frenzy and exploded deep within Kate just as Charles cried out his intense release.

There followed the peaceful aftermath of passion.

"Funny," Kate said when she could finally speak, lightening the intensity of their shared experience. "You don't make love like a preacher."

Charles, who'd been exploring the fine bone structure of her face with his lips, raised up and cocked one eyebrow. "How do you suppose a preacher makes love?"

Kate shrugged, musingly. "Sedately? Spiritually?"

"Oh, I feel spiritual toward you on occasion. Other times the flesh takes precedence."

"Like now?"

"Right now I'm feeling both. Spiritual and physical." He smiled at her tenderly. "Have I mentioned this morning that I love you?"

"I remember you saying something about it a while ago in more basic language. I think I referred to the fact once or twice myself."

"So you did. But have I told you how delightful you are in bed?"

"Well, yes. We touched on that also. I've concluded that you have a decidedly carnal nature."

"Only with you," Charles assured her, his tone laced with humor.

Kate stared into his laughing face and staked her claim with mocking ferocity. "Just see that it stays that way."

RETURNING TO AUSTIN was a return to reality. Kate was dismayed to learn that Charles would be flying to Houston the next morning to stay until the weekend. He was meeting with the bishop to set in motion his permanent assignment at Emmanuel. That decision and Kate's part in it still made her uneasy. Which was probably why Charles had waited until the drive home to mention his upcoming trip.

Next had come the first disagreement of their engagement. Charles wanted to be with her when she told Michael and Clark about the change in their relationship. She insisted it would be better if she sat down with the boys alone.

But Kate hadn't planned on a difficult discussion so soon. Michael was waiting when Charles and she arrived home that evening. From her son's hostile expression, the talk he had planned would be more of a confrontation. Charles's expression hadn't been much more amiable when she'd rushed him out the door to avoid a scene. Now only she and Michael were in the kitchen together.

"I thought you were planning to stay with your dad through Thursday," Kate said, to break the ice.

"I wasn't getting any work done."

"But Kevin was supposed to help you."

Michael stared at her, his expression bleak, telling her with more than words how the two of them had managed. Kate wasn't surprised the scheme had failed. Michael wanted more than Kevin could give, yet it was Kevin's needs that had led to the visit. Both of them were needy.

Kate sat down at the table with a sigh and said, "I'm sorry it didn't work out."

"Yeah," Michael muttered, moving restlessly around the kitchen. Kate knew there was more to come.

"Where were you last night?" he demanded abruptly.

The suddenness of his question unnerved Kate and she fumbled for words. "Well, I . . . Charles invited me—"

Michael interrupted angrily. "I called and called and no one answered. I kept trying all night, but you were never home. I was worried."

Kate felt guilt settling over her like a fog. "Michael, come sit down. We need to talk."

"Do we? You finally have time for me?"

"That's not fair!" Kate flared before she caught herself. "Please, come sit," she requested more quietly, then added with a trace of humor, "You'll wear out the tile." But for once, she failed to engage Michael's sense of the absurd.

Michael sat down across from her, his expression belligerent. He was obviously waiting for an explanation, as though he were the parent and she the recalcitrant child. Kate dismissed that troubling thought.

"First of all," she began placatingly, "I'm sorry I didn't let you know I was leaving town. It happened suddenly. Yesterday was such a beautiful day, Charles suggested we go camping at Enchanted Rock."

"And you went? Just like that?"

Kate thought for a moment. Then answered with the simple truth. "Yes, I did. But I didn't stop to consider—"

"Your own children. What if Clark had broken a leg skiing and needed you?"

"Clark could have called his father. You're being melodramatic, Michael." Inadvertently, she'd poured fuel on the fire.

"Would you call your feelings melodramatic if I'd stayed out all night and you didn't know where I was?"

"That's a different case. You're a child. I'm an adult. I'm your mother."

"Oh, so you finally remembered that," he snapped.

"What is this all about?" Kate asked as calmly as she could. "Why are you so angry with me? Do you really feel I've been neglectful?"

"Well, you haven't been acting much like a mother."

"How should a mother act? Don't I have the right to enjoy a friendship with an adult of the opposite sex? Does that make me a bad parent?"

"A friendship?" The twist Michael put on the phrase brought a blush despite all Kate's efforts. "Is that all it is with Mr. Sheffield? Enjoying a friendship?"

Now they were at the crux of the issue, and there was no dodging it.

"No." Kate gazed squarely at her son. "That's not all. I'm in love with Charles. We're going to be married."

This was not how Kate had wanted to break the news. Michael's stunned expression made him look as if she'd slapped him.

"But...but what about Dad?"

"What about him?" Kate asked, patiently.

"I thought you and he might..."

"What your dad and I had is long since over, Michael. You must know that. He ended it. There's no going back."

"But he needs help!"

"That may be. But I'm not the one who can give it to him. I'm sorry, honey, but that's the truth."

"He's in terrible shape, Mom. I'm worried about him."

"Everyone who cares for your dad is worried about him. But ultimately Kevin has to be the one to see how he's hurting himself. In the meantime, I must get on with my life. Charles and I love each other very much. And he'd like to be a friend to you."

"I don't want his friendship."

"You were beginning to like him."

"The only reason he's nice to me is because of you."

"That's not so!" Kate disagreed, vehemently. "And you know it. Michael." She paused to regain control of her voice. "Charles understands some of the problems between you and me. He'd like to help."

"What have you been doing? Talking to him about me?" Michael asked angrily. "Well, I don't need his help, and I won't live with him." His jaw set stubbornly. "If you marry him, Mother, I'll move in with Dad."

The threat was unexpected. Devastating.

At first, Kate was speechless. Her subsequent anger only added to the confusion.

"Don't threaten me." She spoke harshly. "You're in my custody."

"I'm old enough to choose where I want to live."

"But why, Michael?" Kate's anger turned to pleading. "You know you'd be unhappy. You were only able to stay with Kevin this time for two days."

"I could handle it if I tried. Besides, nobody else cares. Clark's too busy doing his thing. You have 'your *own* life to live.' Well, Dad needs me. I'm not giving up on him. Maybe if I lived with him, things would be different."

All Michael's youthful idealism and broken hopes were contained in his words. Kate struggled against despair.

"I will never agree to your living with your father," she reiterated quietly. "He's not responsible for his actions."

"If you get married, you can't stop me."

"Michael, let's don't talk ourselves into a corner and say things we'll regret. Let's both think about the other's dilemma and see if we can't reach a compromise."

"Are you going to marry Mr. Sheffield?"

Kate gestured futilely. "Michael . . ."

Michael saw his mother couldn't give him the answer he wanted and rushed from the room, effectively shutting her out as he said, "I don't want to talk about it anymore."

CHAPTER SIXTEEN

KATE HADN'T BEEN the only one who faced an unpleasant scene at home. When Charles returned to the parsonage, he found a grim-faced Nolan Eccles with Greg.

"What's wrong, Nolan?" Charles asked, noting Greg's equally bleak expression.

"The word's out that Greg's in town and has turned informant. I'm putting a bodyguard on him." Nolan's eyes met Charles's. "I'm also thinking of moving him somewhere else."

Charles went to sit in a chair before he queried calmly, "Why?"

"For everyone's protection." Nolan bit out the words. "Do I have to spell it out?"

"I guess you do." Charles's tone was mild.

Nolan heaved a frustrated sigh as he did so. "As long as Greg's in danger, you are, too."

"From the very beginning, we knew there'd be an element of risk."

"Well, the odds have just increased. Charles, did it ever occur to you that from a distance you could be mistaken for Greg? You have the same coloring, you're the same approximate height. I should never have let him stay here."

Charles could almost see Greg flinch. He knew Greg had come to think of the parsonage as more than a haven. It had become a psychological safe house where he could confront himself. Charles felt a spurt of anger that his work with the younger man should be jeopardized.

That anger made his response a sharp one. "Nonsense, Nolan. I volunteered my home knowing the danger involved, and the arrangement's worked out beautifully for all concerned. Including you and the case you're building."

Nolan had to agree with Charles's assessment. Still, his policeman's instincts warred with the logic of it.

He was about to voice his doubts when Charles continued, "How close are you to indictments?"

"Close," Nolan admitted. "We have a fair idea of all the players, including a couple of politicians with dubious friends. When we go before the Grand Jury, this town's going to quake and shake. And Greg's testimony is vital. So you see, the other side has everything to lose if they don't find him. They're bound to link him to you eventually, and of course your connection with me is known."

"Eventually is the operative word though. They haven't found him yet, and you admitted from the start the link between Greg and me was nebulous. Look, Nolan, I have to fly to Houston early tomorrow. Install the bodyguard. He can have my bedroom. But don't move Greg until I get back on Saturday and we have a chance to talk this out. I certainly won't be in any danger while I'm out of town, will I?"

"No," Nolan had to admit. Charles sensed Greg relax. At least, he'd bought Greg a little time.

TIME. It fled by or dragged its feet, according to Kate's mood and perspective. She both dreaded facing Charles with Michael's threat and yearned for him to have his arms about her.

All the while an angry, sullen impasse existed between her younger son and her—without Clark there to help diffuse it.

When Kate called her ex-husband to break the news of her engagement, the conversation went poorly.

"I'm going to be married, Kevin."

At the other end of the line there was a long silence. Then, Kevin's strained question told Kate Kevin knew about the man in her life. "To the minister?"

"Yes. His name's Charles Sheffield."

"Have you told the boys yet?"

"Clark's still skiing, so he doesn't know. But I've told Michael. He's not taking it well."

"I'm not surprised." Kevin's tone was pessimistic.

"He says he'll go live with you if Charles and I marry. I don't think that's a good idea."

"What do you want me to say, that Michael can't come? I can't deny him the option. He's my son, Kate."

"It wouldn't work, Kevin." Kate heard the note of panic in her own voice and cursed it silently.

"I don't know that. Just . . . give me time to think. Don't push me," Kevin said roughly.

"I'm not pushing you." But she was. Kate tried to calm down.

Kevin's next words startled her. "I didn't know it was serious between you and Sheffield."

"Why shouldn't it be?" Kate asked, and then Michael's earlier remarks struck her. "After all, you and I have been divorced two years."

"That's not what I meant."

Wasn't it? Hadn't she remained for Kevin a refuge of last resort? The old standby rescuer? Had Michael's fantasies been his alone?

"All right, Kevin. That's not what you meant. You'll have to excuse me, I'm concerned about Michael."

"You think I'm not?"

"Of course you are." She heard the old conciliation in her voice and was suddenly impatient. "There's no point in talking about this now, our plans are still fluid. But I have to tell you I'll fight you if it comes to that."

"We all do what we have to do."

It was a typical Kevin remark, one that left Kate profoundly troubled. If only there were someone with whom she could discuss the deepening crisis. But Lynn was still skiing, definitely not on the cheap, at Aspen. And Millicent was gone.

All Kate's memories of Enchanted Rock were replaced by anxiety, guilt and her fears of what Michael might do. She also dreaded her ex-husband's unpredictability.

Kate had never felt so alone.

She rattled around the office tending to the usual chores, missing Millicent's companionship. There was a January lull before the annual parish meeting. Kate used it to type up the Sunday order of service two weeks in advance. She mailed out the weekly bulletin and waited for Charles to return.

Kate was unpleasantly surprised to find Phoebe waiting for her when she arrived at the church on Friday morning.

"How did you get into the office?" Kate asked, surprised.

"With my key," Phoebe informed her with frost in her voice. "I saw no point in relinquishing it since I'd be coming back soon."

"I see. How is your mother?"

"She's doing much better."

"I'm glad to hear that."

They were circling each other like hostile dogs. Kate's gaze strayed to the clutch of documents in Phoebe's hand.

Phoebe's face reddened. "I left behind some personal papers and discovered I needed them." She went on the offensive. "You've rearranged the filing system. It's difficult to find anything."

"What were you looking for?" Kate asked pointedly. "Perhaps I can help you locate it."

"I've found all I need. Actually, the main reason I came by was to talk to Father Sheffield."

"He's in Houston for the week, but I'll tell him you came by."

"You can also inform him I'll be back at my desk by the middle of next month."

Kate struggled to remain pleasant. "Perhaps you'd better let him know of your plans personally."

Something about Kate's coolness must have goaded Phoebe, because suddenly her venom burst through the mask of civility. "I'll do just that. And I'll tell you, too. Charles Sheffield will never be permanent rector of this church if I have anything to say about it." At Kate's startled look she proceeded, "Oh, yes, I've heard the rumors about his plans to stay. *And* about what's going on between you. I've already written the bishop about this affair you're flaunting. I intend to bring it up at the parish meeting, too."

Kate sucked in her breath, finding it all she could do not to lunge over the desk at the woman.

"I know why he wants to stay in Austin," Phoebe continued before Kate could stop her. "It's not for any love of God. It's fleshly love. Because he thinks he wants to marry you. The Church of England would never allow such a marriage."

Kate looked blank.

"You, Mrs. Hennessey, are a divorced woman."

Kate's face showed her astonishment.

Phoebe asked smugly, "Didn't he tell you?"

Kate shook her head.

"You'd have to go through an annulment. It's a very messy business. No wonder he'd rather affiliate with the American church—it being more lax in its interpretation of the sanctity of marriage."

By this time, Phoebe recognized the extent of Kate's scattered wits. She ended her threat with satisfied fervor. "But I don't intend to let Charles Sheffield use Emmanuel as a way to satisfy his lust. This is my church. I helped found it based on strong spiritual and moral values. I don't intend to see those values dragged in the mud by the very person who should be an example to us all."

Having made her intentions plain, Phoebe swept out of the room, leaving behind an awful silence.

It was broken only by a shaken breath as Kate covered her face with her hands. "Oh, Millicent, where are you when I need you?" she asked aloud, then wondered, Or Lynn? Or Charles?

No. Not Charles. He was the last person she should see. She had to work this out alone. Yet arrayed before her was a series of impossible choices. Any option she explored, someone would be hurt.

Michael. He was already hurting. Their marriage would only underscore his pain.

Charles. Had the Bishop discussed Phoebe's letter with him yet? Did Charles have an inkling of the maelstrom he'd left behind? Kate had told Charles not to stay in Texas on her account, that she was no pastor's wife. How could he hope to work effectively here with rumors of their affair swirling around him?

And what about Kate, she asked herself? How could she face the impossible choices? Well, she knew pain. She wasn't afraid of it. A person just hunkered down and waited it out. Like an internal hurricane. She could, of course, ignore

Phoebe. Ignore Michael's threats. Continue to live in a dream world.

But Kate was made of sterner stuff. For her it was better to face up to reality.

Reality was a relationship that was less than five months old, between two people from different worlds who operated under different guidelines. They'd had no business becoming involved. Kate blamed herself for that. Blamed herself for giving in to forbidden yearnings.

Next time, girl... Next time? No, never again!

There was too much pain. Kate gritted her teeth, fighting the force of it, battling the agonizing vise that was squeezing her heart.

Kate dropped her hands from her face and discovered the papers on her desk were wet from the tears that had dribbled through her fingers. She wiped at them randomly, smearing the carefully typed words.

They'd have to be redone. She'd made a mess.

An unholy, godforsaken mess.

"Kate?"

She looked up to find Charles in the doorway and was stunned by his sudden appearance. He wasn't due back till tomorrow!

"What's wrong? You're crying." Charles started toward her.

Speechless, Kate wiped at her cheeks as she watched him approach. He reached for her, and she scooted back in her chair frantically. Charles stopped in his tracks.

"Who made you cry?"

"Michael says he'll go live with Kevin if we marry."

Charles took in the import of her words and the mood that accompanied them. He went to the answering machine, flipped it on, and moved to the door of his study. "Come inside." He seemed calm enough.

Kate did as Charles asked and he closed the door behind her, gestured toward a chair and went to sit at his desk, taking his time.

By now, several minutes had passed since Kate's announcement.

Still he picked up where she'd left off. "And you believed him?"

"I believe he means to. But I won't let it happen—no matter what."

Charles heard the fierceness that had crept into her tone and interpreted it correctly.

"I see."

His response and the silence that followed pushed Kate into speech. "He was angry that I'd left town without phoning him. There's no telling what he thinks went on between the two of us."

"He probably thinks the truth. That we're having sex. Sex is normal you know, between consenting adults who are in love with each other and intend to marry."

Kate flushed at the baldness of his statement. Charles could read guilt written across her face.

"Those Puritan tendencies getting the better of you, Kate?" he mocked her gently.

"It's not only Michael." Kate's words rushed out. "It's everyone in the church. Phoebe just left. She's written a letter to the bishop."

"One of many she's sent him. The bishop and I discussed Phoebe's problems."

"Phoebe's problems? It's you and me everybody's talking about."

"Most of what they say is kind. You're blowing things out of proportion, Kate. You're underestimating the character and goodwill of my parishioners. At any rate, once we marry, there'll be no more cause for talk."

"Haven't you heard what I've been saying?" Kate asked a little desperately. "Michael won't live in the same house with you. He doesn't accept the engagement."

"That's why I felt we should have discussed it with him jointly. Which is exactly what we'll do next. We tried it your way and it didn't work, love. Now we'll try it mine."

Kate felt totally frustrated. Why was he refusing to admit the obstacles ahead?

"I know why you went to see the bishop," she said, confrontationally. "Why you want to stay and affiliate with the American church."

Charles's eyes narrowed. "Yes? I thought I'd explained that to you already."

"You didn't tell me everything."

"What didn't I tell you?"

"That we couldn't be married in the Church of England. That a divorced woman isn't fit to be the wife of an Anglican priest."

"Who told you this?"

"Phoebe."

He gave in to anger for an instant. "And you let a sick woman like Phoebe poison your mind?"

"It's true, isn't it? What she told me. Just answer me, Charles."

"It's true," he said deliberately, after a fractional pause, "that there would be complications. If we married in the Church of England, you'd have to apply for an annulment. It's also true I wouldn't put you through that. I know you consider your past marriage a real one, however sad its ending. And that asking for an annulment would be like living a lie. Although you do have grounds for one.

"I also admit that loving you and wanting to marry you affected my decision to remain here. Don't you see? There are a multiplicity of reasons that went into my choice.

They're all threaded together like a tapestry. No one factor can be separated out.''

Kate wasn't in the mood to be soothed by his logic. ''I told you I wouldn't stand in the way of your calling. I certainly didn't intend forcing you to live in a strange land, alienated from your faith. You'd end up hating me.''

''Kate...none of that has happened. You're not being rational. And you're giving me very little credit. I've thought this out. I know what I want.''

''Well, I don't!'' she almost shouted. ''I don't know anything anymore. I need time to think. I'm not sure I want my every move scrutinized by an avid congregation. To be made to feel as if I were Mary Magdalene. This thing with the divorce reminds me of why I left organized religion. The petty gossip, the intrigue. The narrow minds cloaked in piety. Why did it have to be Millicent who died? Why couldn't it have been Phoebe?'' Kate clapped a hand to her mouth, horrified by her words.

''We all miss Millicent,'' he pointed out. ''But you're letting Phoebe get to you.''

Kate couldn't answer and jumped from her chair. Charles addressed the back of her head. ''Kate—I never claimed the church was a refuge from the world. It is in and of the world. It shares the common ills of mankind. It embraces both the Millicents and the Phoebes. I can't promise you otherwise.''

''Well, I don't know if I have the stomach for it,'' she said bitterly.

''What are you saying, Kate?'' His voice was very still.

''I'm saying...I don't know.''

''Do you mean you won't marry me?''

Why was he pushing her this way? Backing her into a corner?

''I just...don't know.''

"Are you going to run and hide at the first complication?"

"Maybe!" Kate answered defiantly. "Maybe I'm not as courageous as your wife Sarah. Perhaps I'm a coward. It's better for you to know that now."

"You're frightened because you think you're alone, Kate. That's not the same as being a coward. You just need to remember we're in this together. Our love for each other will give us strength. There's nothing we can't work out as long as we understand that."

"Each of us is alone...ultimately." Kate's words were slurred, her look far away.

"I don't believe that," Charles disagreed quietly. "In fact, I think it's something of a cop-out."

Kate turned to face him. "Is it?" She shrugged despairingly. "I told you to take another look at me. I'm not the saint Sarah was." A spasm of emotion crossed her face. She closed her eyes briefly. "If it just didn't hurt so much," she whispered. "But I can handle the pain."

Charles's patience went up in smoke. He strode across to her in a single motion, taking her into his arms so that she had to face him. "Damn it, Kate! I won't let you do this to us. What about *my* hurting? You don't want to be a saint. You want to be a bloody martyr. Well, I'm sorry, I've already told you I don't fancy that role. I won't let you play it either. Just tell me if you love me?"

"Yes," Kate whispered, "I do."

"And I love you. And yet you won't trust me or yourself."

"I guess that means I've failed you." Kate spoke forlornly.

"Not me. Us."

"I'm sorry." Again, tears were streaming down Kate's face.

"Listen to me and listen very carefully. Will you do that?"

She nodded dumbly.

"We can solve any problem together, if you have faith. In me, in yourself, in the relationship we share. That's all it takes. Faith." He wiped the tears off Kate's cheek with gentle fingers, reminding her of the sweetness in his touch. The ache inside her throbbed dully.

"I have faith in you, Kate." Charles's anger had left him. He spoke with quiet assurance. "I don't believe you'll fail us when you remember how much we care for each other— how much there is to share. You'll find your courage."

He leaned over to brush her lips with his. "You are all I could ever want, Kate, and I think you're very brave. I don't need a saint or a martyr. I need the woman I love by my side." He kissed her again. "My love. Go home. You haven't slept, have you?"

Kate shook her head.

"Don't tear yourself apart with doubts. We'll find a way. Go home and rest. I'll come see you in the morning."

Kate collected her belongings in a blur and drove home by instinct. Once there, she followed Charles's instructions and went to the bedroom where she slumped down on the edge of the bed. After a moment, she lay back against the pillow, turned her head into it and cried until there were no tears left. She slept.

It was dark when she awoke with a start.

Michael!

She'd forgotten him at school.

Kate rushed to the door of her bedroom and opened it. Two male voices drifted down the hall to her.

Clark was home. Of course. He'd been due in today or tomorrow. Michael must have called the house and found him when she didn't appear. Kate sagged against the bedpost in relief. She felt lightheaded, as though she were floating.

In her mind, she tried to piece together the events of the day. That horrible scene with Phoebe with its bombshell ending. The way her thoughts had tangled until they were snarled and knotted. The frightening scene with Charles.

Yet all she could remember clearly was Charles wiping the tears from her face. That one moment erased the last dreadful days. He'd given her his trust. He'd placed their lives in her hands.

Kate looked down. Her hands should be shaking. Instead, they were steady. Capable hands, she thought oddly. Able to throw away happiness or seize it. Unfettered hands. No chains from the past bound them. Dexterous hands. To shape her own future. And yet, by themselves they were incomplete. One should be in Charles's grasp.

Free. Kate was suddenly free. Of doubts and guilt and ambivalence. Free to go to Charles and apologize... explain....

She laughed softly to herself, feeling gloriously happy. Charles wouldn't need explanations or apologies. He understood. All she had to do was go to him.

Once Kate made the decision, her tiredness fled. She realized she wore the suit she'd gone to work in that morning. It had become rumpled and unsuitable for a reconciliation. Something more romantic, maybe? she asked herself. Even a bit sexy? Something that hinted at silken underwear?

Diagnosing from her wayward thoughts that sanity was returning, Kate rummaged through her closet and decided on a clingy gray sweater with a rolled collar and red slacks that did nice things for her curves. She took a quick shower and put on a touch of makeup, then carefully arranged the dove of peace Charles had given her at Christmas.

She could hardly wait to see him. But first she had to brave Clark and Michael.

She found them lingering over a makeshift supper. From Michael's sheepish expression and the serious look Clark wore, Kate suspected they'd been having a momentous conversation—the engagement, no doubt, being the main topic.

They both turned and grinned tentatively when she entered the room. It was the first smile Michael had granted her in days.

"I'm sorry I forgot you today at school." Kate initiated the conversation. "Actually, it's not that I forgot you. But I fell asleep and just woke up a while ago."

"That's okay," Michael mumbled. "When I called home, Clark was here, and he came to get me."

Kate went over to Clark, kissed his hair, and sneaked a hug. "Glad to have you back. How was New Mexico?"

"Super, Mom. By the third day, I was skiing the hardest slopes. Everyone else in the group was too chicken to try them."

Visions of broken legs danced in Kate's head. She squashed them determinedly. "You should have waked me when you came in, to let me know you'd gotten home safely."

"I started to." Clark was having trouble meeting her eyes. "But you looked like you could stand the rest."

She must have looked like death itself sprawled across the bed, to evoke Clark's compassion. Kate sat down at the table waiting to hear his exploits in the snow. But Clark had his mind on other matters.

"Michael tells me you and Charles are getting married. Gosh, Mom," Clark injected a note of humor, "how did you manage that?"

Kate started to answer cautiously, then balked.

"Actually," she fluttered her eyebrows, "I vamped him."

Clark laughed. More importantly, so did Michael. Or at least she'd heard a ghost of a chuckle.

Kate had a speech she'd prepared in the shower. Now was as good a time as any to deliver it. "We haven't actually set the date. I wanted you both to know we'll consult you on it. There are still a few things to be worked out."

"Yeah," Clark volunteered. "Like Michael's being a bozo."

Kate looked at Michael in alarm. Usually that kind of statement from Clark guaranteed an explosion. But once again, Michael surprised her with a sheepish look.

Siblings were amazing creatures, Kate thought. They fought unrelentingly for fifteen years. And then at the unlikeliest moment they established communication. But she wasn't going to analyze the situation or pry into their discussion.

Instead, she stated carefully, "I don't think Michael's being a bozo. He's just not sure where he fits in. Charles and I would like to talk to you about that, Michael, but right now, I need to go talk to him myself. To clear up a misunderstanding. Why don't I bring him back with me?"

"A misunderstanding?" Clark asked. "So that's what happened. When I saw you asleep, you looked like you'd been crying. Was the fight over Michael?"

"No," Kate answered immediately and meant it. "And it wasn't exactly a fight. Let's just say I lost my footing momentarily. It won't happen again."

She settled her gaze on first her elder, then her younger son. "I want you both to know how I feel. I wasn't ever planning to remarry. This engagement has come as something of a shock to me. But it's happened, and I can't—I won't—go back to the way things were. I just want you to understand that my feelings for Charles in no way diminish my love for each of you. All I ask are open minds. Shall I bring Charles back so we can talk together?''

The mulish look of old flitted across Michael's face, but when Kate finished, he nodded silently. Clark winked at her surreptitiously. She'd won a small battle.

Gathering her coat and purse, Kate gave in to her urgency and left, rehearsing another speech as she drove to the parsonage. She could have phoned and announced her arrival, but Kate wanted to see Charles's face. She needed to feel the strength of his arms around her. Maybe that was the reason for the flickering anxiety that interlaced her anticipation. She wanted the scene from that afternoon banished from his mind.

There were lights in the parsonage windows when she drove up, but Charles's car wasn't in the drive. Kate cursed mildly and almost drove on by. But something stopped her. Perhaps Charles had driven the car into the garage for the night. Perhaps Greg was at home and could relay a message. After having come this far, Kate decided to take a chance.

Yet when Kate parked and went to the porch to ring the doorbell, no one answered. She knocked loudly. There was no response.

Greg had probably been instructed not to come to the door. Feeling like an idiot, Kate moved to the nearest window and saw that the pane was shattered. She could feel the crunching of glass on the lawn under her feet. It was her first intimation that something was wrong.

Still, nothing could prepare her for what she saw next.

CHAPTER SEVENTEEN

THE BODY LAY on the tiled floor, a pool of blood thickening beside it . . . no . . .

No!

"Charles!"

The body stirred and groaned.

Kate leaned against the window ledge, fighting the roaring in her head. Then adrenaline began to surge, rescuing her from faintness. Focusing her purpose. Telescoping the seconds.

She rushed to the door and beat on it furiously, all the while shouting Greg's name.

There was no answer.

When Kate turned the knob, the door opened. She ran to Charles's side.

His chest was bleeding. He was only semiconscious and unaware of her presence.

Kate dragged open the counter drawers, found dishcloths and tried to stem the flow of blood, unaware of the broken phrases spilling out of her mouth.

"I'm here . . . don't die . . . Charles, it's Kate . . ."

His face was pale and etched with pain. Yet his lashes flickered at her voice. She thought his hand brushed against her arm. He moaned faintly.

"I've got to get help . . ." Kate whispered brokenly. Saw the phone and punched out 911. Knew a moment of panic when the dispatcher needed the address. She stumbled over Charles's street and telephone number.

Five endless minutes later, the Emergency Medical Service arrived.

"He's been shot," one of the technicians said tersely, as they began their hurried work. "Is this how you found him?"

Kate nodded and pointed to the shattered window, fighting the convulsive reaction that was setting in.

"Luckily the police will be here shortly. They come out on this kind of call."

The medics began an I.V. and placed Charles on the cart. One of them asked Kate, "Anyone else in the house?"

"I don't know."

Just at that moment, Nolan, Greg and a third man hurried into the room. Kate lurched to Nolan's side. He caught her as she stumbled. "Charles has been shot. Through the window."

Nolan braced her with a steadying arm and scanned the grisly scene. He caught one of the medic's looks. The expression he read there made his grasp tighten around Kate protectively.

"Come on, let's get him out of here! Don't wait for the squad car. I'll radio instructions on the way to the hospital."

Nolan's directions were unnecessary. Charles was already being wheeled toward the waiting van.

Later, Kate remembered very little about the harrowing ride that followed. Only the scream of the sirens. The blurred night at the periphery of her vision. And the flashing light of the ambulance in front of them, as rhythmic as a heartbeat, splashing a harsh red glow over the occupants of the police car close behind.

Kate's mind was paralyzed. Thinking brought panic. So her face was stony as she entered the trauma center of the hospital. She answered questions through stiff lips and hovered near the swinging doors through which she'd seen them rush Charles.

She focused on a single thought.

Live...damn it...live...

"Kate, can I call someone for you?"

Kate jumped at the sound of Nolan's voice.

"My...my children need to know. I'd better tell them myself. But the church—Dan."

"I'll take care of it." Nolan's tone was steady, his words matter-of-fact. But beneath his stoic calm, his dark complexion was ashen. "Kate..." His voice faltered and died.

Kate caught hold of his sleeve. "Could you find out what's happening? Charles's condition? Please ask if I can see him."

Nolan nodded and left her side.

Kate moved to the public telephone, fighting the constriction in her throat. Clark answered the ring.

"Clark..."

"Mom?"

"Charles is hurt. I'm at the Emergency Room at Brackenridge Hospital."

"Hurt?"

"He's been shot." Kate's voice wobbled.

"Shot!" From one moment to the next Clark became a man. "Just hold on, Mom. We'll be right there."

Kate stared at the telephone receiver after Clark had hung up, before placing it carefully in its cradle. She turned. Her eyes locked on the double doors that imprisoned her in hell.

She began pacing, her arms folded tightly over her breasts. Moments later, Nolan came through the doors, conferring with a doctor.

"The bullet nicked his heart...lost a lot of blood...he's lucky to be alive...she must have found him almost immediately..."

Their voices halted when they saw Kate there.

"Charles has gone into surgery," Nolan told her, before she could ask.

"Is he...? Will he...?"

"He's in critical condition," the doctor answered Kate's unfinished question. "Other than that, I can't speculate."

"How long will it be?"

"Two or three hours. There's a good bit of repair work to be done. He's a very lucky man you found him when you did, Ms Hennessey. And he's in the hands of an excellent surgeon."

"Will I be able to see him after surgery?"

"As soon as it's possible. All I can tell you now is to wait. Rest if you can."

Kate stared at the clock. It was nine-forty.

Two or three hours...

She made herself walk to one of the comfortable chairs, and sat down stiffly, struggling to contain her edginess.

Greg brought her a cup of coffee, the unknown man who'd ridden with them to the hospital hovering behind him. Kate had forgotten about both men.

"I don't know what to say," Greg began.

Kate put her hand over his, the words barely registering. "I know," she murmured randomly.

"But you don't understand. That bullet was meant for me." There was agony in Greg's voice.

The realization of what he said washed over Kate. Of course! A mistake! The sniper had thought Charles was Greg. The shooting now made a horrible sense.

Just then, the other man spoke. "I'm sorry, Ms Hennessey. My name's Larry Carter. I was put on the case to guard both men. I'm sorry..." Carter repeated inadequately.

"It's okay," Kate instinctively sought to ease their guilt. "I don't blame either one of you. Charles won't either. He wouldn't have wanted it to be you, Greg."

Out of the corner of her eye, Kate saw movement. Her two children had arrived, their eyes searching for her familiar figure.

Kate beckoned to them. They hurried to her side.

Michael's expression was appalled. "Mom, you've got blood all over you!"

Kate looked down. Brown patches marred the soft gray wool of her sweater. For the first time she noticed her hands. Charles's blood was caked along her fingers.

Kate gagged. A cold sweat washed over her. If the policeman Carter hadn't seen what was happening and forced her head between her knees she would have fainted.

"It's all right. I'm okay," she said thickly after a moment, even as Clark returned with paper towels. He'd dampened them and now took her hands in his, wiping them carefully. Carter placed a cool compress against her forehead. She sat up and leaned her head against the wall behind her, refusing to give in to the betraying weakness.

Clark looked up at Carter as he finished his task. "I'm Clark, her son. How is Charles doing?"

"He's in surgery."

"Why would anyone shoot him?"

Kate was aware of Greg who was close by, and answered Clark's question herself. "He was mistaken for somebody else. That doesn't matter now. What matters is..." Kate choked on the words.

She bowed her head again, struggling to keep from flying into a million pieces. And she felt Michael's awkward hand along her back, attempting comfort. The small gesture stiffened her resolve.

"I'm okay," she said once more and meant it.

There was a sudden commotion. Everyone's head jerked up to find two television crews complete with cameras hurrying toward them down the corridor. Other reporters followed. They spotted Nolan Eccles and the questions began.

"We understand there's been a shooting, Lieutenant. A priest. We'd like a statement for the ten o'clock news. Can you give us the particulars? Is it true he's here from England? Do you have any idea who did it? We've heard there was sniper fire. A neighbor said a woman found him. Can we get a statement from her?"

One of them spotted the stains on Kate's clothes. "Miss? Was it you who found him?"

Greg loomed up, Carter behind him. Greg wrapped his arm around Kate's waist and whisked her away. All the while cameras were recording the flurry of movement.

Nolan barked out an order. The reporters became silent and tersely he outlined the bare bones of the shooting, giving nothing away, leaving them frustrated for details. Moments later they filed out of the area, and those inside could see them setting up for broadcasts, framed by the glass doors.

The boys were astounded, Kate was aghast. She'd had no inkling the assault on Charles would be newsworthy. This could blow the cover off Nolan's investigation, and Greg's face would be beamed into a thousand Austin living rooms.

It was one more shock to absorb. Yet oddly enough, after the media had gone, a strange calm settled over the ones who waited.

The minutes ticked by ever so slowly, the plain-faced clock on the wall indifferent in its plodding pace.

Dan came. Nolan had reached him by telephone. After receiving what assurances could be given, he began calling strategic members of the parish so that no one would panic. David and Linda arrived in shock. They'd heard what had happened on the evening newscast. Within an hour there was a small group of parishioners, keeping an anxious vigil.

They were quick to take Kate into their arms, offering what comfort they could. She was with them, yet apart, isolated by terrifying dread.

The night deepened. Kate walked outdoors, hoping the brisk air would brace her, and watched the city closing down to sleep. Only the Emergency Room was bright with light—eternally busy. She turned and slowly went back inside.

Three victims from an automobile crash arrived in a whirl of activity. The police brought in a man who'd been stabbed. Each trauma brought its own assortment of people to wait. As they all were waiting.

Only two weeks ago Kate had been in this same room, keeping another vigil, that one for Millicent.

Kate rose from her chair, beginning to pace again. She was too dazed to be surprised when Lynn showed up, and she accepted Lynn's hug with a thankful murmur.

"Clark left a message on my answering machine." Lynn said in explanation. "We've just flown in from Denver. I came as soon as I heard. What happened, Kate?"

"Charles was hit by sniper fire." Kate's voice was rigidly calm. "He was mistaken for another person—someone he was hiding for the police. It's been on the news, although only a few people know why it happened. Oh, Lynn, he's badly hurt. He's gone into surgery." Kate looked up at the clock. "It'll be at least another hour before we know more."

Lynn led Kate to chairs set apart from the others. "Can you talk about it?"

"I found him, Lynn, just in time. Or he might have...bled to death."

"But he didn't," Lynn reminded her firmly.

"He's in critical condition. They can't give me more than that. Lynn, I said I'd marry him."

"It's a miracle," Lynn whispered reverently.

That brought the smile Lynn hoped for. Then Kate's face clouded. "Yes, but this afternoon I got cold feet and acted like a fool. Oh, Lynn! What if I don't get to tell him what I need to?"

"You will. I believe in miracles." Lynn took a look at Kate's clothing and made a quick decision. "Give me the keys to your house."

Kate did as instructed.

"I'll be back in a jiffy." Lynn squeezed her hand, conferred with Clark for a moment and left.

For the first time, Kate noticed Michael sitting by himself. She went over to him, her maternal instincts stirring. Laying an arm along the back of his chair, she pulled him to her in a brief hug, which he accepted gratefully.

"I guess you're glad Lynn came," he said in a wistful voice. "She's a good friend."

"I'm lucky to have her," Kate agreed. "I'm lucky to have you and Clark, too."

"Yeah. Real luck. To have a jerk for a son."

"You shouldn't say that about your brother."

"Aw, Mom, you know what I..."

Their eyes met. Michael's fell. But not before Kate spied a trace of humor in them.

"Don't blame yourself," she told him, "for something you had nothing to do with."

"I know. But—listen, Mom, I don't dislike him."

"I never thought you did."

"I didn't want anything bad to happen."

"Of course you didn't."

"On your account," Michael ended doggedly. "Why was that guy Greg hiding at Charles's house anyway?"

"Charles was helping him."

"Yeah. He's a real do-gooder. Why couldn't you have found a computer whiz like Hank? We'll probably have strange characters wandering in and out of our lives."

Kate chuckled at Michael's insightful prediction. "Maybe. Probably." The laughter hung in her throat. "I hope so."

Mother and son fell silent, each prey to forbidden fears.

Nolan came up to Kate shortly afterward. Kate sensed behind his grim policeman's face that like Greg and Michael, he was stricken with guilt.

His first words proved that. "Kate, I take responsibility for this."

"Nolan, it isn't your fault. You forget, I was there. From the beginning, Charles was determined to do everything he could to help Greg, even if it meant putting himself in danger. Standing between Charles and what he thinks is right can be..."

"...a formidable task," Nolan ended her sentence with a faint smile. Their thoughts centered on the man whom they both cared for deeply.

Minutes later, Lynn returned with clean slacks and a sweater. Kate went to the washroom and changed, suddenly loathe to handle the clothing she discarded. It reminded her too vividly of the earlier scene.

Then it seemed there was nothing left for anyone to do except walk the halls. Sit awhile. Provide small moments of physical comfort. Sip coffee that was tasteless. Talk randomly. Or ask careful questions trying to piece together the chain of events.

Nolan had called Greg and Carter to the police station that evening for a hurried consultation. They'd driven Charles's car. Charles, who'd taken a cab to the church as soon as he'd returned from Houston, had stayed to work late and, Kate suspected, to wrestle with her doubts. He'd made it home minutes after the other two men had left. That was the reason he'd been alone in the house. Nolan, heeding his instincts, had followed Greg and Carter back to the parsonage to double-check the situation. The three of them had arrived too late.

The comings and goings had all the elements of a French farce, with the sniper arriving at the critical moment. If he knew about Charles's trip and its intended duration—which was a good possibility—and if he'd discovered Greg's hiding place, he'd have been confident the blond man he saw through the window was his intended victim.

Policemen came to the hospital to question Kate and Greg. They conferred with Nolan and Carter. They'd hit it lucky. A neighbor had heard the shot, mistaken it for a backfire, glanced out his window and seen a car racing away. He could identify the car's make and model, for it was a distinctive one. And that was the gunman's second mistake.

BY ONE IN THE MORNING everyone was showing the strain. The control Kate had achieved in piecemeal fashion was wearing thin from continuous stress. The doctor had said there would be some news about Charles in two or three hours. Nearly four hours had passed and still they hadn't heard anything.

She began to wring her hands unconsciously, the agitation building.

When finally a doctor appeared, Kate's knees were rubbery as she rose to face him, Lynn close by her side.

"Ms Hennessey?"

"Yes?"

"I'm Dr. Caldwell. I performed the surgery on your..."

"Fiancé."

Dr. Caldwell nodded. "It was successful. We've patched him up."

Kate started to slump. Lynn caught her elbow.

"Then he'll be all right?" Kate managed to ask.

"He's not out of the woods. The next few hours are critical."

"Can I see him?"

"He hasn't come out of the anesthetic. We're concerned ... because of his weakened condition."

"I must see him." Kate could feel herself trembling. All night she'd been haunted by the remembrance of Charles's bloodied chest, the sight of him lying helpless, near death.

Dr. Caldwell seemed to understand. "Only for a few minutes," he agreed. "Talk to him quietly. Maybe it will help. We'll have a much better prognosis once your fiancé's back with us."

Kate nodded and followed the doctor into the ICU. One of the nurses was by Charles's bedside, speaking his name.

"This is his fiancée," Dr. Caldwell explained. "Let her take over. Maybe he'll respond to her voice."

Kate approached the bed, dodging a welter of tubes and machines. Charles was oblivious to it all; the same face that was so expressive normally now deathly white and devoid of animation.

One arm lying outside the sheet was slack—the same arm that had held her in a passionate embrace. The same hand that had stroked her silkily.

"Are you going to be all right?" Dr. Caldwell asked gently.

"Yes," Kate said grittily and leaned over the bedside, her hand touching his arm, his cheek, his lifeless fingers.

"Charles...it's Kate."

The doctor and nurse moved away leaving Kate alone with him.

"Can you hear me, Charles? Squeeze my fingers if you can." Kate covered her hand with his but felt no movement. She pulled up the bedside chair, willing him to sense her presence.

"Don't think you can get away from me this easily," she groused weakly, and watched for a ghost of a smile.

There was no response.

Kate felt a wave of desolation wash over her and fought against the undertow. If she gave in, if she let Charles go without a struggle, she faced a life devoid of love and hope.

Still grasping Charles's hand, Kate laid her cheek against his shoulder and haltingly, the words came.

"Listen...I'm not sure who You are. I know we've never talked much. But...I need You to hear me now. This man is good. He's real—a great character reference. You'd be an idiot to take him. What good is he to You dead?

"I know...I know. I'm not asking for me. I don't have the right to do that. You and I aren't on the best of terms. But other people need him. People who are friends of Yours. My son, Michael."

Kate's voice faltered for a moment before she could continue. "This...this man's one of Your best investments. How could You replace him? Are You paying attention to what I've said?"

Desperation seized her. "Damn it! You'd better *listen*!"

Kate felt the faintest movement beneath her. Her heart stopped. She raised her head and found Charles's eyes gazing straight into hers. They were a little glassy, admittedly. But a look of amusement was there for her to see.

"I've heard better," Charles admitted in a fuzzy voice that was glorious to Kate's ears. "But for a beginner...it wasn't bad. And it worked. I promise...not to die on you." He moved and grunted with the effort.

Kate grinned at him stupidly. For the first time since the nightmare began, tears started flowing down her face.

"What happened to me?" he croaked.

"You don't remember?"

"Not much."

"You were shot by those men after Greg, and I'm furious with you. You're not safe on the streets. After that line you fed me about living to be ninety-five. The next thing I know you'll contract beriberi."

Kate stopped in the middle of her harangue. Charles was no longer listening, for he'd drifted back to sleep. Realizing the importance of what had just happened, she called out to the nurse and explained that Charles had regained consciousness. She was rewarded with a satisfied smile. Then in typical hospital fashion, the medical team ushered Kate out of Intensive Care, promising her she could return later. A tense mob waited outside in the corridor.

Kate smiled mistily at them all. "He talked to me. The nurse said that's a very good sign."

Excited chatter broke out, followed by tearful hugs and laughter. The next long period of waiting was punctuated with hope and the beginning of relief.

After a time Charles's nurse came out and motioned Kate to come forward. Everyone drew close. "Father Sheffield's come around again. He's asking for you, Ms Hennessey."

This time, when Kate went into his cubicle, she could see for herself that Charles was more alert. His eyes were wide open. She bent to kiss him, overwhelmed with thankfulness.

"You can't catch beriberi," Charles murmured. "It's caused from a vitamin deficiency."

Kate leaned her forehead against his, breaking into help-less laughter. "Which proves," she finally managed to say, "that you're not eating right. You need a keeper. Someone to see you lead a long and uneventful life."

"Uneventful?" Charles asked dubiously, his voice still fuzzy.

"Well...mildly adventurous," Kate relented.

"Did you have someone in mind?"

"Oh yes. The perfect person. I'm resigned to my fate. I seem to be the only one standing between you and catas-trophe."

"Yes," Charles agreed as he brushed the back of his hand against her cheek. "I remember that much. Thank you, Kate, for saving my life."

She caught his hand and held it against her face. "I'm only returning the favor." A new batch of tears was flow-ing. "Charles, thank you for trusting me when I was such an idiot this morning. I almost ruined everything."

"I don't remember this morning," he mumbled. "All I know is now." He frowned, disoriented. "What time is it?"

"Oh, about four in the morning. It's Saturday," she re-alized.

His frown dissolved into a dear smile. "At four on a Sat-urday morning, Kate...you're beautiful."

"Red-eyed, weeping and swollen-faced." She wiped at her cheeks self-consciously. "You're delirious, Charles. I'd better call a nurse."

"Wait..." He caught hold of her. "Don't leave...my condition's precarious." His voice trembled. "I need constant attention. And TLC."

"I'd say you were improving by the minute." Kate stood and kissed him on the nose. "And my time is up. Besides, there are some anxious people waiting for my next report. I'd like to tell them their prayers have been answered."

By this time, the nurse had joined them.

"Well, Father Sheffield. I see you're more alert. Mmm, your color's better. Do you know where you are?"

"Yes. When am I getting out of here?" Charles's question was weak but hopeful.

"Not for a while." The nurse began her routine, checking his I.V., popping a thermometer into his mouth, counting his pulse-rate, recording his blood pressure. "The doctor gave instructions for a private room when you've stabilized. Of course, you'll have to promise to be a good boy and not overexert yourself."

"Grrrmm," Charles growled around the thermometer.

"Don't worry. I'll see to it he behaves," Kate promised.

"Mmmmmm," Charles's tone changed. He was sounding surprisingly healthy for a man who'd just cheated death. But his eyelids were heavy.

"Down, boy," Kate ordered and patted him fondly.

As though following instructions, Charles promptly fell asleep.

CHAPTER EIGHTEEN

IT WAS NOON on Saturday before Charles's transfer out of ICU was complete. But a tireless band of parishioners had spent the entire night and morning at the hospital. Dan and Phil, Nolan and Lynn, Carter and Greg, whom Charles spoke with a moment longer than the others, all filed past his bed. When Greg left, his expression was washed clean with relief.

Finally, Clark and Michael trooped by the bedside, looking uncomfortable with the portentous occasion. Now that Charles was off the critical list, both of them were curious about how it felt to be gunned down. "Like Dirty Harry" was how Clark put it.

Charles, giving in to his baser instincts, gave them a blow by blow account. Kate had to leave the room.

While she was gone she phoned Connie, her mother, and arranged for her to stay with the boys over the next few days. The request necessitated an abbreviated account of the shooting. Kate also gave in to the inevitable, announcing her engagement. Connie murmured something about the answer to a prayer.

Twenty minutes later, Kate rushed back to Charles's room to save him from the ghoulish clutches of her sons. Her fiancé was beginning to look the worse for wear, and she included all three males in her scolding as she shooed Clark and Michael out the door.

Alone at last, Kate settled into the easy chair provided by the hospital and watched Charles drift off to sleep. That easy chair developed character over the afternoon. Kate dozed fitfully. Every time she awoke the memories of yesterday's events returned in vivid detail. She had to get up, stand by the bedside and gaze down at Charles to assure herself he was still breathing.

He woke up at dinnertime chipper and noticeably stronger. By this time, Kate felt like death warmed over. She'd used up her store of adrenaline and was running on sheer nerves. So, at Charles's prodding, Kate made her way to the basement cafeteria for dinner. She bought a local newspaper along the way, when its headlines screamed out at her.

Episcopal Priest Shot by Sniper.

Under the caption was a picture of Nolan Eccles speaking to the press in the hospital corridor. Greg and Kate were right behind him, highlighted by the camera's flash. A snapshot of Charles was inset to one side. Kate skimmed the article, worriedly, over mashed potatoes and meat loaf.

The motive for the shooting was still unclear. However, the reporter had already pieced together certain facts. First, the article mentioned that a "mystery" man with a cop in tow had been staying with Charles, perhaps in hiding. Second, that Charles and Lieutenant Eccles worked closely together on the pilot family project they'd conceived, which had received publicity last summer. The article speculated on Father Sheffield's involvement in a dangerous case—something, perhaps, more sinister than a domestic disturbance.

How much, Kate asked herself, should she tell Charles about his sudden fame when she returned to his room? Nolan was there when she arrived, already in deep discussion with the patient.

"What's going on?" she asked testily when she spied the paper with its headlines on the bed. "Couldn't that have waited a while longer? It's barely been a day. He's had major surgery."

Nolan looked appropriately chastened.

Charles defended his friend against his beloved's wrath. "It's my fault, I made him tell me. I had to know what he'd done with Greg. It seems my shooting has blown the case wide open." He gave her his sweetest smile. "Come here. I've missed you."

At his expression, Kate regretted her burst of temper. It all comes of being cotton-headed, she decided disgruntledly, planting a kiss on Charles's cheek. With his good arm, he pulled her closer and returned the favor, full on her lips.

"Charles...remember...you aren't to exert yourself."

"I think I'm in better shape than you are, sweet. You look somewhat worse for the wear."

"Last night I was beautiful," Kate remembered sadly.

"You still are," Charles said gruffly. "But it's come to me just how much I've put you through. Nolan—see that she gets home and to bed."

"I'm not going," Kate stated stubbornly.

"Kate, I'm out of danger. I'm going to be fine."

"I know. I mean, I know intellectually. It's just that last night's still so vivid. I need to see you like this, be close to you, to replace those horrible memories." She shuddered.

Charles looked patient, but unconvinced. Their disagreement would have deteriorated into an argument if Lynn hadn't appeared at that moment to lend support to his and Nolan's cause. With Nolan's promise to stay the night with Charles, Kate was persuaded to sleep over at Lynn's house and to be chauffeured to the hospital early the next morning.

THE NEXT FEW DAYS passed quickly for Kate. There were long hours by Charles's bedside, patrolling a flood of visitors. Then she'd drive home late at night to fall into bed. Nolan would arrive daily for mysterious meetings.

Charles's condition improved steadily. He was up and out of bed, feeling confined. Kate was nervous at his impatience, urging him to take it easy. When he asked her to bring him work from the office, Kate firmly refused the request.

So she was surprised to find him buried under a stack of papers one evening when she returned unannounced. She'd just spent a few hours at the office reclaiming order out of chaos. Linda, Dan and others were answering the phone at the church, but Kate felt better after an afternoon catching up.

She was not, however, pleased with the scene before her. As she leaned over to kiss Charles hello, she asked, "What's this? You can't be trusted. See what happens the minute my back is turned! What accomplice brought these to you?" She thumped the papers Charles clutched, her tone the same one she used on her children.

Charles looked like Clark or Michael caught in the act. It was an expression she'd seen before, the look sheepish and faintly chagrined.

Amused? Odd.

Kate tugged at the stack he held. Charles's grip resisted her. His look grew more sheepish.

"Charles—this can wait. You're supposed to be resting." She finally wrested the papers away from him and sat down to straighten them. "What on earth was so important you needed to work on it now?"

How very odd.

The contraband material had the weight and look of a manuscript. Kate broke into a knowing smile. "I get it," she teased him. "You're writing a book. You admitted as much to me early on." Her look grew very thoughtful. "Let me guess what it's about. An incredibly scholarly work on the medieval church. Am I warm?"

All this time, Charles hadn't said a word. The enigmatic smile he wore gave nothing away.

Okay, Kate decided, she'd see for herself.

She glanced down at the top sheet. Page 253. Her eyes skimmed to a middle paragraph.

The Austin sun beat down on Jeffries as he waited for the woman to appear. Suffocating waves of heat shimmered off the pavement. Sweat soaked the light suit he wore.

England was never like this, Jeffries thought to himself ironically. Hot and blindingly bright and charged with heated emotions.

You've blown your cool, old chap. Under the Texas sun. You're in love with the lady.

His chief suspect.

No—it was worse than that.

He knew now she was the next victim.

"Jeffries...?"

Inspector Burton Jeffries? Kate fumbled through the pages, scanning them with stunned, disbelieving eyes, reading the proof for herself. As if the author's name on every heading hadn't given him away.

William Fitzgerald.

Carefully, Kate placed the manuscript onto the bedside table. Only then did she meet Charles's gaze.

He was silently awaiting her reaction, his own face a study. Guilt was the most probable candidate for what he was feeling.

As well it should be!

"You are," she began tonelessly, "undoubtedly...the most dangerous...deceitful...underhanded...amoral, unscrupulous, lascivious—"

"Lascivious?"

"*Lascivious*, conniving man I have ever fallen in love with. You tempted me with illicit passion, stole my heart with a smile, tricked me into loving you, bribed me with baubles, coerced me into marriage, threatened me with rock climbing and seduced me in a tent. Then, you very thoughtlessly stopped a bullet, adding gray hairs to my collection."

Kate stopped to take a breath, her indignation glorious. "And now the final perfidy! I agree to give my hand in marriage to a humble man of the cloth. And instead, I find I've pledged my heart and soul to a writer. A *mystery* writer. A moody, temperamental, grouchy... *The* mystery writer!"

"Now, Kate, you know I'm none of those things," Charles ventured gingerly.

"What things?"

"Moody, temperamental, grouchy. At least not very."

"You admit to the others?"

"Yes," he owned meekly and bowed his head. "I've said from the start you were too good for me. I had to resort to underhanded methods."

"Who else in Austin knows who you are?" she asked, steaming.

"Well, Nolan. He's been my technical advisor."

"He knew and I didn't?"

Charles winced. "I feel bad about that."

"So you should!" Now Kate understood Charles's look when she and Nolan had been introduced.

"Other than that," Charles confessed, "only Greg. He found out when he moved in with me."

By now Kate was remembering in exquisite detail earlier conversations she and Charles had had on this subject.

"Those times you let me ramble on! How I wished I could sit at Fitzgerald's feet. How I hero-worshiped you! And you never gave me a cl—!"

"What would you have done if I had?" he broke in.

"I don't know." By this time, Kate was gesturing wildly. "I probably would have been so in awe of you..."

"I rest my case."

"What case?"

"That we needed to get to know each other better before I revealed my alter ego."

"Get to know each other better! How much better would you suggest? When I think about Enchanted Rock...if I'd known...before we made love..."

Charles was genuinely amused. He also had that gleam in his eye Kate knew so well.

"What on earth difference would it have made at that particular moment?" he asked silkily and reached out his hand to her. She walked toward him in a daze. He settled her against his good shoulder so that she was half on the bed, their faces close.

"Tell me. I'm interested," he coaxed. "Would it have stifled your enthusiasm? Increased your inhibitions? We cut through those rather nicely, as I recall."

"I'm not sure," Kate confessed. "I had enough trouble with the idea of your being a minister."

"Exactly," Charles said smugly. "I wanted you all to myself those two days. If I'd told you about Inspector Jeffries, there'd have been another person in that tent. Fitzgerald can get his later," he finished crudely.

"Oh?" Kate's lips curved ever so slightly. "What's he like as a lover?"

"Who? Fitzgerald or Jeffries?"

"Both." She couldn't help adding, "Afraid of the competition?"

"Maybe," Charles acknowledged. "My double life has had its complications over the past several years. Not the least of which was your 'hero worship.' I decided early on it was best to keep my writing a secret, except for a few people. Otherwise, it might get in the way of my work."

"Have you been writing for very long?" Kate asked, finally.

"Not really. Although I must have a gene for it. My mother, if you'll remember, keeps copious journals and pens a weekly newspaper column. But I only got started after Sarah's death. I'd become involved with Scotland Yard while setting up a family disturbance project. The more I learned about police procedure the more intrigued I became. Since my personal life was floundering, writing became a kind of therapy, and Jeffries grew in my mind. The concept's not original, as you know. The Inspector's only one of an ancient and honorable line of gentlemen detectives."

"But Jeffries is the best."

"Ngaio Marsh's fans wouldn't agree."

"Hmmph. What do they know?" Kate caught herself up short. "What am I saying? I should still be furious. Instead, I'm defending you!"

"I tricked you," Charles murmured, roaming her face with his lips and reacquainting his hands with her soft curves.

"Yes." Kate's voice was husky. "I can see you have."

"Kate . . . ?"

"Mmm . . ."

"Do you mind, really? I confess I've been a coward. I didn't want to lose you."

"Fat chance of that." Her breath was warm against his skin. "Actually, I can see certain advantages."

"As there are. You can sit at my feet, or in my lap. Any number of interesting places. I'll reveal all the tricks of the trade."

"You *are* talking about the craft of fiction?"

"What do you think? Believe me, I'm a great editor."

"You'll cut me to ribbons."

"I'll have fun putting you back together again."

Charles's tone changed. "I'm serious, Kate. And I want to say this to you here and now. I find what I do very fulfilling, both in the church and at the typewriter. If marrying you meant having to leave the ministry, I would have done so willingly, knowing there are many ways to serve God. And knowing our marriage is right and good in His sight. You must never feel I've made a sacrifice." He nuzzled her. "I like it here in Austin. And here in your arms. Did I tell you, Jeffries is making the move, too. He also has fallen in love with an American beauty."

"Very convenient," Kate commented, trying not to blush.

"I thought so. Which reminds me. I received a call from the bishop today. The committee has met and the position at Emmanuel is mine. All in all, I'm a lucky man. I'm also, incidentally, a rather wealthy one. The royalties keep rolling in." He sounded almost apologetic.

"Charles," Kate whispered, "you're bribing me again."

"I know. Is it working?"

"I'll tell you in another fifty years."

"Mother!"

The single word held mortified embarrassment. Kate started and turned her head to find Michael and Clark in the entrance to the room, their faces shocked. Evidently, they didn't feel a hospital bed was an appropriate place for necking.

Children could be so rigid.

Charles's doctor, who stood behind them, however, was not above a discreet leer.

Kate scrambled from the bed and surreptitiously straightened her clothing. She smiled brightly at the doctor, feeling her color rise.

"Well," he said heartily. "You seem to be making a rapid recovery, Charles."

The patient grinned. Kate cringed.

"It's time to send you home. How does tomorrow morning sound?"

"Fantastic. I'm going bonkers."

"I can see that."

Kate would have welcomed the chance to slink out of sight. But right now there were more important matters than her bruised sensibilities. "Are you sure, doctor? I don't want him discharged prematurely."

"It doesn't look like there's much question of that," the doctor said dryly.

"But what about his dressings?"

"I'm going to check those now, though the chart shows no sign of infection. You can bring him to my office in a week for an examination."

Kate was still anxious. "Won't he need careful monitoring?"

"I'm depending, Ms Hennessey, on you for that. I'll give you complete instructions."

The doctor cut away the swathes of bandages, while Kate watched bravely. The boys were more avid observers. She could almost see them speculating on what a bullet wound looked like. Kate blanched at its location, but the stitched skin was already puckering into a scar. The doctor pronounced himself pleased and left shortly thereafter.

Now she had only the boys to face. They still looked vaguely disapproving, and it was all Charles's fault.

Kate decided to retaliate. "Michael. Clark. Charles has a confession to make. In fact, we were just discussing it when you came in."

They looked puzzled.

Charles took charge. "What Kate's trying to say is, there's something I hadn't told her. I'm a mystery novelist—like your mother."

"Oh, no," Kate contradicted him, "not like your mother. Charles's mysteries sell. He writes under the name of William Fitzgerald. I have all his books at home."

"Neat."

"Really?"

"Do you make lots of money?"

"Yes," Charles admitted.

Clark and Michael were impressed, mildly. The bullet wound had impressed them more.

"Mom?" Michael's tone was hopeful. "Are you coming home early tonight?"

"I certainly am." Kate realized suddenly that her children needed motherly attention. "We'll leave right now, so Charles can get back to his craft." She kissed him decorously. "I'll be back with the car tomorrow to help you check out."

DURING THE RIDE HOME, Michael and Clark were quiet. It seemed to be a peaceful silence, at least to Kate.

Then Michael spoke, as though he'd been working up his courage. "Mom, I talked to Dad last night about living with him."

Kate's fingers gripped the steering wheel convulsively. "And?"

"He doesn't think it's such a hot idea."

Kate sagged with relief. "Oh."

"Yeah. I think he's right. Actually, we talked about a lot of things. The family. You getting married. About his drinking. He's decided to see a counselor, even check into a hospital."

Thank you, Kevin.

"Dad says later, maybe, I can stay with him awhile, but right now, my home's with you."

Thank you very, very much.

"So I guess I'll have to get used to Charles."

"Will that be so difficult?"

"Nah. He's neat. Dad's a little jealous of him," Michael confided innocently. "But he understands. I even think, in a way, your meeting Charles has been good for Dad. It's made him look at himself."

Out of the mouths of babes . . .

"Dad's seeing some woman, too. He says he wants to give their relationship a chance."

And may you find peace some day as I have done, Kevin. I wish you well.

CHARLES'S SHOOTING had indeed blown Nolan's case wide open. The news media, in its zeal to uncover the motive, saw to that. Once the reporters identified Greg as the intended target and discovered gambling was involved, the racketeers faced not only indictments, but the glare of investigative reporting. Names, places and the extent of the problem became public domain.

Nolan was livid, of course. The complex case he'd so carefully constructed was splattered across the newspaper day after day. But the publicity served as a catalyst. People began to talk. Some of them were other victims. People in the lower echelon in the gambling organization came forward to plea bargain. And when the case came before the Grand Jury at the end of February, Greg's testimony was no longer crucial.

Along the way, Charles's assailant was arrested. He was a two-bit hood who'd owed certain favors. The man's testimony led to the arrest of the head honchos of the syndicate on charges of attempted murder. Whether or not they would be convicted was another matter. But just as important, the local bookie operations had been closed down.

The Arnold family was thriving, Kate realized after a luncheon date with Jill. As soon as they met, Kate could see that Jill was bursting with news.

"Everything's going so well, Kate. I'm confident Greg and I will make it."

"Where is he? I haven't seen him in weeks, and Charles acts mysterious about his location. I didn't think that was necessary anymore."

"It was at Greg's request. He's been in a treatment center, and he didn't want to advertise the fact until . . . well, until he saw how it was going. Greg still has to fight his pride. But he's learned a lot. You know, Greg swears the best therapy he got was from Charles." Jill met Kate's look. "How do you repay a debt like that?"

"Charles already has a down payment, Jill. When you two are back on your feet, he'll have been paid in full."

"Yes, but Greg owes Charles so much—his life, even. And to know Charles almost paid with his. It's made Greg grow up, I'll tell you. I have, too. I love Greg, but I'll never go back to the life we led. We're going to build a new one."

"You've already begun," Kate assured her.

"We really have." Jill shared her news. "Greg's got his old job back."

"What?"

"Yes. He went to his former boss and laid out everything that's happened. He even went into the treatment program he's involved in. When he was finished, his boss agreed to give him another chance. As well he should! Greg's the best PR man around."

Kate smiled at Jill's transparent pride.

"And," Jill continued, "we're looking for an apartment, with Mom and Dad's blessings."

"I'm so pleased for you, Jill."

Jill looked pleased for herself, but she said earnestly, "I know we're not home free. There'll be difficult times ahead."

"But they'll be easier," Kate advised lightly, "if you make sure to have fun along the way."

"We intend to," Jill grinned. "I still think Greg's the sexiest man alive. Which reminds me, I want to hear your news, too. Have you set the date yet?"

THEY HAD. A Saturday in early April. And Lynn was to be in charge.

"But I don't want a big wedding," Kate announced firmly, fancying she had some say in the matter. Lynn dissuaded her of the foolish notion.

"Sweetheart, you owe it to the world after such a romantic courtship."

"Romantic! Terrifying's the way I remember parts of it."

"Danger adds spice to a relationship," Lynn opined. "Not that I doubt yours is already well seasoned." Kate blushed prettily. "And I couldn't be happier for you." Lynn spoke thoughtfully. "This is what friendships are for, you know, the good times as well as the bad."

The two women smiled, remembering all the times they'd both been there for each other. They clinked imaginary wineglasses in a private celebration, sipped the heady brew of joy and hugged.

After a moment, Kate confessed, "I'm so happy, Lynn, it scares me. My life has taken strange turns I couldn't have predicted—it bewilders me when I think about them. Yet sometimes I feel as if everything's been leading to this. To Charles and our life together. It's almost as if the whole thing had been planned."

"Why, Kate, you're sounding positively religious."

Kate's lips curved into an enigmatic smile.

OF COURSE, the couple had private plans of their own to make outside of Lynn's jurisdiction. Charles rushed to finish his work in progress before the wedding, and Kate, in a burst of confidence, completed hers.

Now came the moment of truth. Detective Malcolm had deduced Rebecca was the killer, but he hadn't deduced her motive. And the not knowing gnawed on him, so that he couldn't walk away.

Randolph had supplied the expensive trinkets she'd craved, all the freedom she flaunted. Granted the man was a bastard, still it didn't make sense.

And so he asked Rebecca the all-important question. "Why exactly did you kill your husband?"

Because Randolph was a crashing bore...
Which was better than the motive Kate had given Rebecca. But what the hell, she'd dispensed with the lot of them once and for all. And she couldn't wait to get started on a new story—right after Charles's and her honeymoon.

They'd agreed on the destination, as well as on other important matters, regarding their life together.

"About birth control, Kate. I've decided to take care of that."

Kate had been meaning to bring up the subject herself.

Still, his implied action startled her into blurting out, "Oh, no, you won't!"

Charles seemed taken aback by her vehemence. "But, Kate, it's the simplest way for us to be safe. Surely," he said, sounding amused, "you're not worried my masculinity will suffer."

"Don't be ridiculous," she said huffily and blushed. "Actually, I've been thinking about birth control myself. I'd..." she couldn't quite meet his eyes, "I'd like for us to have a baby."

For a moment, Kate's announcement reduced Charles to silence. But when he finally responded, his tone was firm. "I can't ask that of you, Kate, at this time in your life. With two children of your own and your writing to consider."

"What do you mean, at this time in my life?" Kate's voice rose. "Linda had their baby when she was forty."

Charles sighed in frustration. "That's not what I meant. Kate..." He took hold of her shoulders. "I don't know what you're thinking, but you mustn't worry..." For a rare moment he struggled for words. "What I'm trying to say is, I don't need you to give me a child. That has nothing to do with what I feel for you."

"But I want to have our baby, Charles. I'm feeling the nesting instinct."

"That's normal," he said reasonably, "right before a wedding. The feeling will pass."

"But I don't *want* it to pass! Millicent said you'd make a good father. I want to give you that chance."

"Kate..." he began helplessly, his composure shaken.

"Don't you want to make a baby with me, Charles?" she asked wistfully.

Charles closed his eyes briefly at her words, then opened them to gaze down at her, humorous resignation just masking his intensity.

"Of course, I want to make a baby with you, Kate."

Kate looked sleek. "I knew you'd see it my way."

Last but not least, Phoebe's threats were removed from their lives. Dan enlightened her on that subject one day in the office.

"Speaking in both a personal and official capacity, I want to tell you how pleased I am you and Charles are getting married. Even if it does mean breaking in a new secretary."

"You mean Phoebe's not coming back?"

"No."

For which Charles would be eternally thankful, but Kate was concerned. "I wondered...Dan, Phoebe told me she was going to bring up... certain matters at the parish meeting."

Dan looked understanding. "That's been taken care of. Phoebe didn't bring up anything at the meeting. The vestry met with her first, and we explained that although we understood she had problems with Charles, the rest of the parish was pleased with his ministry and felt Emmanuel had gained a new vitality under his leadership. We also informed her that we couldn't allow her to spread malicious rumors. She left in a rage.

"The next day I received a self-righteous letter declaring Emmanuel no longer a fit place to worship. She was searching for another parish more in line with her standards, beliefs and practices."

Kate felt pity for the unsuspecting parish, but a great well of relief for Emmanuel.

Millicent's mission had been accomplished.

THE WEDDING, when the momentous date arrived, was absolutely lovely. All four hundred guests agreed. The bishop officiated, Lynn was the matron of honor, and Nolan the best man. Wildflowers of the season decorated the sanctuary, and the April sun shone down its blessing.

The bride was beautiful in a street-length dress of palest cream, with simple elegant lines. Even Kate admitted to the fact. Love, she decided, made an excellent facial.

She was also of the opinion the groom was smashing. But then she could have been the least bit biased in that regard.

The day was perfect, except for Millicent's absence.

Once, during the ceremony, just as the bishop pronounced them man and wife, Kate felt a pang of sorrow because Millicent couldn't be with them to enjoy the fruits of her labors. She glanced at Charles, standing so tall beside her. He smiled and squeezed her hand. All at once, Kate knew he'd gleaned what she was thinking, and that he was assuring her Millicent was there.

EPILOGUE

THE CAMP FIRE SPARKED when Charles threw a log on it, sending swirling particles of light into the dusk. He sat down at the picnic table and drew his wife of seven hours into his arms, nuzzling his face into the delicate curve of her shoulder and heaving a deep contented sigh.

The air was cool but milder than the last time they'd camped here, the park more crowded. But they were at the very spot where they'd pitched their tent in January. Charles must have gone to some trouble to arrange it with the park ranger.

"You are a sentimentalist," Kate teased him, fighting an accelerating heartbeat. It had been close to three months since they'd had this kind of privacy, and she was hungry for Charles's lovemaking. From the pace of the pulse in his tanned throat, Charles felt the same.

Still, they had all the time in the world on this night of nights. And Charles's voice was lazy as he asked, "Why? Because I wanted to bring you back to Enchanted Rock the first night of our honeymoon? It was selfishness on my part. I kept remembering your face in the firelight. The feel of you in the darkness. Those memories had to sustain me through some tough times."

"You mean after you were shot?"

"I mean when I was alone in my bed at night."

"I had a few restless nights myself," Kate admitted. She smiled at him shyly and ran her fingers into his hair. "I hadn't expected such a chaste engagement."

Charles grinned down at her and ran his hands over her back, drawing her body closer. "We'll have to see what we can do to make up for that."

She pulled away from him slightly, trying to read his expression in the fading light. "You planned it that way, didn't you? You brought me here, made mad passionate love to me for two days, and then held out for the ceremony."

"An enforced convalescence influenced my decision."

"So you admit it."

"I know you, Kate. After Phoebe's theatrics, with Michael and Clark watching us like a hawk, and me in the middle of a flood of publicity, I decided we could wait. There's nothing furtive about what we feel for each other, and I didn't want us to have to snatch at passion."

Charles's tone was velvet. "I want us to savor it. I plan to spend the next week touring each and every square inch of you."

"I . . . I think that can be arranged. But what about Big Bend National Park? Wasn't that on our itinerary?"

"A mere side trip," he explained and began an exploration of his primary destination, one of his hands slipping under her shirt.

"The kids don't see it that way," Kate pointed out shakily. "They're afraid our going there means we won't get back on the camping trip we promised them."

By this time, Charles was drifting kisses across the planes of her face.

Kate found it harder to speak. "Of course, Mom staying with them in the new house was some compensation."

The thought of Charles's prenuptial purchase diverted Kate's attention for a moment. She'd felt the nesting instinct and Charles had secured her a spacious nest. At the same time, he'd proposed to the vestry they rent the parsonage cottage to a local seminary couple, citing its lack of space.

"I'm still a little overwhelmed with our domicile." Overwhelmed and comprehending for the first time Charles's true wealth. "Did we really need two studies?"

"One for you and one for me." He began nibbling her neck.

"Four bedrooms?"

"Clark's, Michael's, ours and a spare."

"But two living areas?"

"We'll be hosting church functions," Charles murmured abstractedly, having discovered the silky skin above her waist.

"And the swimming pool?"

"For the parish youth groups." But Charles didn't fool her. It was for Clark, Michael and himself. To get through the blazing summers in store.

That thought recalled a bit of news. "I received a lovely letter from your mother yesterday." Kate had already been introduced to his family by telephone and found them as charming as she'd expected.

"Oh?" She'd finally caught Charles's attention, and he pulled away to look down at her thoughtfully. "And what did my mother have to say?"

"It was a welcome-to-the-family letter." One Kate would cherish always. Charles was right, he'd come by his talent honestly. "But your mother mentioned they weren't flying over until fall. Hadn't they planned to come sooner?"

"I thought you'd like time to settle in before entertaining in-laws. Besides, I planned a quick trip over there in July, so you and the boys could get a taste of the old country."

Kate sighed blissfully. All this and England, too.

Charles noted the sigh and whispered in her ear. "What was that in aid of?"

"Oh, nothing."

Charles took her at her word and went back to his previous pursuits—with shattering effect on Kate's thought processes.

She began chattering. "You know Lynn thinks we're crazy to go on a camping honeymoon. Of course, Lynn thinks anything less than heated towels is roughing it."

"Kate..."

"What?"

"You're dithering."

"I know." Kate's tone was comical. "It's just that it's all coming home to me, what happened today. You're my husband."

"I'm working on that."

"And...I'm your wife." She moved her palms over his chest in wonder, loving the feel of him under the cotton shirt. "It's like being given the keys to a candy store. I still can't believe it." She felt the muscles of his arms and shoulders flex beneath her fingers. "I'm not used to having someone to love—just a touch away."

"I'd rather be closer."

"Would you?" she whispered.

"And I'd like to get on with the loving."

"So would I."

Charles took her hand and led her to the tent. As on that other night, he banked the fire while Kate went inside to wait.

But on this night the dusk lingered. The faintest light filtered through the canvas, outlining their figures. They were heady from the wood scent and this special night and the other's nearness. Heady with the gift they'd been given. To trust, to care, to create love.

Love made them one, and they gasped with the pleasure of it. Passion rippled over them, building, intensifying, flooding their senses like a crashing wave that swept them away and then softly, gently washed them onto a far shore.

Charles was the first to speak. He propped himself on an elbow so that he could look down at Kate's face.

"Are you convinced yet?" he asked her huskily.

"About what?" Kate's lashes opened languidly.

"About being married."

Kate's lips curved into a tantalizing smile. "I must admit you're very persuasive."

"So when can I take over my husbandly duties?"

He'd piqued her curiosity. "What did you have in mind?"

"I'd like to read your manuscript. Michael tells me you've completed it."

Kate stiffened and would have pulled away. But that was impossible in such an intimate position, which was probably the very reason Charles had chosen this time and place to broach the forbidden subject.

"Michael's a Judas. He knows I'm not ready to have the famous Fitzgerald critique my efforts."

Charles cupped her cheek with his fingers, his thumb holding her chin so that she couldn't avoid him. He kissed her lingeringly on the lips. "You enjoyed making love with him just now."

"That was different." Kate sought his mouth as it moved away. "I made love with Charles Sheffield, my husband."

"You'll have to get used to the fact they're one and the same."

"That might be difficult to do."

"I'll make it easy," he promised.

"It's odd," she said, staring up into his face. "I'm lying here vulnerable, completely naked."

"Charmingly so."

"And yet I'm terrified of exposing my work to you."

"It's because you lack confidence in it. We'll remedy that."

"The way you fixed everything else?" she asked, smiling. "You've made me feel beautiful, desirable and loved. And very much a female."

"You are very much a female, if memory serves me." He ran a quick check down her body. "Mmm, I knew I wasn't wrong. And I'm right about the book, too." He gazed down at her keenly, waiting for an answer.

"All right," she relented. "You can read it as soon as we get home."

"Good. Now where were we? Ah, yes, I remember."

But the promise Charles had extracted deserved retaliation. Kate held him back when he would have occupied himself with more immediately gratifying husbandly pursuits.

"Actually, I do have a new story line I'd like to talk over with you. Just to get your opinion on how I might approach it."

"Oh?"

"Yes. It's about this woman who works as a secretary. She's led a sheltered, mundane existence and decides one day to taste the pleasures of life. So she goes to work for this man who she thinks is a concert pianist, only to find out that he's a downhill racer. Which he uses as a cover for an international spy ring. The lady falls madly in love with him and offers up her body—"

"And? She offers up her body?"

Kate sighed elaborately. "This is where I thought you might come up with an idea. What do you think so far? Has the story got potential?"

"I think we should enter into a collaboration." Charles grinned down at her.

Kate's warm breath brushed his skin as she raised her lips to his. "Right now, Charles, I have another project in mind."